True of Blood

Bonnie Lamer

ISBN-13: 978-1477405437
ISBN-10: 1477405437

DEDICATION

For Xenia, Zuriq, Quinn, Conor and Jadyn.
The loves of my life.

<u>Other Titles by Bonnie Lamer</u>

<u>The Witch Fairy Series:</u>

True of Blood

Blood Prophecy

Blood Lines

Shadow Blood

Blood of Half Gods

Blood of Destiny

Blood of Dragons

Blood of Egypt

Blood of Retribution

Blood of the Exiled

True of Blood: Kallen's Tale

Blood Prophecy: Kallen's Tale

Blood Lines: Kallen's Tale

Shadow Blood: Kallen's Tale

Blood of Half Gods: Kallen's Tale

Blood of Destiny: Kallen's Tale

<u>The Eliana Brennan Series</u>:

Essence of Re

Exposed

Secrets of the Djinn Series

Marked

Bound

I love to hear from fans! Contact me on Facebook at http://www.facebook.com/pages/Bonnie-Lamer-Author/129829463748061

ACKNOWLEDGMENTS

A special thank you to Dawn Truskowski and Marjorie Bradshaw for going back through this book and making sure that I am using the English language correctly. I hope they're better at it than I am.

CHAPTER 1

I have a television, so I know what a family is supposed to look like, but mine is nothing like that. To begin with, both my parents are dead. Not the kind of dead where you bury them in the ground, say some nice words, cry a little bit and then never see them again. Nope. When they died, they refused to 'go into the light' or whatever it is you're supposed to do when you die. Instead, they came back home. As ghosts. Have you ever been sent to your room by a parent who has no corporeal form? I have and it sucks.

My parents died three years ago in a car accident. We live deep in the mountains in Colorado and the roads here are treacherous on the best of days. But, in the dead of winter after a snow storm, they're almost impossible to manage. When he was alive, my father was the only doctor for a seventy mile area, and one night in January, he got a call from a distraught man whose wife was in labor. The baby was trying to come out feet first. Apparently, there was a lot of blood and other gross stuff that made my dad think it was a good idea to drive on snow covered and icy mountain roads. My mom went with him to help deliver the baby, and to help calm down the expectant father who was becoming more hysterical by the minute.

They did manage to deliver the baby. Dad fixed up the mom so she stopped bleeding and wouldn't get an infection until she could get to the hospital in Denver when the roads were better. While they had been doing all that, the snow had continued to fall. About half a mile from home, my dad misjudged where the edge of the road was, and their car careened over a cliff to a road below, killing them both. Well, their bodies anyway.

Let me tell you, it is more than a little disconcerting to have your parents leave the house with bodies and then come home without them. I think it must be a lot harder on my little brother, Zacchaeus, or Zac for short, though, dealing with the ghost parents thing than it is for me. At least I can remember when Mom and Dad were able to give us hugs and kisses. But, he's only eight and he's having a hard time remembering them as anything but what they are now. I try to make up for it by making sure I hug him every day, but a hug from your sister will never compare to a hug from your mom or dad.

After the initial shock of the accident, I had to start making phone calls. Mom and Dad knew it wouldn't be long until their car was found, and we had to make sure Zac and I could stay together. I was only fourteen at the time, so Social Services would have stepped in and put us in foster homes; at least temporarily. So, the first phone call Dad had me make was to Aunt Barb. In their will, she was named our guardian in case anything ever happened to both of them. She had agreed when it was written, but I'm pretty sure she never expected to become our guardians and move to the mountains with us.

Don't get me wrong, Aunt Barb was fine with it and she's been great, but she's this brilliant scientist who had been working on proving that it was not possible for there to be another plane of existence. Seeing her brother as a ghost put the kibosh on that research project. Not only was she proven wrong, she had to tell her boss that her research had all been debunked. Of course, he didn't believe her at first. Not until she brought him home one night and introduced him to my parents. After she woke him up from his faint and swore him to secrecy, he agreed she should shift the direction of her research. Now, she is working on proving that astral projection is possible. Unfortunately, even with the support of her boss, this is an area of science that is not well respected. Her reputation has taken a beating, but she doesn't mind. She sees the living proof, of course no pun intended, of her research every day. Over the last three years, she has brought home a couple of her most diehard critics but she can't let everyone in the world know that my parents are ghosts. It would cause chaos and we would become the equivalent of sideshow circus freaks.

Fortunately, Aunt Barb is able to do a lot of her research at home, because it's an hour and a half drive to the research facility where she works in Denver. After what happened to my parents, there's no way she would get into her car and drive down the mountain when the roads are covered with snow. At home, she does all the physical stuff my parents can't do, like cooking. Technically, she's our legal guardian, but my parents are still the ones in charge of Zac and me; giving Aunt Barb plenty of time to work in the office/lab area she set up in the heated garage.

Zac and I have always been homeschooled, so I've never really been around other kids. My mom tried to get me active in things like Girl Scouts for a while when I was little, but it was too hard to consistently make the meetings due to weather conditions. So, I've lived a fairly lonely life in regards to friends. Thank god for the internet. At least I've met some nice people my own age online. After my parents followed their IP address back to their computers to make sure they weren't creepy forty year olds trying to prey on kids, that is. Okay, sometimes it rocks to have parents who are ghosts.

It's seven in the morning now on a Tuesday, and Mom has already given me a warning wake up call. I don't understand why if we're homeschooled that we have to get up so early. But when I bring it up, Mom and Dad always say something like it builds character or it teaches us discipline. I believe I have enough character, and I certainly have enough discipline, so I don't think I need to add to it every morning. We've agreed to disagree, but they still get me up early.

"Xandra Illuminata Smith, get out of that bed this instant!" Mom yells from my bedroom door she has just passed through. Uh oh, she's using my full name, so maybe that last wakeup call wasn't the first one. My parents tell me my name means 'defending men from light,' whatever that's supposed to signify, but I think it was just a cruel joke on their part.

"I'm awake," I mumble into my pillow.

"I don't want you just awake; I want you out of bed and dressed. Your aunt has breakfast on the table. It's rude to let it get cold," she says, crossing her transparent arms across her equally transparent chest. I'm not a hundred percent convinced Aunt Barb likes getting up this early either, but she goes along with it better than I do.

I pry my eyes open again and Mom is tapping her foot as if it could still make noise, instead of her toes disappearing through the light blue throw rug on my bedroom floor. "I'm up," I grumble, pushing the covers off and swinging my legs off my bed. I stumble half-awake to the bathroom only to find that Zac has beat me to it. Crossing my legs, I pound on the door. "Hurry up, I'm dying out here."

"Not funny," Mom says over her shoulder as she floats back to the kitchen.

Five minutes later, after pulling my long hair into a ponytail and washing my face, I walk bleary-eyed into the kitchen and am greeted by the smell of fresh pancakes and bacon. Aunt Barb outdid herself this morning. Usually it's toaster waffles and microwavable sausage links or something equally easy to make. She's at the stove in jeans and a black wool turtleneck, with a white apron hung over her neck. The apron is coated in flour and pancake batter. "What's the occasion?" I ask sitting down in front of a plate. I douse my pancakes with syrup and dig in.

Aunt Barb stops in mid-flip of a pancake and raises her eyebrows. The way she's looking at me is making me self-conscious. I feel around my mouth with my left hand thinking I must have some syrup or something on my face. "You really don't know what day it is?" she asks.

I shrug my shoulders as I put another forkful of pancakes in my mouth. Then it dawns on me and I look up at her sheepishly. "Oh, yeah, it's my birthday. I can't believe I forgot. Thanks for the special breakfast, Aunt Barb." I'm seventeen today and I really had forgotten.

Aunt Barb smiles and shakes her head. "You are the only person I have ever met who could forget her own birthday."

I bite my tongue so I don't say that all the days here kind of run together since I don't get out much; so it's easy to forget what the date is. I go outside, of course, but I don't really have any place to go besides taking a walk around the mountain, and the seasons are pretty much winter, winter, winter and a two week summer. Okay, I'm exaggerating, but the days do get monotonous. "I'm just tired. My brain hasn't woken up yet," I say with a yawn.

"Did you study for your anatomy test?" she asks, scooping a slightly burnt pancake off the griddle and onto a plate.

I sigh inwardly. Sometimes it's rough being homeschooled by a doctor. Other kids get to just go over the highlights in subjects like anatomy. Dad not only makes me learn the names and functions of all of the body's systems down to the most minute detail, but also the diseases associated with them and their treatment. "Yeah, and I think I'm developing cataracts from all reading I had to do."

"You don't get cataracts from reading," Dad says, as he floats into the room and gives me a pat on the shoulder. It leaves my skin slightly cooler than it was, even though the sweatshirt I had thrown on over my long sleeved tee and pajama pants I had slept in. One nice thing about living in the mountains – there aren't any fashion police. "It smells good in here, Barb." He floats over to the bacon and inhales deeply. Dad really misses food.

"Thanks," Aunt Barb says, and then quickly flips a pancake that's starting to smoke. Okay, science is her forte, not cooking.

"Morning," Zac says, flopping down into the chair across from me at the kitchen table. "Can I have four pancakes, Aunt Barb?"

Mom, who's been hovering around the stove and trying hard not to remind Aunt Barb to flip the pancakes, because nobody likes a critic, looks at him doubtfully. "I think your eyes are bigger than your stomach."

While Zac is focusing his attention on Mom, I reach over and take several pieces of bacon from his plate, leaving him only one. "Hey! That's not fair," he complains loudly when he turns back around.

Mom gives me a stern look. "Xandra, live and let live – fairly take and fairly give."

Mom's always spouting off things like that. It's like living with the Dalai Lama sometimes. Reluctantly, I put two pieces of bacon back on Zac's plate and he grins smugly at me. Ignoring him, I turn to my dad. "Dad, since it's my birthday and I've had to spend so much time preparing for the anatomy test, can I have an extra day or two for my physics paper?"

Raising a skeptical eyebrow, he considers me for a moment. Finally, he says, "Alright, two more days, but I want an extra page then." Hmm, that didn't work out exactly as I'd planned.

Mom whispers something to Aunt Barb, who then fishes in the pocket of her apron and pulls out a small wrapped box. Turning her ghostly body to me again, Mom has a smile on her face and a twinkle in her eye. "I've been saving this for you. My mother gave it to me when I was your age and her mother gave it to her." That surprises me. Mom doesn't usually talk about her parents, and will become tight-lipped if asked about them. I assume they had some sort of falling out and I don't even know if they're still alive or not.

Aunt Barb sets the gift on the table and I pull at the paper and open the box. Inside is one of the most unusual, and beautiful, bracelets I have ever seen. It's a cord tied in knots and in between the knots are pieces of stone in a variety of colors. "It's pretty, Mom, thank you. What's this stone?" I ask, pointing to a green stone with flecks of red in it.

"It's called a bloodstone," she replies. "The green matches the color of your eyes perfectly. Do you really like it?"

I nod. "It's great."

"Good, I'm glad you like it. I have one more thing for you. It has also been in my family for generations." She nods to Aunt Barb; who then fishes another small box out of her apron and sets it on the table next to my plate of cooling pancakes.

When I open this box, I find a necklace on a similar cord with knots, but this has only one stone in the center. The stone is amber-colored and shaped into a circle with a hole in the center that contains a rust-colored metal. The stone is embedded in a cradle of silver.

"I've never seen anything like this. Thanks again, Mom," I say, as I pull the cord over my bone-straight, long black hair and settle it on my neck. Mom looks pleased as I continue to examine the various stones of my new bracelet and necklace. She has never been one for jewelry, and I know I've never seen them around before, so these presents surprise me. Dad always says Mom is too pretty to need jewelry. I suspect they just don't want to spend the money on it. But, he is right. Mom is very pretty with long curly blonde hair and an oval face. Her eyes are so blue, even as a ghost they're the color of the ocean and shine brightly. Dad also has blue eyes and sandy brown hair like Zac, and he has a stocky build. There must have been some serious recessive genes in their DNA to give me black hair and green eyes. Even the shape of my face is different, with high cheekbones and a slender face. Mom says I'm beautiful, too, but I always wanted to look more like her.

Mom is beaming at me and Dad is smiling at her. Even as ghosts, the love they have for each other is almost tangible. Mom says it was their love for each other, and for us, that anchored them both here to continue to take care of us. I often wonder if I'll ever meet someone with whom I'll experience that kind of love. But since there are no boys in a fifty mile radius of where we live, it certainly isn't going to happen any time soon.

After breakfast, Zac and I do the dishes. I wash and he dries and puts away. We have an unspoken mutual agreement to drag this out as long as possible to postpone starting on our schoolwork. That's one good thing about Aunt Barb not being the greatest cook; the pans she uses usually need a lot of scrubbing to get the burnt food off them.

"Xandra, I can see myself in the Teflon," Mom laughs, as she hovers over my shoulder. "I think it's clean enough." She knows what we're up to but she doesn't usually give us a hard time about it. She thinks a little rebellion in kids is a healthy thing.

Not being able to avoid it any longer, Zac and I trudge into the small room at the back of the house that is set up like a classroom. There's a whiteboard on the far wall, a large desk off to the side of the room, and two smaller desks facing the whiteboard for Zac and me. The wall behind the larger desk that Mom and Dad used to use, when they could actually sit on furniture, is lined with educational books. Everything from math and science, to English grammar and literature, to obscure ancient texts of religion and mythology. I love looking at those. I have a fascination with anything that has to do with magic. When I was younger, I used to wish I was Hermione Granger from the Harry Potter series, though I don't ever admit that out loud.

While I'm taking my anatomy test, Zac gets a lesson in dividing large numbers. He's having a hard time sitting still this morning because we've been snowed in for a week. He hasn't had much of a chance to play outside. When the snow is this deep, it can be dangerous to wander too far from the house and Mom and Dad worry a lot. I remember how it felt when I was his age to have all that pent up energy and no way to release it, so I feel for him. But he is making it hard to concentrate on my test, as he keeps interrupting Mom's lesson with questions and comments.

When he accidently knocks his pencil holder off his desk, Mom gives him a stern look, although I can see a sympathetic gleam in her eye. "Zacchaeus, soft of eye and light of touch – speak you little and listen much." I'm pretty sure she got that one from a fortune cookie. Zac makes an effort to concentrate on his lesson. So I am able finish my anatomy test in peace before starting on a physics assignment Dad had given me.

Finally, it's lunch time and we can take a short break. I usually make lunch for me and Zac. This allows Aunt Barb to work uninterrupted until dinner time. Zac and I head to the kitchen and I make him his favorite sandwich. Peanut butter and jelly, light on the peanut butter and heavy on the jelly. I make myself a turkey sandwich with cheese. It's a little dry with no condiments, but I've never had a taste for mustard or mayonnaise.

"I think the snow is letting up," Dad says, as he floats into the kitchen. "Since it's your birthday, maybe we can play hooky and take a walk later and look for tracks." Zac grins. He loves taking nature walks with Dad and learning how to spot animals. At this point, I think he could track a mountain lion through a blizzard.

"Did you grade my test?" I ask nervously around a bite of turkey sandwich.

"I did and you passed with flying colors like you always do," he says with a proud smile. "I think you'd deserve the afternoon off even if it wasn't your birthday. What do you think, want to go?"

Hmm, tough choice. Slaving away over physics and Dante's version of hell for the next three hours, or trudging through knee-deep snow. It really is a tossup. I don't consider nature and me to be friends. But, Dad looks so excited at the prospect that I can't refuse, even though the thought that as a ghost he can no longer feel the cold runs through the back of my mind. On the other hand, he also can no longer do any of the things he used to love to do outside, like hunt or fish or even chop firewood for the fireplace. For his sake, I try to muster some excitement. "Sure, sounds great."

Dad chuckles at my lukewarm response but chooses to ignore my hesitation. "Great, after you finish up lunch, throw on your winter gear and meet me outside. I'll see if your mother wants to come, too." He floats off in the direction of the living room where Mom is reading a novel on the computer that Aunt Barb programmed to automatically turn the page every sixty seconds. She decides to stay inside and finish up her book.

The nature walk is everything I expected it to be. Cold, wet and miserable. After an hour, I start to get whiny, and by two hours, I'm downright surly. Dad finally gets the hint and we start heading back towards home. After climbing up a particularly steep slope and losing my footing twice, I vow not to leave the house again until July. I'm so excited to finally be at the top that I almost walk through Dad who is staring at the ground with a puzzled expression on his face.

"What's the matter, Dad?" I ask.

"There's people tracks," Zac says excitedly, pointing to a spot about ten feet away where there is a line of tracks in the snow. They do indeed look like human footprints.

"People tracks? Who besides us would be crazy enough to trudge through this snow and get this close to being a human icicle?" Okay, I already admitted I'm feeling surly.

Completely ignoring my icicle comment, Dad says, "That's what I'd like to know." Peering closer at him, he looks worried. The way he's standing so still, as only a ghost can do, and staring with his brow scrunched together is making me nervous.

"Is everything okay, Dad?"

Shaking his head as if to clear his thoughts, he looks back at Zac and me. "Yes, of course. Just wondering why someone would be so far off the trail." The closest hiking trail is over five miles from our house. Someone would have to be seriously lost to find their way here.

He must be thinking the same thing. "Why don't you take Zac back to the house? I want to see where these tracks lead and see if someone needs help." He's totally oblivious to the distress that coming across a ghost, when you are already lost in snow-filled woods and thinking you're going to freeze to death, would cause. But his heart is in the right place. Who knows? Maybe a spirit guide through the woods would be welcomed by a lost hiker.

Zac and I make it back home and I'm finally able to peel off my soaked jeans and gray long underwear, which are unfortunately a necessity at this elevation, and step into a hot shower. By the time

I'm done and come out of my room, Dad's home. He and Mom are in the living room speaking in hushed tones.

"It couldn't be," Mom is saying. "There's no way anyone could have found us here."

"Then how do you explain the tracks suddenly disappearing? Who else could do that?"

What is he talking about? "Dad, what's going on?" I ask, coming into the room and startling them both. If they could turn any paler, I believe they would.

Dad tries to put a convincing smile on his face. "Nothing's wrong. I wasn't able to find the hikers and I'm worried they're in danger."

"What did Mom mean about someone finding us?" I don't miss the guilty look that washes over her face before she puts her own unconvincing smile on. "I was just hoping they would find our house so we could help them, but we're so deep in the mountains that it would be almost impossible. I hate to think of someone being all alone and lost. I think I'll go talk to Barb about getting dinner started." With that, she floats through the living room wall in the direction of the garage and Aunt Barb's lab.

"I think I'll take another quick look around," Dad says, as he floats through the large picture window.

Okay, Mom and Dad have never lied to me before that I know of. But, their explanation just isn't adding up with the conversation they were having. They're obviously not going to say anything else on the subject, though. All through dinner, they both have a hard time looking me in the eye when talking to me, and I'm getting more uncomfortable by the minute. What is going on that they don't want me to know about?

After dinner and dishes, I go to my room and log onto my Facebook account. I get lost for the next couple of hours in my own little cyber world of friends. By the time I come out to get a snack before bed, it's already Zac's bedtime. I stop by his open bedroom door and listen to Mom tuck him in. From the time I can remember, Mom has always sang the same lullabies to us. I used to look forward to them every night when I was younger and needed to be tucked in.

I still love to hear her lilting voice as she sings the songs she claims have been sung to all the children in her family for generations. I stand in the door to listen as she sings softly:

"Deosil go by the waxen moon - sing and dance the Witch's Rune;
Widdershons go when the Moon doth wane, the wolf will howl by the dread wolf's bane;
When the lady's moon is coming new, kiss your hand to her times two;
When the moon is riding at her peak, then your heart's desire you should seek.
Heed the north wind's mighty gale - lock the door and drop the sail;
When the wind is from the south, love will kiss thee on the mouth;
When the west wind blows o'er thee, the departed spirits will restless be;
Heed ye flower, bush, and tree - by the Lady blessed be."

I have no idea what the song means. When I've asked in the past, Mom just smiles at me mischievously and tells me that the important thing to remember from the lullaby is to bind the spell every time, let the spell be spoken in rhymes. Then she says it was a southern wind that brought Dad to her. As far as an answer goes, it's not a very good one, but I can never get her to tell me anything else.

"Will you sing both to me tonight?" Zac asks, yawning widely.

Mom smiles. "You look awfully tired, are you sure you want me to sing again?"

"Uh huh," he says and his eyelids are already drooping.

"Alright, we'll do both tonight." Mom begins to sing softly again.

"*Bewitching Goddess of the crossroads*
Whose secrets are kept in the night,
You are half-remembered, half-forgotten
And are found in the shadows of the night.
From the misty hidden caverns
In ancient magic days,
Comes the truth once forbidden
Of thy heavenly veiled ways.
Cloaked in velvet darkness
A dancer in the flames

You who are called Diana, Hecate,
And many other names.
I call upon your wisdom
And beseech thee from this time,
To enter my expectant soul
That our essence shall combine.
I beckon thee O Ancient One
From far and distant shore,
Come, come be with me now
This I ask and nothing more.

Zac is sound asleep by the time she finishes. I think she only kept singing because of me listening at the door. Even if I can't explain what the songs mean, I'll probably still sing them to my kids someday, too, just because they're so beautiful and comforting. I'll hold off on the cryptic replies, though. When they ask me what they mean, I'll just admit that they don't mean anything, I think as I head back to my room with the apple I just got from the kitchen.

A little while later, Mom comes into my room. She's in pajamas now and I can't help but think how cool it is that she and Dad can appear how they want to appear. They don't sleep any more, but they still appear in pajamas every night. She sits down next to me on my bed where I'm reading. She and Dad have gotten much better at hovering and appearing to sit on things. They used to look like they were sitting inside of them or a foot above them.

"Good book?" she asks.

I shrug. "It's okay."

"I can't believe you're seventeen already," she says, as she presses a cold translucent hand to my cheek. "There's so much I still need to teach you."

"From the amount of homework you and Dad give me, it seems like my brain is already going to burst," I grumble and she smiles.

"I wasn't talking about schoolwork. I mean about life. About mistakes. About destiny."

My brows furrow as I consider what she's saying. "Mom, is this the birds and the bees talk? Because I figured all that stuff out a long time ago. Since there aren't any boys around here for me to make any mistakes with, you really don't have anything to worry about."

"Not your mistakes. Mine," she says quietly. I swear, by the way she's looking at me, if ghosts could have tears in their eyes, she would have them now. She gestures to my necklace and bracelet. "Promise me you will wear these always."

"Mom, you're making me nervous."

With a cheap imitation of a smile, she rises from my bed. "I'm sorry, I don't mean to. I'm just a mother who is having a hard time with the fact that my daughter is all grown up now and I have not truly prepared you for the world. I always thought I had plenty of time. But, now you've reached a magical age and you're unbound; falling into adulthood without any practical guidance."

Somehow, that doesn't make me feel better. "What are you talking about?"

"Nothing we need to discuss tonight. We'll talk more tomorrow." With that, she touches my face one more time and then floats out of my room, leaving me perplexed and a little bit frightened. It's now impossible for me to concentrate on my book as I ponder yet another cryptic conversation with my mother.

As the light of the full moon streams in over my dark blue comforter from the large window that faces out into the woods, I think of a verse in the lullaby Mom sang to Zac. 'When the moon is riding at her peak, then your heart's desire seek.' What is my heart's desire? There are so many things I want. I would love my parents to be corporeal again. I would love to live somewhere that has summer all year long, instead of being almost constantly surrounded by snow or rain. I would love for Zac to have other little boys to play with instead of being stuck in this house most of the time with very little to do. I would like to have friends of my own, to do things with like go to the mall or the movies, instead of being stuck in this house too with very little to do. That last thought tugs at my conscience as I think of the loving household my parents have provided for us. They love Zac and me so much, they chose to forsake an afterlife which promises to be glorious. Instead, they anchor themselves here to make sure we are safe and well taken care of. If we moved off this mountain and around more people, there's a good chance they would be discovered and our family would suffer. Zac and I might even be put in foster homes. It seems ungrateful of me to want more than they have already given us. But maybe Mom's right, maybe I haven't experienced enough of the world at large, and I'm missing out on some important life lessons. That's the thought that lingers in my mind as I fall asleep on the night of my seventeenth birthday.

CHAPTER 2

I wake up antsy and I blame it on my conversation with Mom last night. At breakfast, I can't even enjoy my toaster waffle because she keeps looking at me like something bad is about to happen. This is not like her at all. Even after becoming a ghost, Mom has always been happy and full of life, but today, she looks closer to being dead than she ever has. I can't help but wonder if she and Dad have been waiting for me to be old enough to care for Zac so they can finally move on. With that thought in mind, I push away my plate of frozen waffles and slump back into my chair.

"Everything all right?" Dad asks, looking at me with concern. Even he has seemed nervous this morning and Dad has always been the most laid back person I have ever met. Granted, I haven't met that many people, but still, he never looks nervous.

"Yes," I lie. My parents exchange a look that I can't quite figure out.

"Xandra, honey, why don't we take a break from school today and spend some time together?" Mom says, trying to sound cheerful but failing. "After you finish dishes, come find me in the living room. I'll be reading."

My feeling of dread is getting worse by the minute. Zac and I take as long as possible with the dishes, but since there are no pans to wash, we have them done way too soon. Not being able to put it off any longer, I walk into the living room and take a seat on the overstuffed red couch.

Mom drifts over and sits down with a transparent leg underneath her so she's facing me. "Do you remember the fairy tale you used to love when you were a little girl?"

I shake my head. "Not really."

"Would you mind if I told it to you again?"

"Mom, I'm a little old for fairy tales."

"Please, just humor me," she says with a small smile. I nod reluctantly as my feeling that something bad is going to happen soon increases.

After a moment, she begins to tell me the story:

Once upon a time, there was a lovely Princess who lived in a beautiful white house that was as big as a castle. She had a wonderful life. There was a stable behind the house full of horses that she loved to ride, and she was given everything her heart desired. Her parents, the King and Queen, loved her very much. She could do no wrong in their eyes.

"She had a charming childhood filled with magic. Her mother was a powerful Witch, and after the Princess's seventeenth birthday when her magic was unbound, her mother expanded her magical education from theory to practicality. The Princess already knew that the earth held many secrets and now she learned to use them to draw magic to her to do her bidding. Her mother also taught her to be responsible as she honed her skills, for magic is only to be used for good, never evil. The Princess found she had wonderful abilities, such as performing difficult spells, and she could even move things with her mind. For over three years, she worked hard to become the woman her parents meant for her to be, as she would be Queen someday.

"But as she worked and trained, the Princess grew sadder and sadder. She didn't want the responsibility of a Kingdom of Witches. There was always bickering and challenges of magical abilities; and her parents were constantly under the threat of being overthrown by someone more powerful than they were. The Princess longed to escape the world she had been born into even though she felt guilty for wanting to leave her parents. She knew her destiny was already set in stone. Or so she thought.

"On the night of her twenty-first birthday, the Princess was wandering the woods behind her home, enjoying the almost full moon of the Equinox that would usher in spring. As she stopped to pick a lovely purple flower, she noticed a shadow in the trees. She stood and continued her walk, for she was never afraid of shadows in the night. She had her magic to protect her. After several minutes, it became obvious the shadow was following her. Being the brave Princess she was, she moved toward the shadow to discover what animal was so curiously coming along for her walk. To her amazement, she found a horse as black as the new moon, with obsidian eyes and a glossy black mane she wanted to run her fingers through. She had never seen a horse as beautiful as this one.

“Reaching out a tentative hand, she stroked the horse’s nose. He snorted softly in pleasure and she moved closer to him. He was a powerful stallion with wild eyes and a hard muscular body. As she continued petting him, he began to nudge her with his nose. The Princess finally realized that the horse was trying to encourage her to ride him. Charmed with the idea, the Princess wrapped a handful of his mane in her hand and used it to pull herself up. She sat on his bare back, enjoying the freedom of riding without a saddle. When she was in place, the horse began to gallop.

“The Princess laughed as she enjoyed the feeling of the wind against her face and her long blonde hair streamed out behind her. They rode like this for a long time, the beautiful black steed and her. When they reached a clearing in the center of the woods, the steed slowed and finally stopped. The Princess climbed off his back and picked spring flowers for him to eat as she stroked his neck and back. She couldn’t stop staring at his eyes that danced with intelligence and something else she couldn’t name. She knew she could love this horse more than all others. She hoped she could convince him to follow her home. She knew that her father would purchase him from whoever owned him, for he loved for her to be happy.

“After a while, it was time to return home for the night. She mounted the horse again, and they ran with the wind back to where she had found him. He stopped and nudged her legs with his nose. The Princess took the hint and dismounted. With a final rub of his nose, the stallion rode off into the night. The Princess feared she would never see him again.

“The next day, the Princess returned to the woods and waited, as the moon of the spring Equinox rose in the sky. She was sure the beautiful black horse would come to her again that night, and just as darkness took its hold, she heard him. She smiled as he trotted to her, and laughed when he rubbed his nose against her face. She needed no encouragement this time to climb upon his back. They spent the night together under the full moon and stars in the clearing in the woods once again. The Princess was sad when he nudged her and wanted her to climb on his back so he could bring her home. It was much harder to leave him that night than it had been the night before.

"On the third night, the Princess waited once again, and when she saw him coming toward her, her heart filled with joy and love. He carried her through the dark woods and back to the clearing. When she climbed down from his back, she wrapped her arms around his neck and whispered to him how much she loved him and wished that he would stay with her forever.

"The horse began to shimmer and shake, and the Princess stepped away in fright as she watched his long nose recede and his body grow smaller. His skin lightened and his obsidian eyes became a vibrant green. Within moments, the most beautiful man she had ever seen stood before her. The Princess didn't know what to do as she watched this transformation, for nothing her parents had taught her about magic could explain what had just happened.

"The man smiled gently at her and asked her in a velvety voice not to be frightened. He explained that he had been transformed by an evil Witch, and only the love of a beautiful woman such as herself could break the curse. The Princess's heart filled again with joy. She rushed into the arms of this dark- haired man and felt love blossom inside of her for the man instead of the beast. He kissed her deeply and held her to him, murmuring words of love in her ears."

Mom had stopped looking at me as she spoke. She's staring out the window and she looks sadder than I have ever seen her before. Bringing her attention back to me, she says, "This is where I always stopped the story when you were little, but there was more." She continues on.

"The Princess loved the man so much that she lay with him that evening in the clearing. She shared her love and her body with him. When it was time to return, the man explained that he had to go back to his home to let his family know the curse was broken. He wouldn't be able to take her with him, but he promised to come back for her soon. The Princess returned to her own home and waited anxiously for his return.

“As the days turned into weeks, and then into months, it became apparent that a baby had resulted from that one night in the clearing. With great anxiety and shame, the Princess spoke with the Queen and explained what had happened. The Princess had expected her mother to be angry, but when she saw terror in her eyes, she knew something much darker had happened than a silly young Princess falling in love. Horrified, her mother backed away from her daughter. Then she hurried from the room and came back moments later with the King, who looked angrier than the Princess had ever seen him.

“The King ranted and raved about how the Princess had brought ruin to the world. He even shook her by her roughly by her shoulders asking if she understood the ramifications of her actions. The Princess shook her head as tears began to fall down her cheeks. As her father sensed how truly ignorant his daughter was of what she had done, he pulled her into his arms and hugged her tightly. ‘It’s our fault,’ he said. ‘We didn’t teach you the old laws. Our mistake has become your ruin.’

“The Princess thought her parents were upset simply because she was pregnant, but she soon discovered that something much more sinister had occurred. The King told her of the Pooka, or the Fairy people, who had once spread mischief and evil through the lands. Hundreds and hundreds of years ago, they would attack humans and ruin crops if offerings were not made to them. They grew more and more powerful, and over time, they began to demand blood sacrifices. That was when the Witch King of the time felt something had to be done to stop them. He called for his Derwydd, his most powerful advisor, and they made a plan to force the Fae back into their own realm, for they weren’t from our lands.

“This ancient King tracked the Fairy King with magic when he was transformed into his animal shape, which was a black steed. The Witch King was able to bind him long enough to climb on his back. When the Fairy King finally fought off the binding spell, he bucked and reared and tried everything to get the Witch King off his back. For three days and nights, the Witch King held on as the Fairy King became weaker and weaker, finally admitting defeat. It was then that the two Kings forged a blood oath; an oath that could never be broken, for whoever broke it would die instantly.

“The oath stated that the Fairy King would gather up all the Fairies within three nights’ time, and then escort them back into their own realm. They would never return; the realms would be closed to each other forever. However, if the Fairy King, who could return in his animal form for three nights every year, could convince a true-blooded Princess to fall in love with him and agree to lay with him to produce a child. The child born from this union would have the power to break the bindings holding the Fae in their own realm, letting them once again join this one and wreak havoc on humanity.

"For many generations, no daughters were born to anyone in the royal lineage. Kings married commoners, and magic was used to ensure that only sons were born to make it impossible for the binding to be lifted. The Princess was the first daughter born to a King and Queen for hundreds of years, and the Fairy King seized his chance to finally break the bonds.

"When the Princess's father explained what had happened to the Derwydd of the time, the royal council, or Witan, was called together to determine what to do. By every vote except the King's, it was determined that the baby must die before the Fairy King came back to claim it. With a heavy heart, the King explained this to the Princess. She screamed and cried and begged, but it was no use. The decision had been made.

The Princess was locked in her room that night with two guards at her door to prevent her escape. The most powerful Witch of the Witan was brewing a potion to make her miscarry the baby she had already grown to love with all her heart. The ceremony was to be the next morning.

"The Princess was determined to save her baby. Later that night when the rest of the house was sleeping, she built up her courage and she magically opened her bedroom door. The guards were ready for her. They came towards her, ready to repel her magic with amulets given to them by the Witan. But the Princess wasn't going to use magic. She let the guards get close to her and then she pulled her athame from the folds of her nightgown. She used this sacred knife that was never supposed to be used to draw blood, to stab the guards, giving her the chance to escape. She could not pause to determine if they lived or died. Once it was discovered what she had done, she would be hunted by members of the Witan and sentenced to death. There was no possibility that the Princess could ever be able to return to her home ever again.

"The Princess fled, taking a horse from the stable, for the garage was too well lit and guarded for her to get one of the cars. She rode the horse hard through the woods for uncountable miles until she couldn't push him anymore. Then, she set out on foot. She ran as fast as she could until her chest felt like it would explode. When it became too painful, she would slow to a walk but she kept moving, stopping only for short breaks. She travelled like this for days, keeping to the woods and back country as much as possible. She scrounged for food and slept under trees and in the open air. By the fifth day, she was filthy and weak. She had scratches on her hands and feet, making it impossible for her to travel in the woods any longer. She didn't dare use her magic to heal herself even this far from her home because the Witan could use it to track her.

"It was on the fifth day that the Princess met a handsome man with beautiful blue eyes and kind smile. He was a doctor and he promised he could heal her wounds with science instead of magic. He brought her to his home and listened to her unbelievable tale, and he believed her. As he cared for her physical wounds, he also helped to heal her emotional ones.

The man and the Princess fell deeply in love. He left his home, his state and his medical practice, and they disappeared into the mountains. They were careful not to leave any type of trail behind them. Once there, he helped raise the Princess's daughter as his own, and he loved her more than anything in the world."

Mom's eyes are boring into mine as she says, "And even in death, he loves you still."

Okay, can being a ghost make you go crazy? Because I'm pretty sure my mom has gone over the edge. "Mom," I say slowly, "it's 2011. Do you really expect me to believe that you are some kind of Witch Princess? That I'm half Witch and half Fairy and nobody else in the world has figured out that magic really exists?"

Mom smiles sadly. "Many people know magic really exists, but they keep our secret or they are spelled to forget."

"Okay, Mom, you're freaking me out here. You really believe all this, don't you?" I stand up from the couch to put some distance between us. What do you do when your ghost mom goes crazy?

"Xandra, you have ghosts for parents. How is it that you can't believe magic is real?" She floats up from the couch towards me, but I back away, so she stops in the middle of the room.

"I believe in ghosts because I have to, and because I believe that your ghost form is your soul taken out of your body. I do not believe that people can do magic and make people forget things."

"I know it's hard to take in..."

"Does Dad know you believe this?" I ask, interrupting her.

"Yes."

"And he's okay with it?" Dad's always been a pragmatist. It's hard to believe that he would believe in Witches and Fairies and magic.

"Your father has done everything in his power to keep you safe from my past and your foretold destiny."

"My destiny? You mean it's my destiny to open the gate between this world and the Fairy world? Mom, that's just crazy. Are you sure being a ghost for so long hasn't kind of eaten away at your sense of reality?" I know that sounds cruel and disrespectful, but come on. She wants me to believe in Fairies! Not to mention the idea that my real father could turn himself into a horse. My real father. The one with black hair and green eyes just like mine. Dad's not my real dad. I sink down onto the thick gray carpet in shock.

"Xandra?" Mom says softly.

I don't look at her. I can't look at her right now. My whole life has been a lie. What else don't I know about my parents and their past? "Who are you? Are you really Julienne Smith?"

Mom shakes her head sadly. "My real name is Quillian Vorel Levex, Daughter of King Sveargith and Queen Athear. I am of the Witch line and was supposed to rule over the Witches after my parents. But now, I am branded malsvir and Faessi, evil and a coward, for betraying my people and bringing into the world the possible destruction of humankind."

It takes a moment for her words to sink in. "What?" I squeak. "Do you mean me?"

She moves her head into a small nod. "You were never meant to be born, but I loved you too much to allow them to kill you."

Oh, this is too much. I live in the mountains in the middle of nowhere with the closest person living more than ten miles away. Yet, I'm supposed to bring about the destruction of mankind? "How, exactly, am I supposed to destroy everyone?"

"Your blood could allow the Fairies back into this world, and they will come back angry after being kept away for so long. They will force humans to bow down before them for fear of death."

"Yeah, I think I've read about things like that in a myth or two. But, that's all they were, Mom. They were myths. You can't possibly believe all this. If you do, then you really are crazy." I am beyond disconcerted now and have moved on to angry.

"Honey, I know it's hard to accept..."

"No, not hard to accept. Impossible to accept! I don't know why you want to make me believe this stuff, but it's crazy and I'm not going to do it!" With that, I pick myself up off the floor and walk away from my insane mother. I go into my room, slamming the door behind me. I pace back and forth in front of my bed trying to understand what made my mom go off the deep end. She was fine just a couple of days ago. What is it about me being seventeen that has caused her to go crazy?

After a few minutes, I decide I need to get out of the house, but I don't want to risk being seen and having to talk to Mom some more. So, I put on my dark red jacket, and pull on my black knee-high boots, and I push my bedroom window open. Quietly, I climb out and close it softly behind me. I trudge through the snow, aimlessly trying to shake off the morning I've had. Mom's story keeps nagging at me, begging me to believe it. Which I absolutely refuse to do. It's impossible.

CHAPTER 3

After about an hour of wandering, I realize I've gone quite a ways from home and should probably head back before I get lost. I had pulled on my black hat and gloves that I keep in my jacket pocket, but the cold mountain air can't be held at bay for long. Reluctantly, I turn around and follow my footprints in the snow back towards home. About half a mile from my house, I start to see footprints that aren't mine. Strange. No, stranger than strange. Could this be the same person who left tracks in the snow yesterday?

Stopping, I scan the woods for any sign of movement, but there's nothing except the occasional bird. The bare trees are quiet, not even swaying in the gentle wind that's blowing. Turning back towards home, I keep moving. Dad can come back out and look for the hiker and make sure he or she isn't lost.

I go about twenty feet when a red fox appears in my path about ten yards away. It's just standing there looking at me. Funny, we don't have red foxes at this altitude. A few seconds later, a mountain lion joins the fox. Okay, those we do have this high up, and it's best to avoid them. I stand very still, hoping they will both keep moving and ignore me. They don't. They start walking towards me. I'm pretty sure I'm hallucinating, because as they walk, the air begins to shimmer and their bodies elongate. Their faces change, and soon, they are walking only on their hind legs as the fur from their bodies begins to dissolve. In less than thirty seconds, two very naked people are walking towards me. The woman is tall, probably three inches taller than my five feet seven inches. She has jet black hair and high cheek bones like mine, but the twisted smile on her thin lips takes away any beauty she might possess. The man is also tall, with a large muscular build, and his dark hair is shaved close to his scalp. Both have vibrant green eyes and both look menacing. I take several steps backwards which just makes them laugh.

"Don't worry, Princess, we have come to bring you home," the woman says, and I'm pretty sure she doesn't mean the home I left an hour ago.

Summoning up my courage, I ask, "Who are you?"

"We are Pooka, loyal to King Dagda. I am Olwyn and this is Maurelle. We were given the task of returning you to your rightful home in the realm of the Fae," the male says. Both continue walking towards me as I take a few more steps backwards in the deep snow.

"I already have a home," I say nervously looking around for a possible escape route.

The female, Maurelle, scoffs. "You have been forced to live among the Cowan. This is not a home, it is a prison. You are superior to them and you belong with your own kind."

"Cowan?" I ask. Maybe if I lunge to the left, I can lose them by jumping over the small gorge over there and looping around back to the house from the other side. I surely know the woods better than they do.

"You may refer to them as humans," Olwyn explains.

They are almost close enough to grab for me now. I need to make my move. I fake right and Olwyn grabs for me, but then I lunge left and start running. I can hear them behind me as I run through tree branches. I lift my feet up into a jump over the five foot gorge and lose my footing on the other side. I am not fast enough in getting up and Maurelle catches my coat. Roughly, she pulls me to my feet and hurls me against a tree face first. My head hits it hard and my vision gets slightly blurry. I feel blood at the corner of my mouth, and I'm pretty sure I'm close to losing consciousness.

"You will return with us," she says, wrapping a hand around my neck and lifting me off my feet. But, as she makes contact with my skin, the amulet around my neck shines brightly and she drops me just as quickly as she had lifted me. She pulls her hand to her chest and cradles it as if she has been burned, and she takes a step back from me. She is about to speak when her attention is caught by a raven that lands on the lowest limb of the tree I am leaning against.

Maurelle's lips pull into a sneer. "Kallen."

Trying hard to stay still so as not to bring her attention back to me, I watch as the raven elongates and begins to take on the characteristics of a boy around my own age. A gorgeous boy. Where Olwyn is big and brawny with bulging muscles and is much older, this boy is tall and lean and has the muscles of a large cat. Sleek and strong. His black hair is unruly and his green eyes are piercing. He also happens to be completely naked like the other two. Doesn't anybody feel the cold like I do?

"Maurelle," the boy says as he jumps to the ground. "I will not let you take her."

"There are two of us, Kallen. You cannot fight us both and expect to win," Olwyn says, pulling himself up to his full height which is still several inches shorter than Kallen.

"No, but I can slow you down," Kallen says. From his closed hand, he throws two objects hitting both Maurelle and Olwyn in the chest. Turning to me, he yells, "Run!"

I hesitate for only a second before I realize that whatever he has thrown at Olwyn and Maurelle has them kneeling in pain. I pull myself up, and ignoring the pain in my head, I run as fast as I can, getting cut by branches and brush as I push through them. I'm almost home when I hear the pounding of feet in the snow behind me. I dare to look over my shoulder and I find Kallen getting closer, his longer legs able to carry him faster than mine. Maurelle and Olwyn are nowhere to be found.

Breathing heavily, I slow down and finally come to a stop to try to catch my breath. Kallen slows to a walk and approaches me. I expect my savior to be happy I had escaped, but all I find on his hard, gorgeous face is annoyance. "Why did you not use your magic?" he demands, standing in front of me in all his naked glory.

"I-I don't have any magic," I stammer. Has the whole world gone crazy, or am I suddenly in a parallel universe?

"Of course you have magic," he scoffs. "The amulet around your neck is proof of that."

I look down at the necklace Mom had given me. It's no longer glowing, if it really had at all. I look back up at Kallen and as my eyes travel up his body, a flush covers my cheeks. I've never seen anyone my age naked before. "Don't you have clothes?" I ask, casually trying to cover my embarrassment with bravado and failing miserably.

He crosses his arms over his chest. "I am perfectly comfortable being sky clad."

My brows pinch together in confusion. "Sky clad?"

I didn't think it was possible for him to look more annoyed, but he does. "Clad only by air," he explains.

"You could've just said naked, and around here, we prefer clothes," I say, trying to keep my eyes from wandering any lower than his because they keep trying to.

"You were just attacked by Pooka warriors and you are concerned about my state of dress? You are a silly, ignorant girl."

"Hey, what's your problem?" I demand. He may have saved me, but there's no reason for him to be such a jerk about it.

"My problem," he says through a clenched jaw, "is you flaunting yourself about these woods as if you had not a care in this world. Do you not care if the Pooka take you? Are you in league with them?"

"I don't even know who the Pooka are, but I do know that you're a jerk and I'm going home." I turn around again and start walking through the snow, wishing I could effectively stomp my feet so he would know how annoyed I am now.

Kallen catches up to me and grabs my hand. But he releases it quickly with a hiss. I turn to look at him and I see pain in his eyes like I had seen in Maurelle's when she touched me. I look down at my amulet and it's glowing again. "Why does it keep doing that?" I ask stupidly.

Kallen gives me a disgusted look. "Because it is iron bound by amber bound by silver."

I have no idea what that means. "So?" I say, hoping he will explain.

From the look on his face, he's getting more disgusted by the moment. "Did that Witch of a mother of yours not teach you anything?"

"Look, Kallen, or whatever your name is, I don't know who you think you are, but you need to leave my mother out of this. My guess is, you don't know why it's glowing either or you would just tell me. I am so out of here," I say and continue walking.

I can hear Kallen following. After a moment, he says stiffly, "It is a Fairy repellent."

Yup, everyone has gone crazy. Or just I have and I'm imagining all of this. I really hope it's not that. "There's no such thing as Fairies. Or magic," I add for good measure.

"You do not believe in magic?" He actually sounds surprised.

I'm tempted to turn around just to see a look on his face that isn't contemptuous towards me, but I force myself to keep walking. The sooner I get home, the sooner I can get away from these crazy naked people in the woods. Now there's something I never thought I would ever have to say.

"Your mother has not taught you the ways of magic?"

"Nope, because there's no such thing."

"How could she have been so foolish?" he asks.

I whirl around. "Look, I don't care if you insult me, but that's the second time you've said something nasty about my mother and I'm not going to stand for it. Why don't you go back to wherever you came from and leave me alone."

"You are an ungrateful little snit. Do you not care if you are in danger?"

"In danger from crazy people in the woods who seem to think they're Fairies? Yeah, I care about that. Which is why I'm trying to get out of these stupid woods and back home. So, thanks for saving me back there from your twisted little friends, but now you need to go away and leave me alone."

"It is not that simple," he says.

"My dad has a shotgun and he taught me how to use it."

"Cowan weapons do not frighten me."

Exasperated, I stop again and face him. "Will you stop it already with this LARP stuff or whatever it is you're doing? I don't want to play your stupid game. Especially if I'm some kind of target in it!"

"What is a larp?" he asks with what looks like genuine confusion on his face.

I roll my eyes. "Like you don't know it means live action role playing. Good for you, you stay in character very well. Now, why don't you go find your clothes so you don't freeze to death and then find some other girl in the woods to mess with." Was that a smirk he just tried to hide? I'm beginning to think he enjoys how much his nudity bothers me. Jerk.

"If I become too cold I will either return to my raven form or dress myself appropriately."

Oh, yeah. I forgot about all the shape shifting stuff that happened back there. The pounding in my head must have pushed it from my consciousness. It had to have been some kind of trick. Some smoke and mirrors thing or something. "Well, then why don't you change back into your 'raven form' and fly away," I say, as I start walking again. "Your friends are probably missing you."

"They are not my friends and they will be incapacitated for a while." He has fallen into step next to me now and I have to keep my eyes straight ahead so as not to get the full show of his nakedness. A part of me really, really wants to take a peek, though.

"Why, did you throw a paint ball at them and now they have to play dead for a while?" I ask, not even bothering to hide the sarcasm in my voice.

"No, I threw a Fae dart at them which will keep them in a weakened state for the next twenty-four hours."

"Why not just kill them?" I ask facetiously.

"It is not the way of the Sheehogue to kill another," he says as if this is universally understood. He adds almost under his breath, "Unless it is for the greater good."

"I suppose you get to decide what the greater good is?" The sarcasm just keeps dripping from my mouth. I'm hoping he'll get the hint soon that I don't believe a word of what he's saying.

"Yes."

"Well, good for you. You obviously aren't going to kill me or you would have already, so go away."

"I have not decided that yet."

I steal a glance at his face and he looks perfectly serious. Maybe he really is deciding whether or not he's going to kill me. Great, the first boy I meet in years who's my age and he's a naked sociopath. I need to get out of here and if I make it home I will never, ever, take a walk in the woods again. I'm not letting Zac out of my sight, either. Picking up my pace, I'm relieved when I can finally see my house. "Okay, seriously, my parents are not going to be pleased if they see me walking with a naked boy so you really have to go away, like now."

"I am duty bound to protect you from the Pooka. Whether I like it or not," he adds with a sideways glance towards me.

"That doesn't sound reassuring," I remark. Ten more yards and I'm home.

"It was not meant to be. I am not here of my own will and this is not the course of action I would have chosen if it was for me to decide."

"What would you have decided?"

"I believe keeping you alive is too much of a risk."

Great, I think I may need to get Dad's shotgun out. I'm about to make a cutting remark when Kallen falls to his knees with a grimace on his face. "What's wrong with you?"

"It seems your mother is more intelligent than I originally thought. I am not able to move forward or back."

Could he get any stranger? "What? Like you're stuck?"

With a glower he says, "You are very astute."

"Well, how do you get unstuck so you can go away?"

"He can only move if I set him free," Mom says from behind me, scaring the crap out of me. How long had she been watching us?

I turn to face her and I have never seen her so angry. She looks at Kallen and says, "I will never give my daughter to the Pooka King and allow your kind to roam free in our world." Okay, I'm pretty sure I am having an awful nightmare or I just stepped into a bad sci-fi movie. Allow your kind to roam free? Who says stuff like that? My mother, apparently. I think I prefer her fortune cookie one-liners.

Kallen looks up at her with anger flashing in his green eyes. "I am not Pooka, I am Sheehogue. I am here to protect the daughter you have apparently kept ignorant."

"She doesn't need your protection. She has mine," Mom says in a voice that I know means don't mess with her.

Kallen looks really pissed now. Whatever is keeping him from moving forward must be pretty painful if the grimace on his face is any indication. "It is only a matter of time before your trifling Witch magic fails you. You are no match for Pooka warriors."

Looking back and forth between the two of them, I am strangely curious to see who wins this argument but then another thought hits me. I turn to Kallen. "You don't seem surprised that my mom is a ghost."

Tearing his eyes from my mother, he says, "She is not the first Witch spirit I have seen, nor is she the strongest."

Even in pain he can't resist insulting my mother. "You are such a jerk. Mom, can we go inside now?" So I can pinch myself and wake up from this insane dream world I've fallen into. My head is killing me and I really need some ibuprofen.

"Yes," she says not taking her eyes from Kallen. When we are at the back door, she says to him, "I will free you this one time but if you try to cross this threshold again, I will not be so kind. Earth, water and air combine, protect my home, protect what's mine. Allow this foe so evilly charmed, who sought us out, to leave unharmed." Kallen falls backwards into the snow as if pushed by a strong wind. I turn around quickly not wanting to see more of him than I already have, though in a different situation I don't think I'd mind. Great, now I'm having lustful thoughts about the naked sociopath. I steal one more peek at him before I hurry into the house. Out of the corner of my eye as I close the door, I'm sure I see a raven fly away.

CHAPTER 4

"Jim!" my mother calls as soon as we are safe in the house.

My father comes through the wall into the living room. "What is it?" he asks having picked up on the emotion in my mom's voice.

"They're here," she says simply.

My father turns towards me and there's genuine fear on his face. "No, they couldn't have found us. Not so soon after her birthday."

Frustrated that I'm not waking up from this stupid nightmare, I decide to play along. "Who couldn't find me and why would they want to?"

My mom's face is full of guilt. "It's as I explained to you before you left. I should have prevented you from being able to leave the house alone, especially not after your father found those tracks. But, I just couldn't let myself believe they were near. You have to promise not to do it again."

I throw myself down on the couch. This is getting beyond ridiculous now. "You're all crazy," I say, crossing my arms over my chest.

Hovering next to me, Mom says gently, "I'm afraid not. Xandra, you are half Witch and half Fairy, and the Fairies want to take you to the Fae realm so you can open the passage between their world and ours."

Standing up, I glare at her. "Are you listening to yourself? Do you know how insane you sound? Oh, and you just had to wait until my seventeenth birthday to tell me all this. And by a huge coincidence, that's also when the Fairies come looking for me because they want to kidnap me. Well, you know what? I'm sick of this stupid conversation! My head hurts because some crazy 'Fairy' threw me into a tree. I've been forced to talk to insane naked people in the cold snow- covered woods that I hate, and my ghost mother is telling me she's a Witch and oh, by the way, so am I. I don't know why you all are conspiring to make me think I'm the crazy one, but I'm not going to listen to any of it anymore. I'm going to take an ibuprofen and go back to bed, so I can wake up from this nightmare and forget all about this!"

I stomp out of the room and go into the bathroom. I grab the bottle of ibuprofen from the medicine cabinet and swallow two down with a cup of water. I go into my bedroom and slam the door shut. I kick off my boots and shrug out of my jacket, throwing it towards my closet. I climb into bed and pull the covers up over my head to block out the light.

It takes me a while, but I do eventually fall asleep. Probably not the best idea since I might have a concussion from hitting that tree so hard, but I don't care. I need an escape from the madness and sleep is the only one I can think of. I assume Mom and Dad would wake me if they were concerned about my head injury.

When I wake up, it's dark outside and my stomach is growling because I missed lunch. I force myself to get out of bed even though my head is killing me, and I go into the bathroom to splash some cold water on my face. It's still sore. I have scratches on the left side and a nice bruise is starting to form on my cheek. I definitely look like I was hit by a tree.

When I reach the kitchen, Aunt Barb is already cooking dinner. When she looks up from the stew she's stirring, she gasps. "Xandra, are you alright?!" She puts her spoon on the stove, making a huge mess that I'll have to scrub off later. Okay, I'm just a tad bit grumpy.

Aunt Barb puts her hand on my chin and turns my face so she can examine my left cheek. She touches it in various spots which hurts like heck. "Ow!" I complain when she pushes on my cheekbone.

"I don't think it's broken, but you're going to have a nasty bruise. What happened?"

"I got into a fight with a tree and it won." I don't know if Aunt Barb is privy to all the strangeness that occurred earlier. If not, I'm not going to be the one to fill her in. I still don't know if all of it was real or just a huge figment of my imagination. Until proven otherwise, I'm going to go on the theory that the entire morning was the result of a concussion-induced delusion.

"You need to be more careful, if you had been knocked unconscious you could have frozen to death," Aunt Barb says, picking up the spoon from the stove and going back to stirring the stew. So, I guess Mom and Dad haven't filled her in. More proof that it didn't really happen.

"Do you need some help?" I ask her. "I could start the biscuits."

"That would be great." She lifts up a spoonful of stew and tastes it. She grimaces and puts the spoon back in the pot, then adds more bay leaves. It looks like dinner is going to be mostly biscuits for me if the face Aunt Barb makes is any indication of how the stew is going to taste.

"Where's Zac?" I ask, taking the frozen biscuits from the large freezer in the pantry. We keep it as full as possible because we don't know when the next good weather will come so we can make it down the mountain to a grocery store.

"He's in his room playing video games, I believe." She tastes the stew again and seems a little more pleased with the taste.

I take the biscuits out of the package and spread them out on a cookie sheet, and put them in the oven Aunt Barb has already preheated. "Where are Mom and Dad?"

"I'm not sure. I haven't seen them since this morning." That's not unusual since Aunt Barb spends most of the day in her lab.

"Is it dinnertime yet?" Zac asks, coming into the room with his DSi in his hands. He doesn't look up from his game as he plops down into a chair.

"Soon," Aunt Barb says. "Why don't you go wash up."

Zac looks at his hands. "I'm not dirty," he whines.

Aunt Barb gives him a stern look. "When you have the ability to see germs without the use of a microscope, then you can decide if you're dirty or not. Until then, humor me and go wash up."

"Fine," Zac grumbles, as he gets up and heads off to the bathroom. Aunt Barb smiles after him. He is pretty cute as far as little brothers go.

Twenty minutes later, the three of us are seated at the dinner table ready to eat, and still no sign of Mom and Dad yet. That's strange, they never miss dinner. They consider it family time. It's not until halfway through the barely edible stew that they finally show up, and they both look worried. Great.

"Everything okay?" Aunt Barb asks.

Dad steals a glance at me before he answers. "Everything's fine right now," he says. Did he take a lesson from Mom in cryptic speak?

Aunt Barb doesn't look convinced, but she lets it drop. "I'm going to need to head into Denver as soon as the roads clear. I believe I've had a breakthrough. But, I need the equipment in my lab there to confirm my findings."

"I believe the forecast said we're supposed to have a warming spell in a day or two, which should make the roads passable," Dad says. "Maybe Zac could go with you. He's been cooped up here for too long."

My Aunt Barb looks surprised, but Zac gets excited immediately. "Can I go, Aunt Barb? Please!"

Aunt Barb looks at my father, who is trying hard not to let any emotion show on his face. "Um, yes, I suppose so." She turns her attention back to Zac. "I'm not sure how much fun you'll have at my lab, but maybe we can spend the night at my apartment in the city and do a little ice skating or something."

Zac's eyes light up. "Yeah, that would be great!"

I catch my dad mouthing 'thank you' to Aunt Barb and she gives him a slight nod. She obviously knows something is up, but she's going to ask him about in private, not in front of us. I'm always amazed when they do things like that. Like I'm not going to pick up on what they're doing. I'm not blind or an imbecile.

I decide to make some waves. Turning to Aunt Barb, I say, "I would love to go into Denver and do some shopping. Can I go, too?"

Out of the corner of my eye, I see Dad shaking his head no. Hesitantly, Aunt Barb says, "Um, maybe I can take you on the next trip." She's starting to look frazzled. She knows she's in the middle of some sort of family issue, but she's not sure what it is or who's side she should be on.

Mom finally floats into the room and she looks almost haggard. Aunt Barb gives her a questioning look and Mom shakes her head, looking pointedly at Zac. So, I guess we're keeping the craziness from him. That's probably a good idea. No sense in sharing the family psychosis with the eight year old.

Dinner seems to take forever. When Zac has finally scraped his bowl clean and shoved the last of his third biscuit in his mouth, he asks, "Can I be excused?"

"Yes," Mom says with a smile. As soon as he leaves the room, though, the smile disappears. Turning to me, she asks, "Xandra, how are you feeling?"

"My head hurts," I answer around a spoonful of stew.

Mom nods. "I'm sure it does. You should take some more ibuprofen. How are you feeling about everything else?"

I look at her blankly. "You mean the crazy nightmare I had this morning? I'm choosing to ignore it."

"Xandra, honey, it wasn't a nightmare."

Pushing my chair back from the table, I stand up. "I have a lot of studying to do and I need to finish that physics paper Dad assigned me. I'll do dishes later." I leave the room before any of them have a chance to say anything else.

In my room, I boot up my computer. While I'm waiting for everything to load, I walk over to the window to look out at the snowy trees under the full moon. It really is pretty and peaceful here. Well, until today that is.

On a tree about twenty feet from the house, I see a raven sitting on a low branch. It seems to be staring back at me. Narrowing my eyes, I open my bedroom window. "Shoo!" I yell at it, but it just keeps staring at me. I look around my room for something to throw at it. I find an old tennis ball I like to bounce against the wall when I'm really bored. I throw it at the raven, missing it by only a foot, and it still doesn't move. It continues to stare as if daring me to throw something else.

Searching my room again, I decide to throw a dart from my dartboard. The tips are plastic, not metal. So, even if it was to hit the raven, it probably wouldn't hurt him. But he doesn't know that. Taking careful aim, I throw the dart. The raven is forced to fly out of its way or it would have been a perfect bullseye. I smile smugly at him when he finds a perch several branches up.

Satisfied with myself, I close the blinds and sit down in front of my computer. I go to Facebook instead of working on my physics paper and chat with some of my cyber friends, trying to block out the insanity that has become my life. I bet none of them have a raven hanging around outside their bedrooms babysitting them. Especially not one that can turn into a gorgeous, naked Fairy.

At the thought of seeing Kallen naked, a blush creeps into my cheeks. That wasn't exactly how I'd imagined meeting a boy my own age. Despite his rudeness and sociopathic traits, he is still the best looking boy I have ever seen. I've never even seen a movie star or model as hot as he is.

After about an hour, I'm curious enough to see if he's still there. I lift up a slat in the white blinds and peek out. Sure enough, he's still sitting in the tree watching me. Can't he take a hint? I let go of the slat and find my boots and coat I had taken off earlier. When I have them on, I open the window and slide out.

When I'm just a few yards from the tree, I say in a loud whisper, "Go away you stupid bird!" The raven continues to stare at me. I pick up a stick and throw it up into the tree forcing the raven to move again. If ravens could give people dirty looks, this one would be. His annoyance is clear as he flaps his wings and fluffs out his black feathers as he lands on a higher branch. Looking around, I find a bigger stick. I throw this one with perfect aim and I hit his wing before he has time to fly to another branch. I smile smugly at him again and then I look for another stick.

When I turn around, prepared to throw it, the air begins to shimmer and the raven's body begins to elongate and change, until it once again becomes Kallen sitting on the branch. Kallen who is still very much naked. "Good lord, will you please put some clothes on?" I complain.

Kallen gives me an eye roll, but the air around him shimmers again. Now, he is wearing a pair of black pants that fit him snugly from his waist to his feet. He leaves his chest and feet bare. Looking haughty, he asks, "Are you planning to throw things at me all night?"

"Are you planning to stare at me all night?"

Looking indignant, he says, "I am keeping sentry in case Maurelle and Olwyn decide to return."

"Then shouldn't you be watching the woods instead of me? You won't be able to see them if your back is to them," I counter.

"I do not need to see them; I will sense their presence when they are near. I am more concerned that you will do something foolish and cause yourself to be in even more peril than you already are."

"Gee, thanks. Glad to know you think so highly of me."

"I did not say I think highly of you. I think you are rather foolish and naïve."

With a frustrated sigh, I say, "I was being sarcastic."

"And I was being honest."

"Yeah, well, you can keep your honesty to yourself. Why don't you fly off and go look for those other two crazies and leave me alone."

"It makes more sense for me to wait where they are sure to come, than try to find them in a sea of trees. If you had any common sense, you would have figured that out on your own."

"Do you always talk like that?" His lack of contractions is getting on my nerves.

Looking confused, he asks, "Like what?"

"Like you're going to get an E in English if you don't speak as properly as possible."

"I have no idea what you are going on about. My English is nothing less than perfect, as is my grasp on all Cowan languages."

"You speak other languages?"

He eyes me with disdain. "It is important to the Sheehogue that we are able to communicate with all lower life forms. Whereas most Cowan only care to communicate with those in their immediate vicinity."

Now it's my turn to roll my eyes. "Will you stop with this Cowan and lower life form crap?"

"How would you rather I respond to your questions if you will not have me speak the truth?"

"It may be your idea of the truth, but it's not mine. Here on earth, we believe everyone is born equal."

He smirks. "Your history does not uphold your claims. Where do you believe the realm of the Fae to be, if not on this earth?"

"Actually, I don't want to know where the realm of the Fae is, I just want you to go back there."

"And leave you with only a Witch as protection? That would ensure the destruction of the Cowan."

"Again with insulting my mother? She seems to be able to keep you at bay, so what makes you think she can't keep those other two away as well?"

He looks at me as if I'm the stupidest creature on earth. "Fairies are able to attune themselves to the magic of Witches. It is only a matter of time until I am able to shake off the effects of this flimsy shield, and walk right up to your house, as if it is not even here."

Wow, that actually sounds kind of cool. But if he's serious, then safety could be a huge concern. If I choose to believe all this nonsense, that is. So, that must be why Dad wanted Aunt Barb to take Zac down to Denver. He knows the Fairies are eventually going to be able to get to the house. I wonder why he didn't want me to go, too, then.

"Xandra!" my dad says sharply from behind me, as if thinking about him made him appear. I jump, feeling as if I've been caught doing something bad. "You need to come back inside." Looking at Kallen, he adds, "Leave my daughter alone. She wants nothing to do with your kind."

Kallen is looking at Dad with surprise on his face. "A Cowan spirit." Looking back at me, he says, "Your mother's magic may be stronger than I initially believed. It takes a powerful Witch to bind two souls to this plane."

I want to ask him more about it, but Dad is getting impatient. "Xandra, go inside. Right now."

Reluctantly, I do what I'm told. With a last look over my shoulder at Kallen, I walk past my Dad and go back into the house through the door instead of my window that I crawled out of. Dad follows a second later.

"What were you thinking conversing with that monster?" he asks as I take off my coat and boots.

"I don't think he falls under the category of monster, Dad."

"Xandra, don't be smart with me. Your mother and I are very worried that this Fairy has found you. You need to be more careful."

I've had it with them treating me like I should know what the hell is going on, and then expecting blind obedience from me. I yell in frustration, "You know, it probably would have been easier to deal with if I hadn't been hit with everything in one day. I'm so confused; I don't know what to believe. I'm worried about the fact that my parents, who always expect me to tell the truth, have lied to me my entire life! At least that Fairy doesn't seem to have a problem with answering my questions and telling me the truth, even if I don't like what he's saying!"

Dad looks taken aback. "Your mother and I may have kept things from you, but we've never lied to you."

"Really, Dad? Then how come I have black hair and green eyes when the rest of you have blonde hair and blue eyes? You're the one who taught me about genetics. I probably should have figured it out then, but I was a little slow on the uptake because I stupidly assumed that you and Mom had told me the truth about you being my dad." The pained expression that washes over his face stops my tirade and makes me want to shrivel up and die. Yeah, I'm angry and hurt, but I don't need to take it all out on him.

"There's more to being a father than genetics, Xandra. In all the ways that matter, I am your father," he says quietly.

I don't think I could feel any worse. I desperately wish I could take my words back. Sighing in aggravation, I say, "I know, Dad. I'm sorry. I didn't mean it." I really wish I could hug him right now, because words just don't seem enough to make him believe I really, truly am sorry. "You've been the best dad in the world. I didn't mean to imply that you weren't. I'm just scared and confused. But mostly, I'm angry that no one told me any of this stuff before now. Not that I really believe it all, but still, it's a little much to have thrown at me all at once."

Dad smiles sadly. "I know it is, honey, and yes, we should have told you sooner. But, it just never seemed like the right time."

Mom, who must have heard me yelling, floats next to him. "We are sorry for that," she says quietly. "If you must be angry with someone, be angry with me, because I was the one reluctant to tell you."

My anger is beginning to quiet and curiosity is taking its place. "What I don't understand is why this is happening all at once."

"It's because of your seventeenth birthday," my mother explains. I look at her blankly until she continues. "When a Witch is born, his or her powers are bound because a child using magic is a very dangerous thing. The magic of a child is wild and uncontrolled and the risk is too great. That is why each child is bound until the age of seventeen; the year that signals the last year of childhood and the move towards adulthood. Witches believe this is when one's maturity has reached the point of being able to control the magic. This is the reason the Fairies waited so long to come after you. They know this is our custom and they need your Witch magic to be unbound for it to work with your Fairy magic in order to open the Fae realm to ours. For it was Witch magic and Fairy magic that locked it away." She's having trouble meeting my eyes as she continues. "I was stupid and naïve believing that we wouldn't be found. I had no idea the Fairies were just lying in wait for your birthday to come and go."

She looks so miserable that I can't be mad at her anymore. "It's okay, Mom. But what do we do now? He," I say pointing outside towards Kallen, "said it would only be a matter of time before he can walk through the shield, or whatever it is you put up."

Mom nods. "He's correct. I am a very powerful Witch, but even my magic does not have the ability to keep the Fairies away from you forever."

"Then what are we going to do?"

"Your father and I have been discussing it. I had always assumed that I would be able to protect you, but my powers are diminished by being a spirit. We need to come up with a better defense and I'm not sure yet what that is."

"You can let me go," Dad says quietly. "Keeping me here is a drain on your power."

"No!" Mom and I both cry together. "Dad, that can't be the answer." Looking at Mom, I ask, "What about my power? You say I'm half Witch and half Fairy. Doesn't that mean that I should have some sort of abilities to defend us against the Fairies?"

Mom shakes her head. "Your powers are too new. You need to grow into them and learn to use them as they come." Turning to Dad with eyes burning with love, she says, "I will keep you here as long as I am here. I could never let you go." I didn't know until now that it is Mom keeping them both here as ghosts.

The depth of emotion passing between them is both beautiful and uncomfortable to watch. "Isn't there anything you could teach me?" I ask, breaking into their moment.

Mom turns her attention back to me. "I have given you some protection. The bracelet and the amulet you are wearing will provide some defense against the Fairies."

I nod my head. "The amulet glowed when the Fairy touched me. He acted like it burned him."

Mom looks pleased. "Don't take either of them off. The amulet was forged long, long ago by some of the most powerful Witches who ever lived." With a grimace, she adds, "If I had heeded my mother's direction when she told me that, then all of this never would have happened."

I wonder if she really means that. "Then I never would have been born."

Mom looks shamed by my words. She lays her ghostly hand on my cheek, and the coolness of it feels good against my bruise. In a strong voice, she says, "I would not change a thing. I would choose the exact same path as I did before to bring such a beautiful, intelligent and loving daughter into this world." I'm not sure I believe that, but I appreciate her saying it.

"Xandra, will you please go make sure that Zac is getting ready for bed? Your mother and I need to talk."

I look at Dad warily. "You're not going to try to convince her to let you go, are you?"

Mom shakes her head. "You needn't worry. He would never be able to persuade me of that."

Giving them both a skeptical look before I leave the kitchen, I go off in search of Zac. He's in his room and he already has his pajamas on. "Hey, munchkin. It's time for bed."

"Already?" he whines.

"Afraid so. Mom will be in in a little bit to say good night, but I'm going to tuck you in tonight."

"Okay," he says as he climbs in bed. "Are you going to sing to me?"

I smile. "Sure, anything you want." I spend the next twenty minutes with him singing and telling stories until his eyelids start to get heavy. Mom finally comes in and she looks worried. But, she's smiling for Zac's sake. I let her say good night to him and I slip out of his room to go to mine. I grab some pajamas and decide a hot shower might be able to calm my nerves a bit.

I stay in the shower until there's no more hot water. When I can't take the cold anymore, I turn off the water and step out to towel myself off. I pull my pajamas on and wrap my long hair in a towel to help it dry. Back in my room, I open the blinds to see if Kallen is still outside. He is and he's back in his bird form. When he sees me, he tilts his raven head to the side and looks at me strangely. Geez, hasn't he ever seen a person with a towel on her head before? I close the curtain and finish towel drying my hair and then brush it out. When all the snarls are finally out, I lie down and try to read, but my mind keeps wandering making it impossible to concentrate. In frustration, I turn off the light and try to go to sleep.

Mom comes in a little later to check on me and I pretend to be asleep. I just can't bring myself to talk any more today. I already have too much to digest, and I'm afraid that she's just going to keep adding to it. Eventually, my overloaded brain quiets. I'm able to fall into a light sleep, but I have terrible dreams all night about Fairies attacking me.

CHAPTER 5

I wake up early the next morning feeling like I hadn't slept at all. I pull on some jeans and a dark green turtleneck, and then pull another long sleeved gray cardigan over it. The cold makes layering a necessity. Mom and Dad are in the kitchen when I wander in for a bowl of cereal, since it's too early for Aunt Barb or Zac to be up yet.

"Couldn't sleep?" Mom asks as I pull a bowl from the cupboard.

"Not much," I reply. I grab a box of Fruity Pebbles™ from the pantry and get the milk. I'm too tired to speak in anything other than monosyllables. Mom and Dad seem to pick up on that and they leave me to my cereal for a few minutes.

Breaking the silence, Dad peers out the window and says, "I can't believe he's still there. He hasn't moved all night."

"He thinks he's protecting me," I say around a mouth full of fruity goodness.

Dad looks at me with a dumbfounded expression; his translucent mouth hanging open. "He's protecting you?" He looks over at Mom. "I thought the Fairies wanted to take her back to their world?"

"They do," Mom says. Reluctantly, she adds, "But this one says he's not Pooka and that he's here to protect her from them."

"Do you believe him?"

Mom shakes her head. "No."

I swallow the last bite of my cereal. "I do." Both of my parents look at me like I've lost my mind. Yeah, like I'm the one who seems crazy after all the stuff they've said over the last couple of days. Well, maybe I am crazy because I'm starting to believe some of the stuff they said is true.

"Why do you believe him?" Mom asks.

I shrug as I stand up to put my bowl in the sink. "Because he hates what he's doing, but he won't go, even though I keep asking him to. Plus, he saved me from those other Fairies in the woods yesterday."

"What other Fairies? I thought he was the one that pushed you against the tree. You mean there are more of them here?" Dad is so angry now that he almost has some color in his face.

Honestly, for the first time in my life, I don't care if my parents are upset with me. None of this is my fault. "Yup. There were two Pooka warriors who tried to kidnap me yesterday and Kallen stopped them."

"Xandra, you should have told us this yesterday," Mom scolds. "We need to know these things so we can protect you."

"There was so much going on, I guess I forgot." That sounds lame even to me. But it's the truth.

Dad looks at me as if I have the sense of a two year old who just tried to stick her hand in a light socket. "You forgot that you were attacked by two other Fairies?"

Color creeps into my cheeks. "It was a rough day," I mumble, barely loud enough for even me to hear it.

Dad starts to say something, but Mom cuts him off. "Jim, she's right. It was a rough day yesterday and we really didn't give her a chance to tell us what happened. We just assumed that the Fairy who got snared in my protection spell was the one who attacked her." Dad still looks like he wants to say something but he presses his ghost lips into a straight line and doesn't.

A loud cawing from outside saves me from having to say anything else. Mom and Dad both rush to the window to see what the racket is about. "Oh my god," Dad says quietly.

I look out the window myself and see Kallen shed his raven body for his human one. What does it say that I'm already not impressed with it? I think the last couple of days have made me numb to the weird and supernatural. I'm pleased, but I'll admit just a little bit disappointed that as he finishes transforming, he clothes himself in something other than air.

He eyes the three of us through the window and motions towards the woods. I'm pretty sure he's trying to tell us that Maurelle and Olwyn are coming. "Um, Mom, do you know what to do when two Pooka warriors attack?"

Mom turns her attention back to me. "What?"

"I think the other two Fairies are on their way."

For the first time in my life, I see my dad look scared. That's not comforting. At least Mom looks more determined than scared. Looking at me, she says, "Xandra, go to your room and stay there."

"Um, wouldn't it be safer if I stayed by you?" Being alone in my room just doesn't seem all that safe to me. What am I going to do by myself if they make it through Mom's protection field, or whatever it is?

Mom looks like she's going to insist I go to my room, but after a hard stare, she relents. "Fine, but you are to stay behind me, and for no reason are you to step outside. Understood?"

I nod. I'm starting to get a sense of how dangerous all this really is. I don't think I'm going to handle it well at all. Right now, hysteria seems the way to go, but I'll try to keep it under control as long as I can. I barely even notice that my breathing has increased and my hands are shaking. How did my life flip upside down so quickly?

"Jim, please get Barb and Zac. Bring them in here." Dad nods and passes through the wall towards the garage. A minute later, a very confused Aunt Barb joins us in the kitchen and Zac comes trailing in after her. He doesn't look concerned at all, so Dad must not have told him anything.

With a severe look over her shoulder warning us to stay put, Mom floats through the outside wall just as Maurelle and Olwyn come into view. They are still in their animal forms, but Mom seems to be able to tell what they really are as she faces them down. Kallen has climbed down from his perch in the tree and is facing them as well. He's holding a small satchel that I hadn't seen before. He must've had it stashed somewhere because it looks too big for his raven form to carry.

As they near, Maurelle and Olwyn shimmer out of their animal form and I hear Aunt Barb gasp behind me. Zac reacts like an eight year old boy. "Whoa, that's so cool!"

"What the hell are they?" Aunt Barb asks when she finds her voice again.

"Fairies," I tell her and there's more panic in my voice than I would like. She looks as doubtful as I did when I first heard Fairies existed.

We can't hear what anyone is saying, but Maurelle's mouth is twisted into the sneer she wore when she was attacking me. Kallen has turned towards the other two Fairies and he has something clasped in his hand. Olwyn looks at him warily for a second, and then he tries to plaster a confident look on his face. They are obviously ready for Kallen and his Fairy darts this time. I wonder if they have some sort of defensive magic for them.

Aunt Barb apparently can't stand not being able to hear what's going on, so she leans over the sink and pushes the kitchen window open. Dad gives her a worried look but she ignores it. We all lean towards the window, straining to hear what we can.

Olwyn is turned towards Kallen. "If you throw another dart at me, Sheehogue," he says this as if it's a dirty word, "I will kill you where you stand."

Kallen looks unfazed by the threat. "Just because you are the Pooka King's runner does not mean you are more powerful than I am."

Maurelle turns her attention to Kallen instead of my mother. "I am sure King Dagda will be surprised to hear his favorite nia has turned Brathadóir. We will be sure to inform him when we bring him your body."

Kallen's lips twist upwards, but it looks more like a snarl than a smile. "King Dagda may have you on a leash like the dog you are, but he has always known my position on reopening our world to this one. I will not allow it to happen."

Olwyn grins and his teeth look like they didn't quite transform all the way from his mountain lion self. His incisors are long and sharp. "I will take great pleasure in proving you wrong."

As the three Fairies pass their barbs back and forth, my mother is whispering something. Just as Maurelle turns to face her, my mother raises her arms and something explodes from the ground. Small pieces of what look like rusted nails rain down on the Fairies, and everywhere they graze or puncture their skin, large bloody welts appear. Since Maurelle and Olwyn are closer to her, they're hit by most of the shrapnel. Kallen, who must have been paying some attention to my mother, tries to take cover right before the explosion. He is hit by only a couple of stray nails. Taking advantage of the fact that Olwyn and Maurelle have both once again been brought to their knees in pain, he flings what he has in his hand towards both of them. A large explosion of black smoke engulfs them both, and when the smoke clears, they are both gone.

"Wicked!" Zac says loudly from next to me. I had forgotten that he was watching all of this. Probably wasn't the most responsible thing on any of our parts to let him do that. What if something had happened to Mom?

Dad must've had the same thought, because he turns to Zac and says, "Zac, why don't you sit at the table and play with your DSi?"

"Aw, Dad," Zac whines. But, he trudges over to the table as if his feet are covered in lead and makes a big show of sitting down, folding his arms on the table and resting his chin on them. I can't help a small smile for his fine dramatics.

Looking back out the window, I see Kallen sink to his knees as he holds his hand to his side. He must have been hurt worse in the explosion than he originally let on. Ignoring Mom's instructions to stay inside, I open the back door and run out into the snow. I stop about five feet from him. Mom yells at me to get away from him, but I ignore her.

"Kallen, are you alright?"

I can tell from the pained look on his face that he's not, but he turns a stony face towards me and through gritted teeth he says, "I am well enough."

I snort. "Liar."

He narrows his eyes and attempts a contemptuous look at me, but his eyes betray him. Turning back towards Mom, who is almost next to me now, I say, "We have to help him."

Mom shakes her head adamantly. "This could be a ruse, Xandra. They may have planned this so that we let our guard down. We can't do that."

I give her a sour look. "So, we're just supposed to leave him out here to suffer? I don't think he's faking his injuries, and he did make the other Fairies disappear." Looking back at Kallen, I ask, "Where did you send them, anyway?"

"They have been sent back to the passage to the Fae land. If the passage was open, they would have been thrust through it. The best I could do was having them start from the beginning. Their injuries will stall their return." He says all of this through a clenched jaw, as he holds his hands to his side.

A line of blood begins to seep through his fingers and I whirl around towards my mother. "How can we leave him when he's obviously hurt so badly? Haven't you always taught me to be compassionate? Where is your compassion?"

"Xandra..." Mom starts but I cut her off.

"No, I don't want to hear that this could be a trick. He's fought those other two off twice now. I think we need to give him the benefit of the doubt. Please," I add for good measure. I'm not quite sure why I'm fighting to help someone who so obviously dislikes me, but it seems like the right thing to do.

Mom looks torn as she looks back and forth between Kallen and me. Finally, she lets out a long sigh, even though as a ghost she doesn't really breathe. "Earth, water and air combine, protect my home, protect what's mine. This Fairy who claims a friend to be, if there is no trace of treachery, shall pass unharmed through this Witch's charm, but if his heart is not true, his course of action he shall rue."

I don't know what I expected; maybe smoke or shimmering or something to indicate that Kallen would be able to pass through the shield that had stopped him yesterday. But all I get is a big nothing. There is no way to tell if the spell worked or not. I give Mom a questioning look and she gives me a small tight nod. She doesn't look at all pleased, but she makes a gesture with her hand for Kallen to come to the house.

Kallen looks just as unhappy as I approach him and he leans away from me. And he called me an ungrateful snit. I put my hands on my hips. "Do you want help or not? My dad's a doctor, he could tell me what to do."

Kallen scoffs. "When is the last time he treated a Fairy?"

Okay, he does have a point. "I'm sure between him and my mom they can figure something out."

Kallen gives a doubtful look to my mother. I can tell she's just itching to take back her spell that will let him come into the house. His side must be getting worse because his face contorts in pain. He nods once and attempts to rise to his feet, which is obviously difficult. I reach out to help him up.

He yells, "No!" just as my mother says, "Xandra, don't touch him!"

When my hand touches his bare skin, he hisses loudly and falls back to the ground. The amulet around my neck glows brightly, and I realize the mistake I've made. I can't help a Fairy if I'm wearing a Fairy repellant. I start to take it off, but Mom puts a cold hand on mine. "No, go get your Aunt Barb and she can help him. You mustn't remove the amulet."

Reluctantly, I nod and I walk towards the house. Aunt Barb must've heard Mom because she is already pulling her boots on to come outside. She walks through the snow to Kallen and she kneels down next to him. She gingerly puts an arm around his waist and puts his arm that isn't pressed against his injury around her neck. He's about ten inches taller than she is, so it's awkward, but she manages to slowly get him to the house.

"Where?" she asks Mom. Her voice is strained from exertion.

"On the couch."

Aunt Barb helps Kallen to the couch and he slumps down onto the overstuffed cushions. His face is pale and blood is still trickling through his fingers. "Thank you," he says to Aunt Barb. He must be in pain because his voice has lost some of its haughtiness. He didn't even complain about a lowly Cowan helping him.

After a moment, I realize I am staring at him, and when his cold green eyes find mine, I blush and turn to Mom. "What should we do?"

"I need you to go into the kitchen and pull down the plastic box on the top shelf. It has all of my healing herbs and flowers in it."

Mom has healing herbs in the pantry? The things I don't know about my parents just keep adding up. Trying not to feel like I have been betrayed yet again by being kept in the dark, I nod stiffly and go to retrieve the box. I hear Mom ask Aunt Barb to get a pan of warm water, a bowl and some clean towels.

I have to use the step stool in the pantry to get the box down. It's on the very top shelf and pushed all the way to the back behind some old camping supplies. No wonder I never saw it before. I push the lanterns and the metal plates and silverware aside that we haven't used since Dad died. He was a lover of camping. Aunt Barb, not so much.

The box is heavier than I thought it would be. I bring it down the ladder and take off the lid to gaze into it. The plastic box is sectioned off into a bunch of compartments and each one is filled with some sort of plant or herb, and each one is giving off a distinct and strong odor. Individually, they probably smell fine, but all together? It smells a little bit like the compost pile we have in the woods behind the house. I quickly put the lid back on and bring the box into the living room.

Kallen is still on the couch and Dad is examining his wound. Looking up at Mom, he says, "I've never seen anything like it. It's as if a hole was burned straight into his body. It's about three inches deep from what I can tell. What did you throw at them?"

"Iron," Mom says. "It's poison to a Fairy and has the same effect as a hot poker would on a human. As soon as it touches them, the iron begins to burrow inside, damaging tissue, organs and even bones it its path."

"How did you do it?" I ask. Mom's a ghost, how did she throw something at the Fairies?

"I have Witch's bottles buried all around the house. It's just a matter of releasing them."

Kallen looks at Mom with some degree of respect as she says this. Obviously, she had planned ahead for some things, and apparently it's a good defense, but I have no idea what she's talking about. "What's a Witch's bottle?" Kallen doesn't look at me with respect when I ask this. His expression is condescending and annoyed.

"Have you not taught her anything?" he asks Mom.

Mom narrows her eyes and gives him a hard look. For a second or two, I think she's going to hex him or something, but she chooses to ignore him instead. Turning to me, she explains, "A Witch's bottle is similar to a small bomb, but it can only be called forth by the Witch who created it. It's rather simple in design. A glass bottle is filled with whatever you need, in this instance I wanted to ward off Fairies so I filled it with iron nails, and then you add your urine to claim the bottle as your own. Then, you can set it aside or bury it until you need it. You call it forth with a simple incantation."

Okay, the ick factor of this conversation just increased by a million. "You threw iron nails and urine at them?" Gross.

Ignoring the fact that I am thoroughly disgusted, Kallen turns to Mom. "Are you wortcunning?" he asks. Mom nods her translucent head as she looks into the box. She has made her long blonde hair appear to be pulled back in a ponytail so it doesn't fall into her face. I don't know if she had to, or if she is just trying to seem as alive as possible.

"What does wortcunning mean?" I ask. Okay, if Kallen gives me one more of those looks, I'm going to poke him in his side. The injured side. It's not my fault I wasn't taught any of this stuff.

Mom looks up from examining the things in the box. "It means knowledgeable in the use of herbs and flowers for healing and magic."

"Oh." Let's add that to my list of things I'm ignorant about, too.

Mom is all business now. Turning to Aunt Barb, she starts giving her instructions. "Barb, please pour about a cup full of water into the bowl. Then I need you to take a pinch full of angelica, willow, vervain, and mugwort." As she says each name, she points to the compartment containing each. "When you have them all, use the blood stone to pound them and stir them together." She points to a stone that looks exactly like the one on the bracelet she gave me, but bigger. "This should be a strong enough unguent to start the healing process."

Before I ask, she turns to me to explain. "An unguent is a magical healing salve. The herbs and flowers will aid in healing and the blood stone will stop the bleeding." I nod stupidly as if this is all making sense. What happened to good old fashioned medicine? It seems like some stitches and antibiotics would be better than some herbs stirred together by a rock, but I bite my tongue so I don't say that out loud. A quick look at Dad tells me he's doing the same.

Mom is giving more instructions to Aunt Barb. "Pack as much of the salve into the wound as you can and then use one of the towels you got to cover it." Turning to me, she says, "We need to create a saka to begin the healing."

Okay, I think she and Kallen are just making up words now. Exasperated, I say, "You know I don't know what a saka is, or how you create one."

Mom looks properly chastised. "I regret that I did not teach you these things. I just wanted you to remain innocent as long as possible."

"That worked out well," I mumble under my breath. Louder, I say, "What do I need to do?"

"A saka is a joining together of mana." More of the new vocabulary from Mom's library of stuff I didn't need to know until now. Hmm, am I bitter much?

"What's mana?" I see Kallen roll his eyes. I am so tempted to hit him that I have to join my hands together to keep from doing it. He would make a great scapegoat for my building resentment at being kept in the dark.

"Mana is the spiritual power that Witches gather from the earth. Each of us has the ability to hold a certain amount within us. The more powerful we are, the more mana we can hold and the more powerful our magic is. When a large amount of mana is joined together, such as through two Witches binding their mana for the same end, it is called a saka."

"Okay, but I still don't know what to do."

"We need to join hands. Then, I need you to concentrate on the salve, willing it to heal him." I'm just now noticing that Mom refuses to say Kallen's name. I wonder why? Does she hate Fairies that much?

Moving closer to Mom, I hold my hand out and she closes her ghostly hand around it. My hand instantly becomes cold. "Close your eyes and imagine his wound healing."

I do what she tells me. In my mind, I think of my anatomy lessons and imagine the organs and tissue in the location of his injury knitting themselves back together, as if the searing of the iron was occurring backwards. I'm able to push everything else from my mind and the image becomes clearer. I can see the torn cells as they once again become whole and I see them again form muscle and bits of fascia, I see the bones knitting together as if they had never been touched. Finally, the skin becomes whole, pushing the salve from the wound.

I am so engulfed by these images that I don't hear the gasps and murmurs from the others in the room. The cold touch of Mom's hand is gone. She must have dropped my hand because I wasn't doing it right, and it was easier to do it without me. Slowly, I open my eyes, nervous to hear what I was doing wrong now.

Dad and Aunt Barb have backed up so they are now standing about five feet from the couch. I'm not sure what their expressions mean, but they kind of look scared. Kallen and Mom are looking at me as if I just sprouted a second head or something. Putting my arms akimbo, I ask, "What? What did I do wrong?"

"Wrong?" Mom asks. She sounds surprised. "Xandra, you didn't do anything wrong. You did it exactly right."

"Then why are you guys looking at me like I'm a freak?"

Kallen answers first, but he answers with a question which is always so annoying when you want answers. "Has your mother explained to you why the pairing of a Witch and a Fairy is forbidden?"

"I think it's pretty clear that no one has explained much of anything to me," I say as I cross my arms over my chest.

I can't figure out the expression on Kallen's face. The only expressions I've seen so far have been annoyed and more annoyed, but now he seems to be trying to keep his face blank of emotion. "Because it has always been feared that the pairing would unleash a creature who was too powerful to be stopped by either the Witches or the Fae."

I am going to ignore the fact that he just called me a creature. Putting my hands back on my hips, I sigh heavily. "So?"

Slowly, Kallen uses his hand and pulls the towel covered in salve from his wound. Or, I should say, from the area where his wound was a moment ago. He looks pointedly at his skin and then back to me. My brows furrow together in confusion. "Okay, it's gone. Isn't that what was supposed to happen?"

Mom shakes her head. "A healing salve takes time to work. It's a difficult process to reconnect tissue, especially tissue that has been burned, because it becomes a matter of creating new tissue, not just knitting tissue back together. It should have taken days for this type of healing to occur with saka energy being directed towards it several times. The fact that he has been healed completely after one saka is unheard of."

I still don't understand what the big deal is. "Well, you said you were a powerful Witch."

Mom shook her head. "I didn't do this."

Apparently, from the expressions on their faces, I'm being really dense. "Then who did?"

"You."

I look at Kallen's skin and then back to Mom. "Uh uh, no way. I don't know how to do that."

"I channeled your mana and focused it where it needed to go, but once it found its purpose, I had to let go. I'm not a strong enough vessel for the amount of mana you were sending through me."

This is getting ridiculous. There's no way I did it. "So, let me get this straight. Even though I've never done a magical thing in my entire life, suddenly I'm this super Witch who can heal someone instantly? Sorry, I don't buy it."

Mom looks at me with a gentle expression, as if she's about to talk to a small child. "Your powers were bound until after your seventeenth birthday, remember? There was no way to tell how powerful of a Witch you'd be."

I notice Kallen's being conspicuously quiet as my mom tells me these outlandish things. I'm sure he's just dying to negate her theory. "Will you please tell her that I had nothing to do with this?"

He still has the blank expression on his face. "I do not recall much from before the Fae world was closed off from this one, I was quite young. But I do not recall hearing of a Witch who was this powerful. I do know that no one in the Fae realm ever tells stories of the pairing of a Witch and Fairy. As I said before, the product of this union might be able to wield too much power and influence." He isn't looking at me like I have either power or influence.

Regardless, the full meaning of his words seeps into my mind slowly through my exasperation. I'm about to start another tirade about how impossible what they're saying is, when another thought hits me. I turn back to Kallen and give him a hard look. "What do you mean, before the Fae world was closed off? Didn't that happen hundreds of years ago? Or was that another lie?"

His expression still doesn't change. "No, that was not a lie. I have no reason to lie to you about this."

This is too much. "Are you trying to tell me that you're like three hundred years old or something?"

"Three hundred and sixty seven." He says with a straight face.

I've had it. My brain is going to explode. Who knows, maybe that's what they're trying for. I just can't figure out why they all want me to think I'm crazy. Whatever the reason, it's working. "I can't take any more of this insane conversation." Turning on my heel, I stalk out of the room and for the second time in two days, I slam my bedroom door closed behind me.

Mom apparently isn't willing to leave me alone this time. Within seconds, she is coming through my wall. I wish they made locks that could keep ghosts out. I cross my arms over my chest and glare at her. "Mom, I'm not talking about this anymore today."

"Xandra, honey, you can't hide in your room and pretend that none of this is happening. We need to make plans. Your father is already having Aunt Barb and Zac get together what they need for an extended stay in Denver. Now we need to figure out what to do with you."

She says that like I'm the one causing the problem, but I don't pounce on her 'what to do about you' part of what she said because talking about Dad and Aunt Barb reminds me of something. "Why did Dad look scared when Kallen was healed?"

"Because when you were channeling your mana, your hair was blowing like it was in a strong wind and your aura was visible. It's green, by the way, with clouds of orange."

"Great, the colors of my aura clash," I mumble. I can't even get that right. I sigh and sit down on my bed. "Mom, why are all of you doing this to me?"

"Because seventeen years ago, I loved you too much to not bring you into this world. I'm truly sorry that you are now suffering the consequences of my decision."

Ghost mom guilt. It doesn't get any worse than that. And when she puts it that way, I do sound kind of ungrateful about her giving up everything for me. I look up at her. She looks so sad that it seems strange there aren't tears on her cheeks. With another big sigh, I stand back up. "What do you want me to do?"

She reaches out her cold hand and touches my face. "You are a strong and powerful Witch, Xandra, and we need to teach you how to use that power."

I have no idea what that is going to entail, but it does sound better than physics. "Is there going to be homework?"

Mom smiles at me over her shoulder as she glides through the wall. "Some."

I feel a little embarrassed about my dramatic exit a few minutes ago and I can feel my cheeks turning red as I reenter the living room. I have a hard time meeting Kallen's cold green eyes. He hasn't moved from the couch and I'm not sure if that's by his choice, or if Mom threatened him.

After I sit down in the leather recliner that Dad used to love lounging in, Kallen turns his eyes to Mom. "You do not mean for her to remain here, do you?"

Mom looks at him with disdain. "Where else would I teach her?"

"Perhaps it is not her Witch magic that she needs to concentrate on," Kallen challenges. Whoa, is he saying that I have Fairy magic, too?

Mom isn't able to respond because Zac comes into the room with a full blown pout on his face. "Mom, do I have to go with Aunt Barb? I want to stay and see the Fairies."

"There's one right there and you can see they're not that special," I tell him with a simpering smile towards Kallen. Good thing he can't shoot Fairy darts with his eyes or I'd be in trouble.

Mom floats down and bends her legs so they don't go through the floor until she's eye to eye with Zac. "Yes, you have to go with Aunt Barb. You'll be much safer there if the bad Fairies come back."

His little brows come together. "I thought Fairies were nice, like in the stories." I can't help a snort which earns me another glare from Kallen.

"Just like all people aren't nice, neither are all Fairies," Mom explains with a warning look at me not to add my commentary. "It'll just be for a little while. I promise."

"As long as she is here ignoring the fact that her Fairy magic is stronger and more effective, she will not be safe," Kallen says, crossing his arms against his still- bare chest, drawing my attention to his strong arms and serious six pack abs. He looks really good for a three hundred and sixty seven year old. Unfortunately, he catches me checking him out and he looks at me disdainfully. I'm back to wanting to hit him again.

Mom gives him the warning look now, and then brings her attention back to Zac. "Zacchaeus, I need you to go get some of your things together that you want to take with you. Not too much, just the things you really feel you can't live without for a few days." She shoos him out of the room and then she turns to Kallen. "My daughter and I can handle whatever your Fairy friends can dish out."

"Including an exorcism?" Kallen asks snidely.

I jump up and point a finger at him. "Don't you dare threaten my mother!"

Kallen looks unfazed. He completely ignores me and continues to talk to Mom. "I am merely pointing out the course of action Maurelle and Olwyn will take. When they do, your daughter will be left with no one to teach her all the things she should have been taught years ago. She does not know even the most basic magic."

Mom crosses her translucent arms. "What are you suggesting?"

"That she is removed from this," he pauses as he looks about the room with derision, "home, and goes into hiding until her magic is strong enough for her to defend herself. She obviously has the power, she simply needs the control."

"Hello! I'm still in the room. Don't talk about me like I'm not." I really, really dislike him. I don't think he could be a bigger jerk if he tried.

Kallen brings his eyes to rest on me. "I am assuming it is not your decision whether you remain here or go into hiding. Therefore, I am speaking to the person who will make that decision." I was wrong. He could be a bigger jerk.

Mom narrows her eyes at him. "Where, exactly, do you think she should hide and with whom?"

"As my blood is pure, not tainted as is Maurelle's and Olwyn's, I would be able to shield her presence from them. I could even prevent them from sensing her Witch magic, which is how you were so easily located. It was simply a matter of following your particular flavor of magic."

"You can taste magic?" I ask.

Kallen inclines his head and speaks as if he's talking to a small child. "It is simply a figure of speech. I will try to be more precise with my words so you may understand their meanings." That's it. I pick up the throw pillow at the end of the couch and I take its name literally. I throw it at him, hitting him in the head. He glares at me but doesn't throw it back.

I turn to Mom to tell her there is no way I am going anywhere with him, but she is completely still and looks stricken. I don't think she knew Fairies could sense Witch magic. Especially not Witch-specific magic.

"What have I done?" she asks no one in particular.

CHAPTER 6

"Mom, are you okay?" I ask.

When she turns to me, there is real fear in her eyes. "I led them right to you. I should have given up all of my magic when I ran away with you, but I thought if I was far enough away from my parents it would be safe."

"It's okay, Mom. You didn't know." I don't like seeing her so scared. She's supposed to be the one protecting me right now. I look at Kallen out of the corner of my eye and he's watching Mom with self-assured eyes as the reality of the situation sinks in for both of us. Maybe she can't protect me.

"Mom, we can figure something out. Maybe my magic is strong enough to repel them." I don't believe this, but right now, I would say anything to wipe that look of fear off her face.

"Your magic is wild and untamed. You would probably do more harm than good," Kallen says, as he continues to stare at Mom.

"Gee, thanks for the support and encouragement," I say facetiously.

"I was not being…" he began.

"I know, that was my point. Couldn't you at least pretend to be a decent guy for maybe ten minutes or so, or would that ruin your reputation in the Fairy homeland?"

He tears his eyes from Mom to look at me. "Would you have me tell you lies? I could paint a pretty picture where your mother somehow saves the day with her magic that does not begin to compare to that of the Fae. I could tell you that you will all live out the rest of your lives, or afterlives," he says pointedly to Mom, "in these mountains and sunshine and happiness will abound."

I try to ignore his condescension. "Why are you so sure that Mom's magic isn't strong enough?"

"It is as I already explained to you. Fairies have the ability to absorb a Witch's magic, if you will. The more that is absorbed, the less the Fairy is affected by that Witch's magic, until it no longer has any effect whatsoever. Maurelle and Olwyn may be tainted, but they are older than me by several hundred years. They are strong."

"What do you mean by tainted? And don't roll your eyes at me. There's no reason why I should already know the answer."

Kallen almost looks amused. Wow, who would have thought that could happen. "You are correct; the Fae world was closed many years before your time so there is no reason for you to be well informed of our history. Tainted means there is Cowan blood in their lineage. It can be extremely difficult for a full-blooded female Fae to conceive when paired with another full-blooded Fae. Some of the older Fairies chose to look to the Cowans as a way to ensure their Fairy blood was passed on. When the worlds were separated, they brought these children into the Fae realm, but this tainted blood made the children born from these unions weaker. Their magic is not as powerful, nor are their Fairy senses. That is why I can detect Maurelle and Olwyn if they are near, but they cannot detect me unless I show myself to them as I did when they came upon you in the woods."

"So, by tainted you mean they're weaker." Look at me stating the obvious. At least, I thought it was obvious. I'm wrong.

Kallen inclines his head. "No, by tainted I mean they are lesser."

I shake my head in disgust. "You are so full of yourself. I haven't seen anything about you that would make you such a superior being. A jerk Fairy is still just a jerk."

Kallen ignores me and says to Mom, "Will you ignore the truth and leave her here, damning all the Cowan to a world of servitude and pain?"

I roll my eyes. "Really? Dramatic much?" I turn to Mom. "Mom, less than an hour ago, you didn't trust Kallen enough to let him in the house, and now you're going to believe every word he says?" Turning to Kallen, I add, "I seriously regret talking Mom into letting you in. We should have left you out there with the hole in your side. You haven't even said thank you for being healed by us lesser beings."

If I didn't know better, I would almost say he looked a little contrite. "You are correct, my apologies. I thank you both for the kindness of healing me, and your hospitality for allowing me into your home." Wow, was that a glimmer of humility shining out of his dark soul? Nah, couldn't be.

A thought hits me. "If Fairies are so much more powerful than Witches, then how did a Witch better your King and banish him back to your world?"

"He had the help of a powerful Sheehogue. We choose to honor all life forms, even lesser ones. The Pooka treatment of humans was unacceptable."

"Gee, your compassion and sensitivity overwhelms me."

Ignoring me, he continues, "A powerful Sheehogue obtained hair from the tail of King Dagda when he was in his animal form. She used this hair, and hair from the Witch King, to create a binding spell so neither King could use their magic. They were reduced to using their physical strength and endurance. The Witch King was the stronger of the two, and King Dagda was forced to return to the Fae realm embarrassed and angry. You can understand, I am sure, why his return to this realm would be accompanied by death and destruction after being humiliated as he was."

"You know what you haven't explained?" I ask, hating to admit that it's taken me this long to think of this. "If this King Dagda was supposed to be the only one who could come to this realm, how are the three of you here?"

A shadow falls across Kallen's face, but is gone before I can even be sure it was there. "When your mother lay with the Fairy King," he begins, and I am icked out by the thought of Mom 'lying' with someone. Oblivious to my discomfort, he continues. "The exact terms of the blood oath became murky. It became possible for someone in possession of a physical aspect of King Dagda to enter this world. But each time he does this, it weakens his own magic."

"You mean like his hair?" Okay, I think I'm finally catching on to how this stuff works. Kallen inclines his head in acknowledgement of my statement.

If that's the case, then I think maybe we did make a huge mistake by letting Kallen into the house. "Okay, then that explains how Maurelle and Olwyn got here. I'm assuming the King gave them some of his hair or something. But how did you get here? It doesn't seem likely that he gave you anything so you come here to protect me from those two." My voice is accusing and angry, and I take an unconscious step to put myself between him and my mom.

"The same Sheehogue who created the binding spell was able to send me through to this realm without the knowledge of the King."

"How convenient. So this Sheehogue just happened to still have a piece of the King lying around? It seems that the King would have been pretty careful about keeping all of his physical aspects to himself. Wasn't he pissed at the Fairy after he or she bound him like that?"

"He was not pleased, but he had agreed to the binding spell."

"Huh? Why?"

"Because he was confident he would better the Witch King. It was a great blow to his ego that he was not able to do so."

"And even though you hate humans and Witches, you took it upon yourself to come here and save us all?" Right, like I believe that.

"As I said, Maurelle and Olwyn are strong, even with their tainted blood. It had to be a true-blooded Fairy who followed them to this realm. I took the burden upon myself."

I roll my eyes. "You are such a liar."

Finally, Mom finds her voice again. "Xandra, we can't discount what he's saying just because we don't like it." She turns to Kallen. "Would you be willing to take a blood oath?"

"That would, of course, depend on the oath."

"Would you be willing to protect Xandra as you would your own life?" Mom asks him.

Without hesitation, Kallen says, "Yes."

I am so not liking where this conversation is going. "Uh, Mom, what are you thinking?"

She turns to me with sad eyes. "I am thinking that the best way to protect you may be to let someone stronger, someone who knows the ways of the Fae, protect you."

"Mom, no! I've known him for what, a day? I've known you my whole life. I would rather take my chances with you than with someone who so obviously hates me like he does!"

Kallen lifts his brows. "I do not recall telling you that I hated you."

I give him a dirty look. "Maybe not in those words, but it comes through loud and clear in everything else you say." Turning back to Mom, I plead with her. "Please, send him back outside and let's do what you were always planning to do. You protect me."

Mom looks torn. She's having trouble meeting my eyes with hers. "I think his plan may be better. I need to discuss all of this with your father." She disappears through the living room wall, leaving me standing there with my mouth hanging open in shock.

I don't know whose life I've fallen into, but this can't possibly be mine.

CHAPTER 7

Whirling around to Kallen, I stomp towards him. The closer I get, the more he eyes my amulet. Good, I should touch him again just for the satisfaction of removing the smug expression from his face. I'm just inches from him when I stop and stand akimbo. Through gritted teeth, I practically growl at him. "Why are you really here? I don't believe for a second that you care that much about the fate of humans or me."

"On the contrary, I am quite concerned about your fate."

"Right. What's in this for you?"

"The knowledge that I have prevented the destruction of a lesser civilization." He actually says this with a straight face, but the gleam in his eyes tells me that is far from the real reason.

I'm about to say something else when Mom and Dad float through the living room wall. Mom has a determined look on her face and Dad has a worried one. He floats to my side and places his cold hand on my shoulder in a show of support. "Julienne, there has to be another way. We can't put our daughter's life in the hands of a complete stranger." Finally, someone is taking my side.

"Jim, I don't see that we have any other choice. I just don't know enough about the ways of the Fae. The knowledge was not passed down to me. I don't know if that is because it's lost, or if my parents were planning to include that in my education at a later time." I can see some lingering guilt in her eyes about how she left her parents.

Dad looks long and hard at Kallen. Finally, he asks, "What would you do to protect my daughter?"

What? He's seriously considering this, too? "Dad, no! What is wrong with you guys? You were the ones who told me not to talk to strangers, let alone go off with one. Yet here you two are saying I should do both."

Kallen once again ignores my complaints. "I believe it would be best to keep her in the mountains where she could practice her magic without drawing attention to herself. I would be able to shield our path from detection by Maurelle and Olwyn."

"You mean live outside? In the snow?" Yeah, like that's going to happen!

Kallen has that disdainful look on his face again. "You are half Fairy. Living in the open air should come naturally to you."

"Yeah, well, apparently I didn't get that gene. What's your plan – to live in caves and eat berries from trees?"

"If we are lucky enough to find a cave that would provide adequate shelter from precipitation, then yes."

Seriously, this is not my life. I can't really be standing here discussing living in caves with a Fairy. And my parents are on his side. Definitely an alternate reality.

Mom still has that determined look on her face. "Xandra, if he takes a blood oath to protect you and he fails, he will die."

Well, there is that I guess. But that's still not enough for me. "How can you seriously be floating there telling me I'd be safer with Kallen when you can't even say his name?"

Mom looks confused. "What?"

"Not once since we brought him inside have you called him by name. If you trust him so much, then how come you barely look at him or talk to him and you don't use his name?"

"Xandra, that's nonsense. I have no problem calling him by his name."

"See, you did it again! You said him instead of Kallen."

"She will not speak my name because it will lessen the effect of her magic on me," Kallen says from the couch.

I think Mom is just as dumbfounded as I am. "What do you mean?" I ask him.

Kallen looks at me evenly as he explains. "It was probably taught to her when she was very young, as it always was with Witches, that calling a Fairy by name lessens the effect of her magic on that Fairy. She may not even realize she is doing it, as it was probably repeated so often to her when she was young, that it became a natural defense. Apparently some of the old teachings have held true."

Turning back to Mom, I ask, "Is this true?"

Mom gives me a half shrug. "I do seem to have trouble letting his name pass through my lips."

Angry, I whirl back around to Kallen. "So what you're saying is that every time I have said your name, it has lessened my ability to use whatever magic I may have against you?"

I don't miss how he has to keep his lips from curling up on the sides. "That is a reasonable assumption. Your Witch magic may not have such a strong effect upon me now."

"But since my mom hasn't said your name, her magic is still pretty powerful against you, right?"

He inclines his head. "That is correct. For the time being, anyway."

"Good." I march over to the couch and before he understands what I'm going to do, I touch his bare chest with my hand and my amulet flares into a blinding light. He flings himself back so hard, he knocks the couch over and does a somersault as he hits the floor. Scrambling to his feet, he backs away a few more steps and glares at me. "You do realize that is tremendously painful?"

I smile sweetly. "Yup."

"Xandra, that wasn't nice," Mom admonishes, but there isn't any real chastisement in her words. Looking at the way she's now trying to keep a smile off her face, I think she found it as funny as I did.

Trying to look as innocent as possible, I say to Kallen, "I was just trying to determine if your theory was correct." He doesn't say anything; he just picks up the couch as he watches me warily, his anger seething from his pores.

"How long do we have until the other two recover from their injuries?" Mom asks him.

Swinging his eyes to her, he says, "Assuming they brought powerful healing herbs with them from our realm, I would say no more than two or three days at the most. That would give us a decent head start."

"What do you mean, head start? I thought you were powerful enough to keep them from finding us?" I knew it was all lies.

"I can keep them from locating us magically, but they are not stupid. They will assume that I will keep you in these mountains."

"If that's true, then why stay here?" Is he stupid or what?

Once again, he looks at me with condescension. "Where else do you propose you should learn to control your magic? Perhaps in the very large city down the mountain filled with Cowan? What do you think would happen to them if they were caught in your uncontrolled magic?"

"There are other places in the world besides these mountains that don't have very many people around," I huff.

"Travelling to those places would take up valuable time which could be spent on your training," Kallen countered.

I'm really getting tired of the way he has an answer for everything I say. "I don't want to go with you."

He crosses his arms over his chest, covering the red mark that is still there from when I touched him. "I am not overjoyed by having the task of training a headstrong and ignorant young girl, but it seems that fate has ignored both of our desires."

"Xandra," Mom says softly. "I think it's for the best." The look on her face tells me that she's made her decision and there won't be any talking her out of it. Arguing more would be pointless.

"Fine, I guess I'll go pack," I say sullenly as I stomp out of the room. Immature, yes, but it makes me feel better regardless.

In my room, I stop and look around at my things. What do you take when you're going off into the mountains in the middle of winter to learn magic from a jerkwad Fairy? One more failing in my education thus far, I guess.

Going to my closet, I open the sliding doors and dig around on the floor until I find my camping backpack way at the back. The one that I was hoping to never to use again since Dad didn't think it was safe to make us go camping with him if he wasn't corporeal. I set it on my bed and start pulling things out of my drawers. I throw in several pairs of heavy wool socks and a couple of pairs of gray long underwear. Yet again a time in my life where climate wins out over fashion. I am able to fit in three pairs of jeans, three turtlenecks and three heavy sweaters and several pairs of underwear. It's hard getting the zipper closed but I finally manage.

Just as I finish zipping it, Mom and Dad come in my room. "I'm busy packing," I tell them. I'm still not done sulking yet.

"Xandra, you understand we're doing this because we honestly think it's the best thing for you, right?" Mom asks. I look at her and I can tell she really believes that. Dad is trying to look supportive next to her but it's obvious he's still not a hundred percent sure about this plan.

I pick up my backpack that already has my sleeping bag rolled up and attached to the bottom of it and walk past them. Over my shoulder, I say, "Dad, what should I pack besides my clothes?"

"Xandra, can we please talk about this?" Mom asks.

I shake my head. "You've already made the decision so there's nothing to talk about. If you think you're going to get me to believe that this is the right thing to do, you might as well not even try. I think this plan stinks. You're basically giving me to a stranger who for all you know could be a homicidal maniac who's going to kill me as soon as we're out of sight." I open my bedroom door and walk out without glancing back.

I carry my backpack to the kitchen pantry. Using the stepladder, I collect some of the camping gear I had moved aside earlier to get Mom's box of plants. I bring down two sets of metal dishes, a lantern, a flashlight, and a small kerosene cook stove and I put them all in the appropriate side and front pockets of my backpack. When I come out of the pantry, Mom and Dad are standing there looking shell-shocked. They don't say anything and neither do I.

"For what it is worth, I am not a homicidal maniac." Kallen is standing in the doorway of the kitchen leaning on the frame with his arms crossed over his bare chest. His head almost reaches the top of the doorway.

I tilt my head and give him a dirty look. "Like you'd admit it if you were."

He ponders it for a moment and then smiles. "I concede that point to you."

"Great," I mumble. I walk around Mom and Dad to bring my backpack into the living room. Kallen is still in the doorway so I glower at him until he moves, which he eventually does. I don't miss the humor in his eye. Glad he thinks this is so amusing.

Once in the living room, I drop my backpack to the floor and drop into the recliner to wait for whatever horrible thing is going to happen next. Maybe we could round up some poisonous spiders and snakes to put in my sleeping bag just for the fun of it. Okay, I'm not handling this well at all, but who would?

It takes several minutes before my parents float back into the room. This time, Aunt Barb is trailing behind them with a small ceramic bowl and a knife in her hand. Okay, maybe it's not snakes or spiders but it definitely looks as if things are going to get worse. "What are those for?" I ask her.

My mom answers for her. "For the blood oath. You and he will be bound with your lives to the promise that is set forth with your blood. As I said before, if he fails you, he will die."

"I hope it's slow and painful," I murmur under my breath. Apparently, Kallen heard what I said if the dirty look on his face is any indication.

Mom chooses to ignore my comment and she has Aunt Barb set the bowl down on one of the dark wood end tables. Turning to me, she says, "You need to put several drops of your blood in the bowl." She indicates to Aunt Barb that she should give me the knife.

"You want me to cut myself?" I ask in disbelief.

Mom looks at me gently. "Just a few drops are all that is needed. If you just prick your finger with the tip of the knife, it will be enough."

Reluctantly, I take the knife from Aunt Barb. She doesn't look any more thrilled about the idea than I do. I use the knife to jab the tip of my finger before I have time to think about how much it's going to hurt. Immediately, a large drop of blood gathers on my fingertip. "What do I do with it?" I ask Mom.

"Simply let it drip into the bowl. Now, please hand the knife to the Fairy."

I hand Kallen the knife. He takes it and pokes his finger. He then puts his finger in the bowl and mixes his blood with mine. I don't know if that was what he was supposed to do but Mom doesn't say anything so it must be.

Turning to Kallen, Mom says, "You must speak the words of your oath aloud."

Kallen nods once. "I swear by this blood that I will protect Xandra Illuminata Smith's life as I protect my own."

Mom looks pleased. She closes her eyes for a moment and when she reopens them, she begins to speak. "Bound by blood, moon and tide, by this oath you must abide. If by traitorous heart you deceive, or by lack of courage you mislead, count that breath to be your last as the earth will claim its next repast."

Again, I can't help but be disappointed by the lack of anything happening when Mom says a spell. It seems like the blood in the bowl should at least boil or something. How do you know a spell works if you can't see any physical proof of it?

Kallen is the first to speak. “We should go while the sun is still high.” Mom nods in agreement.

Wow, I really have to do this. All the while I was getting my things together, and even when I poked my finger, in the back of my mind was the assurance that my parents would never ever send me out into the mountains with Kallen. But from the pained looks on both of their faces, it seems that is exactly what they plan to do.

Not able to meet my eyes, Mom turns to Aunt Barb. “Will you please help Xandra gather as much food as the two of them can carry?” Aunt Barb’s mouth drops open. “Please?” Mom asks again.

“My old backpack is in the hall closet. They can use that,” Dad says unhappily. Everything about him right now screams that he doesn’t want me to go, but nothing about him says that he’s going to argue the point. Aunt Barb finally nods numbly and goes to search for the backpack to fill it with food.

Again, this can’t possibly be my life.

CHAPTER 8

The goodbyes were long and tearful. Mom and Dad hugged me the best they could without pressing their spirit bodies through mine. Zac was confused and angry and for some reason resentful that he couldn't go with me. For him, this is just one big adventure. What I'd give to be eight again so I could believe that, too.

It's now just past two and Kallen and I have been trudging through the snow for two hours heading farther up the mountain. My feet are freezing and the cold January air has frozen the hairs in my nose. Even my eyeballs are cold. To make things even more enjoyable, Kallen hasn't said a word to me since we left my house.

I can't take the silence any more. "Shouldn't we be going around the mountain instead of up it? We'll be like sitting ducks up at the top." Oh, look, another glower from Kallen. What a surprise.

"We are throwing the runners off our trail. By going up first, we confuse their sense of smell as the thinner air carries less of our scent."

I knew he was lying about being able to shield us from the other Fairies. It's not until Kallen stops abruptly and I narrowly avoid running into him, that I realize I said that out loud. Looking down his nose at me, he says, "One of the first lessons you should learn is that you cannot rely completely on magic. Learning to protect yourself using your wits is just as important. This is assuming you were blessed with any."

Okay, now I'm mad. I push my heavy backpack off my shoulders and let it drop in the snow. I point a finger at his chest coming just millimeters from touching him. He takes a step back but I follow. "I am so sick and tired of you saying mean things about me! You haven't even given yourself a chance to get to know me. You just assume that because I haven't been taught any of this crap that I'm stupid. You need to back off or the only thing you'll be able to teach me is how to get mad enough to shove this amulet down your throat!"

He actually seems speechless for a moment. His mouth opens and closes several times before any words come out. Finally, he says, "I may have been a bit harsh in my judgment based on your ignorance."

"May have been harsh? You've been a giant ass is what you've been." I stand there glaring at him for several moments before he speaks again.

"What is it that you wish me to say?"

"I want you to say you're sorry and that you'll stop being such a jerk since we're apparently going to be spending a lot of time together."

Inclining his head slightly, he says, "I apologize." He doesn't really look like he understands what exactly he's apologizing for, but that's probably the best I'm going to get. I pick my backpack up and try to get it back on my shoulders but it's so heavy that I almost fall down when I try to put my arms through the straps. Aunt Barb had helped me put it on before we left.

"Allow me," Kallen says stiffly and instead of helping me put it on my back, he takes it by the top strap being careful not to come into contact with my hand and starts walking again. He's so tall, the backpack doesn't even touch the snow. I stand there dumbfounded for a moment. It's such a surprise that he's doing something nice for me that I don't know how to react. After a moment, I continue to follow him up the mountain and we slip back into our uncomfortable silence.

As we continue to walk, Kallen occasionally adds a piece of clothing to his ensemble. When we first started out, he was only in the black pants he put on this morning and a pair of what looked like moccasins. They were leather and laced up the front. After a while, he added a long sleeve dark blue shirt and it went on like that until he was wearing a heavy coat, knee high boots, and a hat and gloves just like me. A big part of me is glad that he can be affected by the cold more than he had originally let on. I couldn't help a smug smile every time he added a new piece of winter wear.

By five o'clock, I am exhausted and a little nauseated. It's been a long time since I've been at this altitude and it's taking its effect on me. Even Kallen seems to be slowing down and breathing heavier as we keep ascending. For the past three hours, our conversation has consisted of things like 'watch out for that rock' and 'careful of this branch.' The climb has been significantly better with him carrying my backpack, though, which he still has in his hand.

"Kallen," I call. He's about twenty-five feet ahead of me. He stops and turns around. "I need to take a break. I'm tired and I'm hungry."

He looks like he wants to argue but after a moment he nods. "It looks like there is a place just up ahead where we can stop." I give him my first genuine smile since I met him.

As he promised, about fifty feet ahead there is an overhang with a small concave area underneath it. Kallen drops both backpacks and from the one he started out carrying, he pulls out two small camp stools. They only sit about twelve inches off the ground but it's better than sitting in the snow. I sit down and unzip the part of the backpack with food in it. Out of the corner of my eye I can see Kallen struggling to sit on the small chair. He looks like a giant trying to sit in a chair made for a child. I pull a couple of granola bars out of the backpack and toss him one when he's finally as comfortable as he's going to get. He looks at it like he doesn't know what to do with it.

"I take it you don't have wrappers in your realm?" I ask amused at his confusion.

He looks up at me. "No, our food is prepared more naturally than yours."

"You rip it open like this," I demonstrate by opening my package. He does the same to his and takes a bite and chews. He doesn't seem to hate it since he takes another bite.

"Can I ask you something?" I ask tentatively. We seem to have some sort of truce going on that I don't want to mess up with my ignorance but it's been bugging me.

"Yes."

"What did Maurelle mean when she said that you were the Fairy King's favorite nia and that you had turned Brathadooer?"

Kallen smiles sadly. "The term is Brathadóir, which means traitor. I am the King's nephew and have often been accused of being his favorite regardless of our differing philosophies."

I didn't see that coming. "Does that mean we're cousins if he's my father?"

"Not by blood, simply by hand-fasting." I'm about to ask him what that means but he continues, "That is equivalent to what you call marriage. My mother's sister is the King's Queen. We do not share the same ancestry."

For some reason, that makes me really happy but I don't want to think too much about why, so instead, I ask, "If you've been branded a traitor, what will happen when you go home?"

His face becomes a blank page. "That is of no concern."

My brows come together in consternation. "How can that be of no concern? Surely the King's going to be really pissed at you."

"Perhaps you should eat more. I would like to travel for several more hours this evening." Okay, that wasn't subtle at all. Obviously, it's not something he wants to talk about.

"So, you're not going to answer my question?"

"No."

"How come you get to know everything about me but I don't get to know anything about you?"

He gives me a smile with just a hint of haughtiness in it. "Because I am not the one who needs to learn to use my magic."

He has a point but it's still not fair. I try a different tack. "Are you really three hundred and sixty-seven years old?"

"Yes."

"Are you hand-fasted or whatever you said?" Where did that question come from? A hint of color flows into my cold cheeks. Is that amusement in his eyes over my discomfort?

"No, I am not."

"How come?" The words just keep tumbling out of my mouth of their own volition. "After so many years it seems like you'd find someone you like."

Kallen shrugs. "I am still considered quite young. It is not unusual for someone my age to not have done so. You must also remember there are fewer and fewer full-blooded Fae so it can be difficult to find one who shares my same status."

"So, you'll only marry someone who's a full Fairy?" Why can't I let this drop?

"Yes."

"Sounds like you're going to be pretty lonely when you go back." I wait for him to comment but he doesn't. He stands up and walks out from under the overhang and looks out over the trees. I can't think of anything else to say at the moment so I take his advice and eat another granola bar.

It's full dark and difficult to see by the time Kallen decides we should stop for the night. At some point over the last few hours, he changed direction and we had started heading west instead of up. So at least I'm able to adjust to the constant altitude, but I have never been so physically tired in my life. Dad's camping trips were nothing compared to this.

I'm already missing my family like crazy. I've gotten over a lot of my anger and I've moved on to being glum. I've never spent time any time away from my parents or Zac and now I don't know when, or if, I'll be able to see them again.

I'm not sure if I'm happy or annoyed when Kallen finds a small cave for us to spend the night in. I hadn't been serious about living in caves. "What if some animal is hibernating in there?"

"Then we will be very quiet," Kallen remarks and I'm pretty sure he's laughing at me.

"You're enjoying this awful little adventure, aren't you?"

"I will admit that I do enjoy the outdoors, yes."

"Where do you live when you're in your world?"

He raises his eyebrows, "Remember, this is my world. I am simply from another realm."

"I'm not sure I understand how that works."

"If we successfully keep you from entering my realm, you will never need to understand."

"Did you take lessons from my mother in being vague and cryptic?"

A smile dances around his lips. Maybe the fresh air is good for his disposition. "Your mother kept a lot from you, but I believe she may have had good reason for being vague. Your destiny was not one to be shared with a child."

"So now you think it's okay that she didn't teach me anything about magic?" I ask as I shine my flashlight around the shallow cave looking for any sign of animals. Thankfully, it's empty.

Kallen shakes his head and the smile falls from his face. "No, I do not think she was right in keeping you ignorant of magic. Even if your powers were bound, she could have been teaching you many of the principles of magic that would have been helpful when your unbinding occurred."

A thought trickles into my frozen brain. "You mean things like 'live and let live' and 'fairly take and fairly give'?"

Kallen tilts his head and stares at me curiously. "Yes, that is a basic tenet of white magic. The principle being that when magic is called forth, a drain is put on the earth. Eventually, the magic must be released back so it can return to its natural state or an imbalance occurs. For instance, the clothes I have on. I called upon the magic flowing in the earth to create them but when I no longer need them I will let the magic go and it will return to the earth until it is called once again. Practitioners of black magic do not follow this creed, so they generate imbalances."

"What happens if there's an imbalance?"

"The earth becomes unstable and reacts violently. Imbalances have caused some of the worst natural disasters."

"I thought global warming did that?" Kallen stares blankly at me. "You know, the ozone is deteriorating and our shield from the sun is getting thinner and thinner."

"Most of that I believe is caused by your Cowan-made chemicals, but imbalances can occur both above and below."

I'm impressed he's answering my questions without making me feel like an idiot. "Thank you," I say.

He looks thoroughly confused now. "For what are you thanking me?"

"For not treating my ignorance as stupidity."

He looks down at his hands which are dangling between his knees as he sits on his heels to get a fire going in the little cook stove. I don't think he's going to respond but after a long moment, he says without looking up, "Again, I apologize for my earlier behavior. I am afraid you are not the only one coming to terms with the situation we find ourselves in."

Wow, that was a real apology. I'm stunned into silence. This new and improved Kallen is going to take some getting used to. I watch him start the fire and then I warm my cold hands against its heat.

We sit this way for quite some time before Kallen breaks the silence. "We should rest for the night. We will begin again at sunrise." He removes my sleeping bag from my backpack and begins to unroll it.

An embarrassing thought occurs to me, we only have one sleeping bag. "Um, where are you going to sleep?" I ask as color floods my cheeks and even I can hear the slight panic in my voice.

Kallen looks up from what he's doing and he has a hard expression on his face. "You need not worry; it is not my practice to take the innocence of half-breeds."

Hey, there's the Kallen I know and am growing to hate with a passion. "I wasn't implying that you were."

He raises his eyebrows and snorts in disbelief. Answering my original question, he says, "I will sleep in my raven form. That will make better use of the space we have."

When he finishes with the sleeping bag he stands up. He has to stoop because the cave is not tall enough for him to stand straight. I figure he has to be at least six foot six. I wonder if they have basketball in the Fae realm.

His voice pulls me out of my reverie. "You will want to avert your eyes. I know it offends your sensibilities when I am sky clad."

Great, now he's acting like I'm a prude. Okay, maybe I am a little bit of one. I don't think it's wrong to expect someone not to walk around naked. "Whatever," I grumble as I move to my sleeping bag. I put my back to him as I pull off my boots and my jeans that are damp from the snow. My long underwear is still dry, thank goodness. By the time I crawl into my sleeping bag, he is already a raven. He caws loudly and then flies out of the cave leaving me alone. Maybe it wouldn't have been so bad for him to share my sleeping bag with me. Every little sound is making me think a wild animal is coming back to claim its home and I'll admit that his presence did make me feel safer. It takes a while for me to relax enough to fall asleep.

It feels like only a couple of minutes have passed when I am woken up by a howling sound. I open my eyes fearing a mountain lion has found me, but I can't make out any animal eyes in the small amount of light that is streaming in from the still almost full moon. After a moment, I realize it was the wind that woke me up.

A flutter of wings startles me as a very ruffled raven flies into the cave. The air around it begins to shimmer and I try to inconspicuously avert my eyes until he becomes himself again and has time to put on clothes. Yup, I'm a prude.

"You may look now." Apparently, I wasn't inconspicuous enough.

Kallen is dressed the same as he was before he changed into his raven form and the thought that he's hot, even though he's all bundled up, flows through my mind and I squelch it before it has time to take root. Yeah, me and the three hundred year old Witch and human hater. Like that's going to happen.

"It appears we may be here longer than I anticipated," he says and I can hear the frustration in his voice. "The weather has taken a turn." He sits down near me and leans his back against the rock wall of the cave.

"I can hear that," I say and I snuggle deeper into my sleeping bag. The air temperature in the cave has probably dropped twenty degrees since I fell asleep. Thank goodness my sleeping bag is made for mountain climbing. It was designed for temperatures as cold as twenty below zero.

There is no chance I'm going to be able to go back to sleep with the wind as loud as it is. Neither Kallen nor I say anything as we listen to the storm. A loud crashing noise makes me sit up straight.

"I believe that was a t-tree falling, nothing to worry about," Kallen says through his chattering teeth. He is folded in on himself as much as possible trying to get warm.

"Okay, it's ridiculous that I'm in a nice warm sleeping bag and you're freezing to death." I sit up and unzip my coat until I can reach the cord holding my amulet. Kallen watches warily as I pull it over my head. It's still good to know it scares him at least a little bit. I lay it down on the ground next to me. "Come here."

"I'm fine," he says but a violent chill shakes his body proving his words to be lies.

"Stop being stubborn and come here." I unzip my sleeping bag until it is open enough for him to crawl in. He hesitates for a moment more, but he finally gives in to his need for warmth. His boots magically disappear and he crawls towards me. I lay down on my side to make room for him. As he tries to fit himself in, it becomes apparent that the only way the sleeping bag is going to cover all of his height is if we're spooning. I try to not let my discomfort show as I feel his body pressed full length against mine as he zips the bag back up.

Feeling the need to say something, I state the obvious. "You're cold."

"That was the point of you inviting me inside your warm cocoon." He slips one arm underneath my head and the other rests on my waist. I'm not sure what to do with my arm so I hug it close to my chest trying not to let any more of me touch him than what already was.

His breath tickles as he whispers in my ear, "You have nothing to worry about. Remember, I am only here for your body heat, not your body."

I turn my head so I can see at least part of his face. "Is ten minutes a day the most you're allowed to be a nice guy and the rest of the day you're required to be as big of a jerk as you can be?"

To my surprise, he chuckles. "So it would seem." He shivers and pulls me closer to him and I have to lay my arm on his to accommodate the shift. He took off his gloves before he joined me and his hands are like icicles.

"How long do you think the storm will last?"

I feel him shrug. "It came on quickly so I am hoping it will blow over just as rapidly, but as I am sure you know from living in the mountains that is not always the case."

I groan. "We could be here for days."

"Which is why it was a good idea to follow a less than obvious path. If we are not able to move from here, we are still difficult to find even without magical help."

"Fine, you win. You're smarter than me. Are you happy now?"

He chuckles again. "As I am three hundred and fifty years older than you I certainly hope I have garnered more intelligence than you have in your seventeen years."

I turn so I can see him again, this time shifting my body as well as my head. "If you believe that, then why do you keep getting so annoyed with me when I don't know all of the things you do?"

He sighs. "I am afraid patience is not one of my virtues."

"You have virtues?" I can't help but ask and I'm rewarded with a frown.

"You seem to fling barbs just as readily as I do."

Great, he's right again. I look at him sheepishly. "Sorry, I guess I do."

Some of my hair had fallen across my face when I turned. Kallen lifts his hand and pushes it back. "You have the eyes of a Fairy. Your beauty belies the Witch's blood that flows through your veins."

I'm beginning to get uncomfortable and I don't know how to respond. "Your ten minutes are up for the day, remember?" I whisper.

He smiles. "I believe it is after the midnight hour. I am allowed ten minutes for this new day." His face moves closer to mine and my eyes grow round as saucers because I'm sure he's going to kiss me. But he doesn't. Instead, he whispers in my ear as if he had heard my thoughts, "Do not worry, I do not kiss Witches."

I can't believe I fell for his nice guy routine again. I intentionally elbow him in the stomach as I turn back onto my side and push his arms away from me. As if I even wanted to kiss him. "I'm surprised you're cold, your ego is big enough to use as a blanket." He laughs which makes me even madder.

"Good night, Xandra. Pleasant dreams," he says and I can still feel his shoulders shaking as he laughs at my expense.

CHAPTER 9

At some point I managed to fall asleep. When I wake up I'm happy to see that the storm has passed and the sun is shining. Kallen is still sleeping which surprises me. I thought he would pop awake like a rooster at sunrise.

My shifting to look outside must have woken him because he begins to stir next to me. With sleepy eyes, he yawns and says, "I did not figure you to be an early riser. I assumed you would be lazy and want to sleep until noon."

I give him a sardonic look. "You and your compliments, my heart's all aflutter." He laughs and begins to unzip the sleeping bag to set us free from our confinement.

As I crawl out and begin putting my boots on, I say over my shoulder to him as he stretches as much as the cave will let him, "You know, it's nice to find that you actually have a sense of humor but are you able to laugh at anything besides me?"

He grins at me. "You should feel proud; I have not found anything as amusing as you in a very long time. You are bringing back a part of me I had thought was lost."

"Glad I could help," I grumble as I roll the sleeping bag back up.

It only takes a few minutes to gather everything up and get the backpacks ready to go. The last thing I pick up is my amulet. I hesitate. Is Kallen going to think I don't trust him if I put it on? Ultimately, I decide I don't care because I don't trust him and I slip it over my head. Kallen narrows his eyes but he doesn't say anything. What, he thought I was going to leave it in the cave?

I pick up my backpack to put it on but Kallen takes it from me again. I can't decide if he's being chivalrous or implying that I'm too weak to carry it on my own. His expression is blank at the moment which doesn't help me figure it out. Whatever, he can carry it if he wants. I'm not going to complain.

The sun is bright as it reflects off the snow and I pull my sunglasses out of my jacket pocket and put them on. I notice moments later that sunglasses magically appear on Kallen's face as well. We have another silent morning as we trudge who knows where through the snow.

"Aren't I supposed to be practicing my magic?" I ask testily as I lose my footing because of a snow covered rock and land on my butt for the third time since we left the cave.

Kallen looks back at me and I can see that he's trying not to laugh as he walks back to where I am. I glare at him from where I'm sitting and when he's close enough, I throw a handful of snow at him. That takes him by surprise and he just stares at me for a moment, which gives me time to throw another snowball, hitting him in the head. Oh, good shot me.

Shaking the snow from his hat, he asks, "Are you enjoying yourself?"

I grin up at him. "Yes, at the moment I am. Don't you know how to have fun?"

He narrows his eyes. "In this little game of yours, am I supposed to retaliate in kind?"

"That's how a snowball fight usually goes, yeah."

"Alright then." But he doesn't reach down to pick up any snow and I frown up at him for being such a stick in the mud. Until a huge pile of snow from the tree I'm sitting under falls on my head. I'm almost completely covered in snow and it's Kallen's turn to grin.

I start to get mad at him for cheating by using magic but a different thought hits me. "Can I do that?"

Kallen shrugs. "I do not know," he admits.

"Wow, there's something you don't know? Isn't your head going to explode now from the devastation to your psyche?"

Ignoring me, he says, "Seeing as you are half Fairy it is likely you are able to do some of the things I am. The Cowan Fairies are able to do a lot of things a true- blooded Fairy can, but not all. Your Witch's blood may allow you to do more than they can."

"So a Cowan Fairy wouldn't be able to make the snow fall off the tree?" I ask as I stand up and brush the snow from my pants.

Kallen shakes his head. "No, Cowan Fairies are not able to perform magic by just thinking about what they want to do. They must use incantations or spells similar to how Witches perform their magic."

I frown. "But I saw Maurelle and Olwyn change from their animal forms to human without the need for an incantation or a spell."

He shakes his head again. "What you saw was them thinking the spelled word that had been recited in their incantations which allowed them to assume their animal form and then be released from it."

"So they can't just change form at will like you can."

"Correct."

"So how do we see if I can make snow fall from the trees?"

He looks pointedly at my chest and color washes into my face but I feel stupid when he says, "You will need to remove your amulet for me to help you learn how."

Okay, it was one thing to take it off last night when it was my idea, but taking it off because Kallen tells me to is completely different. I want to say no. I look at the trees and then back to Kallen weighing how great my desire to learn is against keeping my control over him not being able to do anything to me. Finally, I sigh and take it off, putting it in one of the pockets of my backpack.

"I am glad I passed whatever test you were putting me through in your mind before removing your amulet," he says dryly.

I really wish I wasn't too old to stick my tongue out at him because he has this insane ability to make me want to do just that. Instead, I take the high road. "What do I have to do?"

He takes off his gloves as he answers. "We are going to do something similar to what you did with your mother to heal me but instead of joining our mana to make a saka, I am simply going to act as a channel for your mana, or magic as the Fae call it, to flow through so I can direct it to where it needs to go. This is how Fairy children are taught by their parents."

I'm pretty sure he just called me a child but I ignore it. I take off my gloves and I hesitantly put my hand in his when he reaches for me. He raises his eyebrows and looks at me expectantly until I give in and take a firm hold of his hand. "Better," he says. "Now, you need to envision what you want to do as you pull the magic into you. Fairy magic is drawn from the earth the same way that Witch magic is only it is wilder and stronger. It is easy for Fairy magic to go astray if you do not keep a tight hold on it."

That sounds scary. No wonder he wanted me to be away from people while he teaches me. Closing my eyes, I imagine that I can feel a force being drawn into me from the earth. I imagine it filling me as if I was an empty vessel and when I can't hold any more, I imagine that force spreading out to the tree in front of me and shaking the snow from it. I have no idea if it's working or not but I feel strangely at peace and I want the sensation to last forever.

A hand grasps my face roughly under my chin. "Open your eyes, dammit!"

Good lord, does he always have to ruin my happy moments? Slowly, I open my eyes and the feeling of peace that I had plummets down through my body until I feel it seeping back into the earth leaving me feeling incomplete and colder than I was before.

"Ouch," I say as I realize that Kallen is squeezing both my hand and my face. "Stop it," I manage to say despite his tight grip.

"Is it gone?" he asks and I look at him like he's crazy. He sighs heavily. "The magic, has all of it left you?" I nod my head and with relief obvious on his face he lets go of both my hand and my jaw at the same time.

"What is the matter with you?" I demand with my hands on my hips.

He tilts his head and makes a gesture with his arm for me to look around us. I slowly pivot and as I do, I realize that I was successful in making the snow shake down from the tree I had been thinking about. But then I also realize there is no longer snow on any of the trees for as far as I can see. My mouth drops open. Kallen must have lied when he said he wasn't going to join his magic with mine. Annoyed, I turn back towards him. "What did you do that for?"

His face contorts into a look of amazement and not in a good way. "What exactly is it you believe I did?"

"You used your own magic. How are we going to know if mine works if you don't let me try?"

His look of incredulity slowly turns into amusement and he begins to laugh. At me. Again. "Just what's so funny about you not letting me use my own magic?"

He tries to sober up as he shakes his head in wonder. "I did not use a drop of my magic. I had a hard enough time reining in yours. It burned through me so hot and fast that I almost wasn't able to hold onto it."

"Right, like I believe that."

He shrugs. "Believe it or not, neither makes it less true. But we do need to work on your control. You were lost. It took several attempts on my part to bring you back."

I don't understand what he means. "Lost?"

He nods. "As I explained, Fairy magic is different than Witch magic. It is purer, not forced. Because of this, it can create a sense of oneness with the earth. It can be difficult to let it go."

I nod because now I understand what he means. "It was peaceful."

He smiles. "Yes, it can be."

Looking around again, I ask, "Did I really do this?"

"Yes."

"You really didn't use any of your own magic?"

"That is correct."

"Wow."

"Shall we continue on our way?" Yup, there's the buzz kill whose name is Kallen.

"Sure."

We go for a long time before Kallen says anything to break our silence. I swore to myself that I wouldn't end it this time and I don't. He stops abruptly and I almost walk into him. "Here," he says.

"Here?" It's as if he was talking to himself in his head and then said the last part out loud and I'm supposed to know what he's talking about.

"This is where we will set up camp."

I look around. All I see is snow and trees and ridges. Nothing about it is screaming 'stay here!' "Why here?"

"Exactly," he says with a smile.

I shake my head as if it will bring clarity to this conversation. "What?"

He just smiles which is starting to infuriate me now. "Come," he says and I'm tempted to tell him no. Instead I cross my arms over my chest and watch him walk away while I stay put.

Finally noticing that I am not following him after he goes about twenty feet, he turns around and gives me an impatient look. "Come."

"I'm not a dog."

Confusion washes over his face. "I do not recall implying that you are any type of canine."

"Come," I say in a crude imitation of his deep voice. "That's how you call a dog."

Annoyance is now back on his face. "Would you rather I say, oh, please, my Fairy Princess, will you grant me the honor of accompanying me so I may show you to our new abode?"

"You're a jerk."

"So you have said." His annoyance is quickly turning to anger. He turns away from me and continues walking towards wherever it is he thinks we're going to stay. There is no way I am going to sleep out in the open and he's crazy if he thinks I am.

After a moment, he disappears behind some trees and I'm suddenly very alone. I either follow him or try to find my way out of here. Since that's not likely to happen, I guess I have to follow him.

After about ten feet, I see why he stopped. I have no idea how he saw it from the path we were on. Behind a clump of trees and a stony crag, there is a cave that was invisible from where we were. I carefully step over rocks and a narrow ledge and find Kallen already setting down the backpacks and pulling out a lantern. Even in the bright sunshine, the cave is pretty dark.

"How did you notice this?" I ask assuming that he had used his magic.

"Because of the ice," he says not lifting his eyes from the lantern as he sets it down and begins removing some food for lunch.

"What do you mean?"

Finally, he deigns to look up at me. "The ice at the opening of the cave, I caught the sun reflecting off it."

Okay, he just doesn't want to admit that he used magic so I move on. "This is where we're going to stay?"

"Yes."

"For how long?" How long can we possibly live in a cave in the mountains? We only have food rations for about a week not to mention the temperamental weather at this altitude.

He looks up at me again and says dryly, "For as long as it takes."

Having a conversation with him must be what it was like for the followers of Buddha when he was alive. He seems to only be able to answer questions with Zen-like simplicity. "And how long do you think that will be?" I push.

Setting the food he was pulling out down, he stands up and crosses his arms over his chest. I'm impressed he found a cave that he can actually stand up straight in. "How long do you intend to take to learn to control your magic?" he asks.

What a stupid question. "I don't know." He raises his eyebrows and stares at me until understanding sinks in and color floods into my cheeks. If I don't know how long that will take, he can't tell me how long we'll need to stay here. I don't care; he's still being a jerk.

For something to do other than stare back at him, I kneel down in front of my backpack and take my sleeping bag off it. I bring it to the far side of the cave and unroll it. By the time I'm done, Kallen has the small cook stove out and is warming a can of soup. My stomach begins growling as soon as I smell it.

He doesn't say anything while he stirs the soup and when it's hot enough, he pours it into two bowls. He hands me one and we eat in yet another of our uncomfortable silences. I better learn how to control my magic quickly because this is going to drive me insane.

"Why don't you have wings?" I ask trying to fill the silence.

He looks at me as if I'm stupid. Again. "Because I am not in my raven form."

I roll my eyes. "I mean right now when you're not in your raven form. I thought Fairies had wings."

He looks like he wants to say something rude but he doesn't. Instead, he actually answers my question. "That was a legend started a very long time ago because some of the Fae's animal forms are birds, such as mine. When we are not in our animal forms, we do not have wings."

"Oh." I'm actually disappointed. It would be cool to find out he had wings that could pop out of his back any time he wanted. "Do I have an animal form?" I'm not sure I want him to say yes to this. I'm torn on the whole half animal-half person thing.

He nods. "You should, but it will be a while before you discover what yours is. As you begin to use your Fairy magic more, your magic will decide which animal best suits you."

"Okay." I hope it's something that flies. With my luck I'll probably be a fish and when I change when I'm not around water I'll drown on air. I really hate all this magic stuff right now.

After lunch, Kallen brings our bowls to the snow around the cave and uses some to wash them out. Hmm, he's a lot more domestic than I would have guessed. I have a hard time keeping any number of teasing thoughts that cross my mind from popping out of my mouth so we don't get into another verbal sparring match. At least I've learned something over the last couple of days.

"Are you ready?" he asks from behind me.

I turn around to look at him. "Ready for what?"

He looks at me as if I'm dense and says slowly, "To practice."

I would like to practice pushing him over a cliff but I don't say that out loud either. Instead, I simply say, "Yes."

He gestures for me to go ahead of him and we walk out of the cave. I stop after a few feet because I don't know where he wants me. He seems to get that and he walks ahead of me a few more feet and then stops. He has taken off his hat and I can't help but notice that his black hair gleams in the sunlight and is just the right length to run fingers through. Whoa, still not going there so I don't know where that thought came from.

Turning to me, Kallen says, "We need to start with something smaller than you tried before. We don't want you to inadvertently start an avalanche."

For a moment I think he's joking but his face says otherwise. Hey, great way to make me nervous I grumble to myself, but apparently I did say that out loud because his lips are starting to curl up at the sides. Great, he's laughing at me again.

"I had intended to start with the tenets of Witch magic and work up to Fairy magic, but I do not think that is going to be possible. Your Fairy magic seems to want to be dominant so it will be important for you to learn to control it before we try any type of spell or incantation."

My brows knit together as I consider what he said. "How do you know so much about Witch magic?"

"Because the best defense is knowing the tricks of your enemy," he says matter-of-factly.

"So you really do consider Witches your enemy? Where does that leave me then?" I ask defensively.

"It leaves you half Fairy and we are wasting daylight by having this conversation."

I give him a dirty look but I say, "Fine, what do you want me to do?"

Checking to make sure I hadn't put the amulet back on since he last touched me, Kallen offers me his hand. I take off my gloves and shove them into the pocket of my coat and then place my hand firmly in his. He curls his fingers around mine and I swear I feel a tingle up my arm.

He must not have felt anything because he's all business. "I would like you to focus on simply bringing the magic from the earth inside of you. I do not want you to direct it anywhere. I just want you to hold it." I nod and close my eyes.

I imagine that I am an empty vessel again and I can feel the magic trying to fill me up. I let myself revel in the peace it brings. I truly am one with the earth at this moment. I feel as if I am holding the very essence of life inside of me. I don't ever want to let it go and I give myself over to it completely.

The next thing I know, I am lying in the snow and Kallen is on his knees next to me panting. What the hell? He looks like he's going to be sick. When his eyes meet mine I can't read them. He just looks at me stonily as he attempts to catch his breath.

Finding my voice, I ask, "What happened?"

Angry, he says, "You attempted to burn me from the inside out." I sit up and cross my arms and glare at him until he explains further. "You channeled too much magic to hold yourself so you pushed it inside of me and I had to force it out with my own magic. You kept pushing and as our magic worked against each other, my body was caught in the cross fire."

"That must be why my head hurts," I say and he looks at me as if he really couldn't care less that I have a headache. "Should we try again?" I ask and I don't even want to know what thought is going through his mind at the moment. I'm positive it's not at all flattering towards me.

Instead of saying what's on his mind, he sits back in the snow and asks, "How did you know about the give and take of magic?"

It takes me a minute to remember what he's talking about. "Oh, you mean the expression that Mom would always use when she was trying to impress upon my brother and me the importance of sharing."

"Did she use any other clever expressions?"

"Lots of them," I say and he looks at me expectantly so I wrack my brain to think of another one. Any other time I can ramble a bunch of them off but now it takes me a couple of minutes to think of one. "She liked to say 'soft of eye and light of touch - speak ye little, listen much.'"

"A lesson you apparently never learned," he says dryly. I refuse to rise to the bait so he continues. "It appears that your mother may have indeed impressed upon you many of the tenets of Witch magic and in turn, many of these tenets can also be applied to Fairy magic. For instance, soft of eye and light of touch means that magic is delicate, it must be handled carefully. When using it, you must learn to listen to the earth because it will tell you if you are taking too much, or perhaps more correctly said, more than you can control." He says this last part while looking at me pointedly before he continues again. "We need to do this again and you have to try harder to sense how much magic you are channeling. Do not take more than you can handle."

Four hours and seven attempts later, I still don't have a good handle on controlling how much magic I pull from the earth and each time we try, Kallen takes longer and longer before he's willing to try again. I suspect that forcing my magic out of him is even more painful than he had originally implied. It's not even dark yet when he decides we should quit for the night.

He doesn't say much when we settle back into the cave to make our dinner. The food we brought is simple and doesn't require a lot of fuss to prepare. I look over our rations with concern as I consider how poorly I did today.

Right after dinner, Kallen shimmers into his raven form without warning and flies away. Great, alone in a cave in the mountains. Again. Have I mentioned that this cannot possibly be my life? Taking advantage of his abrupt absence, I do a quick sponge bath with some wet wipes I brought and change my clothes. It feels great to be in a new pair of underwear. I keep expecting Kallen to show up just as I'm changing so I move as quickly as I can. I needn't have worried, though, because three hours later he still hasn't shown up. I stay up reading from a book that Mom had given me before I left; her grimoire she called it. It's full of spells and incantations as well as instructions for making amulets and talismans so it holds my attention for a long time but by ten o'clock, I can hardly keep my eyes open any more. I take off my boots and coat and slip into my sleeping bag. I'm able to fall asleep much quicker than I was the night before.

I'm woken up abruptly by Kallen as he straddles my sleeping bag with his knees by my hips and his hands on either side of my head. I just stifle a scream as I realize it's him. "What are you doing? Get off me."

He has the strangest expression on his face. "You are not stronger than I am. You can't be. I am full-blooded Fae and you are a half-breed."

I glare up at him. "So you've said several times. Will you get off me now?"

"I do not know how you are doing it."

"Doing what?"

"There is no one in the realm of Fae who is stronger than I am save the King and my grandmother. That's why I had to come."

"Good for you. You still haven't gotten off me." Good lord, is he drunk or something? Hmm, I wonder if Fairies can get drunk.

Bringing my attention back to him by putting his hand on my jaw as he had this morning, he says, "This power of yours, it must be some kind of trick."

I am beyond angry now. There is no way I'm going to let him get away with this behavior. My amulet is still in my backpack so the only thing I can think to do to get him off me is to use the earth magic I've learned to draw on. I close my eyes and reach down through the earth and I get the now familiar feel of the magic flowing into me. Instead of trying to hold on to it, to control it, I push it outward and I feel it leave me with the force of a tornado.

"No!" Kallen yells and I feel him wrap his arms and legs around me and we roll about five feet from where we were. I open my eyes to tell him to get the hell off me again but I close my mouth as I realize why he had done what he did. Half of the cave has been buried in rock from what looks like a massive rock slide. My eyes find Kallen's and the green of his eyes is so intense they appear to be glowing. I have never, ever, seen someone as angry as he is right now. And he's wrapped completely around me.

"I gave up my world to save you and this is how you repay me," he growls and the next thing I know his lips are on mine. Great, my first kiss and it's a result of anger and control instead of passion. That's par for how things have been going so far this week. Using my hands instead of my magic, I push against him and he immediately ends the kiss. He looks at me as if he can't believe what he had just done.

Well, neither can I. In fact, I'm betting I'm unhappier about it than he is. So much for that not kissing half-breeds crap he gave me last night. "Get off me!" I yell and he scrambles to his feet.

"What the hell is wrong with you?" I continue to yell as I stand up shedding my sleeping bag and back away from him but as a rock near the entrance of the cave shifts I realize it's probably a good idea to keep my voice down. No need to cause another rock slide. "Well?" I ask in a quieter but not less angry voice.

"You almost killed us by using magic you cannot control," he accuses as he stands up as well.

No way am I going to let him shove all the blame towards me. Through a clenched jaw, I whisper harshly as I poke him hard in the chest with my index finger, "I wouldn't have had to do anything if you hadn't attacked me."

He knows this was all his fault. But does he own up to it? No, he turns feather and runs away. Or flies away, actually. Great, he makes the mess and he leaves me to clean it up. Have I mentioned how much I'm growing to hate him? I pull my boots on to protect my feet not only from the cold but also from the small rocks that are now strewn about the cave. It takes me about twenty minutes to round up all of our stuff and arrange it on the side of the cave that isn't full of rocks. I also check the rest of the cave to make sure it's not going to fall down, too. It seems solid so I slip my boots back off, pull my amulet on over my head and crawl back into my sleeping bag but that's only for warmth. There's no way I'm going to be able to fall back to sleep any time soon. Instead, I grab Mom's grimoire and use my flashlight to continue reading.

I must have fallen asleep at some point because I wake up to sunshine and Kallen sitting against the wall of the cave staring at me. When he realizes I'm awake, he stands up abruptly and says, "I will wait outside for you to be ready to practice." Not even an indication that an apology is coming.

I intentionally take my time eating my granola bar, savoring every bite as I imagine him outside in the cold waiting for me. It had started to snow at some point during the night and I hope he'll be covered in it by the time I get out there. I'm disappointed to find that he's not when I finally exit the cave half an hour later.

He doesn't say a thing about how long I took. He simply takes his gloves off, makes them disappear and holds his hand out to me. I reach out and take his hand and he immediately snatches his back with a hiss as a bright light glows from my under my coat. I forgot I had put the amulet back on. Really, I did.

Still, he doesn't say anything. He simply waits for me to take the amulet off and walk back to the cave to put it in my backpack. His face is blank when I come back out. I hold my hand out to him and he takes it without even checking to make sure I really left the amulet in the cave.

Without asking him if he's ready, I close my eyes and draw from the earth. As the rush of being one with the magic consumes me control doesn't enter my mind. It's not until I end up in the snow on my back again that I let it go. Kallen has the dry heaves several feet away from me. Eew.

When I sit up, he realizes that I'm conscious and he stands up. He looks pale but he holds his hand out to me. "Again," is all he says.

I try this time to control it but it's so hard. I've never experienced anything that makes me feel this good. So, of course, I end up on my back in the snow again. This time, Kallen is too.

Immediately, he stands up and holds out his hand. "Again." He's almost as pale as Mom and Dad now and I don't think it's a good idea to try again so soon but I doubt he cares about my opinion.

Taking his hand again, I repeat the process but it's different this time. This time I feel him pushing against my magic, pushing it back into me and he's right, it burns like hell when his magic starts to push through me, too. I let my magic go and drop to my knees still holding Kallen's hand as he pulls his magic back.

He pulls me to my feet. "Again," he says.

I glare at him before closing my eyes and pulling. Before I'm able to bring forth much magic from the earth, his magic is inside of me, burning me and I try to let go of his hand but he won't let me. "Fight," I hear him growl.

Fine, if he's going to be an ass about it. Trying to ignore the pain, I pull. I pull harder than I have any other time. I willingly pull on the earth not to fill myself but to fill both of us. I feel his magic ebb and I keep pushing. I can feel him trying to defend himself as his magic struggles to keep mine from entering him. The point where they meet is like boiling lava and neither of us wants it inside of us. As the pressure builds and the magic has no place to go, it has no choice but to go outwards. I hear a loud explosion and the next thing I know, I'm flying through the air. I feel my head and back hit something hard and then everything goes black.

CHAPTER 10

"Xandra," I hear a deep voice say. I like this voice, it's soothing. "Xandra," it says again and I want to wrap myself up inside of it. But as I become more conscious I start to feel the pain. My head feels like it's going to explode. I open my eyes slowly and the sun burns into them forcing me to close them again.

"Go away," I mumble because now I realize the soothing voice is Kallen's. I'm not even sure if I said it loud enough for him to hear me but I push at him with my hand to make sure he gets the point.

"Xandra, I need to see how badly you are hurt. You hit a tree when our magic threw us apart.

"Like you care," I grumble.

"I care very much, now please, open your eyes."

Wow, he just said please. And it actually sounded like he meant it. Must be my head injury playing tricks on me. "Go away," I say louder and push at him again with my hand but he doesn't budge.

"You must open your eyes. I do not know what healing you will need if you do not let me assess your injuries."

"You hate me, why would you want to heal me?" My voice is getting stronger as I wake up more but I still don't want to open my eyes. The sun hurt my head too much.

"You are stubborn and obnoxious and difficult to manage but I do not hate you."

I crack my eyes a little bit. "With all that sweet talk, you must be a hit with the Fairy women."

I see relief wash over his face. "Your injuries must not be great if you can still disparage me so."

Opening my eyes but still squinting against the sun, I try to push myself to a sitting position but as soon as I try to sit up a sharp pain in my back tells me I should lay back down. I hiss in pain as I go back to my original position. Kallen looks concerned again. "I believe you may have a broken rib."

"Okay, does that mean I can close my eyes again? The sun is really bright."

Was that almost a smile on his face? "Yes, you may close your eyes. I will be right back." As soon as he says it, I slam my eyes closed and I don't care where he's going or what he's doing as long as I don't have to move again anytime soon.

Kallen's back way too quickly for my liking. I feel him kneel down next to me and then he starts pulling up my sweater. My eyes fly open regardless of the brightness of the sun. "What are you doing?"

"I need to put the salve over your wound." He says it matter-of-factly but I don't miss the hint of embarrassment in his eyes as he tugs my shirt up almost to my breasts so he must be telling the truth. I try to lift up to make it easier, but that causes more pain and I really don't need more.

"Lay still," he tells me as he rubs something wet and sticky on my side. "There is the possibility of the rib puncturing your lung if you move the wrong way."

That's enough to make me lie perfectly still. After Kallen gingerly rubs the salve on my skin, he lays his hand over it. I feel heat coming from his hand. Not heat like we were burning each other with earlier. This is a warm, pleasant feeling and my skin begins to tingle under his touch. "That feels good," I can't help from saying.

The corners of his mouth lift up into a small smile. "This is what it feels like when you do it right."

"Oh," is all I can think of to say to that. I close my eyes again and lay still until he lifts his hand.

"How do you feel?" he asks.

I slowly lift from the ground and surprisingly, there's almost no pain. I sit up and tug my shirt down to where it's supposed to be. "It feels good."

Kallen nods once and stands up. "You should rest. Do you need help getting to the cave?"

The look on his face clearly tells me that he hopes my answer is no. So, that's what I say. "No, I can manage." I push myself up off the ground ignoring his outstretched hand and I stand up. I walk slowly back to the cave. The more I move, the more my body tells me how sore it's going to be for a while. I'm relieved when I finally reach my sleeping bag and I can lie down again. Within minutes, I fall asleep.

The sun is still out when I wake up but it's much lower in the sky. Night is just around the corner. I look around the gloomy cave but there's no sign of Kallen. I spend a second wondering what he did all day while I was asleep, but then I realize that I don't really care. I'm relieved he's gone. Between last night and this morning, it seems that our interactions just keep going downhill faster and faster.

My stomach growls letting me know I'm starved since all I had eaten today was the granola bar. I move to where I had put the food last night and a twinge in my back lets me know I'm still not fully healed. But considering all that a doctor would have done for me was tape it and then tell me that it would be painful for a month, a little twinge of pain doesn't seem so bad.

I open a can of chicken noodle soup and light the small cook stove. The heat feels good against my hands as I hold them out towards it. The soup only takes a few minutes to heat up and I pour it into a bowl and bring it back to the sleeping bag so I can wrap myself back up at least up to my waist. I really, really hate the cold. Overall, though, I think I've been a pretty good sport about it since we started on this demented little journey of ours.

When I'm done with my soup I rinse my spoon and bowl out in the snow making sure the snow is white first. This is, after all, the home to many animals. I put the bowl back with the other dishes and crawl back into my sleeping bag. There is no way I'm going to look for Kallen. I'd be perfectly content not to see him again until tomorrow. Next century would be even better.

I try to read from Mom's grimoire but my head starts to hurt again so I set it aside and close my eyes. I plan to just rest for a few minutes but when I open my eyes again, it's full dark outside. I move to stretch my stiff body and I see small beady eyes staring at me. I shriek and move away from it. It takes me a moment in the dark to realize it's just Kallen in his raven form. "You scared the crap out of me, you stupid bird."

Unzipping my sleeping bag and climbing out of it, I start to pull my boots on. The absolute worst part of this trip? It's not the fighting with Kallen, not the lack of decent food or entertainment, no, it's the fact that I have to go outside and pee in the snow. The raven cocks its head as it stares at me and I throw a glove at him making him fly to the other side of the cave. It's bad enough when he stares at me when he's in his human form, excuse me, his Fairy form, but when he's a raven it's just downright spooky. I keep expecting him to say 'nevermore.' As I lace my boots up, I look at him and quote, "For we cannot help agreeing that no living human being, ever yet was blessed with seeing a bird above his chamber door."

Kallen cocks his head to the other side clearly not getting the reference. "Funny," I say as I stand up, "you're about two hundred years older than Edgar Allan Poe yet you've never heard of him. You've missed out on a lot being locked in the Fae world." With that, I step out of the cave to relieve myself somewhere amongst the trees. Yea, loving my life right now.

I was hoping that Kallen would have taken the hint and flown off while I was gone, but he is still in the cave when I come back. Only now, he is back to looking like himself. Great, just what my headache needed.

I don't say anything as I sit down on my sleeping bag and cross my legs underneath me. I pull Mom's grimoire into my lap and use the flashlight to begin reading because the lantern he had lit in my absence isn't bright enough. Kallen has his back to the cave wall with his legs bent up and his arms resting on them. I can feel him staring at me no matter how hard I try to ignore him.

"I am sorry," he says quietly. I'm not sure what exactly he's apologizing for, it could be any number of things that have happened since I met him. I continue to ignore him and read the grimoire until he says, "I am sorry I kissed you."

I slam the book closed and glare at him. "Out of all the things you could have been sorry about, that's what bothers you the most? But of course, you must feel dirty since your full-blooded lips touched those of a half-breed."

He stands up and looking down at me from his immense height, he says, "I am sorry that I kissed you when I was angry. You deserve better than that." Before I can think of anything to say in response, he walks out of the cave into the snow.

Since I had slept most of the day, I'm not in the least bit tired. I read for a while but my mind keeps wandering and I can't concentrate. Since this all started, my mind has been bombarded with so much information that I'm in brain overload. Putting the grimoire aside, I spend a few minutes just staring out at the snow that began falling again a short while ago. So pretty yet so freaking cold. When is this nightmare going to end?

The snow keeps falling and it's getting thicker and thicker until I can't see anything outside of the cave. Despite myself, I'm worried about Kallen being out in this weather. It's really easy to lose your bearings in weather like this in the mountains and end up freezing to death because you can't find your way to shelter. I'm actually relieved when he comes in a few minutes later.

Standing just inside the cave, he shakes the snow from his head and face then he takes off his hat which must be soaked from the wet snow and I can't help being impressed as it just disappears from his hand. When am I going to learn cool stuff like that? Since I haven't been able to gain even the tiniest bit of control over my magic, probably never.

"I do not believe this is going to let up any time soon," he says conversationally as he sits down across from me.

"Me either." Apparently, we're going to just ignore everything that's happened between us. That's fine with me.

"How is your rib?" he asks unzipping his jacket. The black shirt he has on underneath it is tight and highlights his lean muscular chest. Why couldn't he be ugly so I'd stop noticing things like that?

"It's better. It's just the tiniest bit sore."

"I am glad."

Okay, where do we bring this conversation now? What else is there to talk about other than the weather and my rib? "What did you mean when you said you gave up your world?" Whoa, that came out of my mouth before I even knew my brain was thinking it. So much for light meaningless conversation.

Kallen's face becomes stony and he turns away from me to look out at the snow. "I was angry; I said things to try to hurt you."

"Why were you angry?"

Kallen sighs and turns back towards me. "Must we do this?"

"Do what?"

"Analyze everything that has happened. If I give you a blanket apology for all of my behavior since the time we first met, can we simply move forward?"

I study his face for a few minutes but I can't read anything about what he's thinking or feeling. I wish I had a poker face like his. Realizing this conversation isn't going to go anywhere, I say the only thing left to say. "Yes."

He nods and relief washes over his face. "Have you learned much from the grimoire?"

I nod. "Some. I'm still having some trouble with the words. Sometimes it's like reading a different language. I've heard some of them before in songs my mom would sing to me but I still don't know what they mean."

He raises his eyebrows questioningly and says, "Such as?"

I narrow my eyes. "You're not going to make fun of me for not knowing this stuff, right?"

A small, very small, smile touches his lips. "I will be on my very best behavior."

I doubt that but I still ask, "What do deosil and widdershons mean?"

"Deosil means clockwise and widdershons means counterclockwise. You mentioned your mother used to sing songs to you that had these words in them? You could sing one and I could attempt to decipher it for you if it is related to Witchcraft."

I shake my head. "I'm a terrible singer."

Kallen smiles again. "I doubt that. What else do you have to do on a snowy night in a cave in the middle of nowhere?"

I eye him warily trying to determine if he's serious or not. I'm not in the mood for any of his criticism. Okay, why not. The worst he can do is laugh at me and I'm getting used to him doing that. So, I begin to sing:

"Deosil go by the waxen moon - sing and dance the Witch's Rune;
Widdershons go when the Moon doth wane, the wolf will howl by the dread wolf's bane;
When the lady's moon is coming new, kiss your hand to her times two;
When the moon is riding at her peak, then your heart's desire you should seek.
Heed the north wind's mighty gale - lock the door and drop the sail;
When the wind is from the south, love will kiss thee on the mouth;
When the west wind blows o'er thee, the departed spirits will restless be;
Heed ye flower, bush, and tree - by the Lady blessed be."

"The Witches' creed," Kallen remarks. "What an interesting way to teach it to you without telling you that you are a Witch."

"As I look back at all the crazy things Mom said when I was growing up, I'm realizing she did that a lot."

Kallen nods in agreement and then he begins to explain the song. "Deosil means clockwise and when making a ritual circle a Witch should move around in a clockwise direction when the moon is past the new and growing, or waxing, towards a full moon. Widdershons, or counterclockwise is the way to move as the moon wanes toward a new moon."

"What is a ritual circle for?" I wish I didn't have to keep letting him know just how ignorant I am, but on the other hand, that's certainly not from my own doing.

Surprising me, he doesn't have a hint of condescension on his face when he explains. "A ritual circle is drawn by a Witch to keep interfering forces out when he or she is working a particularly complicated spell. It can also be used to hide oneself. The circle becomes a place resting between realms and cannot be crossed from either realm if the Witch is strong enough to hold it."

Okay, I know he's going to mock me for this one. "Are there really werewolves?"

He shakes his head and smiles. "No, but an old wives' tale says that wolves enjoy eating wolfsbane so if you follow the sound of their howling you will find that particular plant. The simple truth is the plant thrives the best in the same environment as wolves do. Wolfsbane is often used as a poison."

"Which is why it is dreaded, okay, I get it. What about kissing your hand to the lady times two?"

"During the new moon, a Witch's power is at its weakest and she must double her efforts if working spells at this time."

I smile. "You're kind of like a walking encyclopedia of Witch knowledge. So when it says when the moon is riding at her peak, then your heart's desire you should seek it means that the best time to perform Witch magic and have it be the most successful is during the full moon."

Kallen nods. "That is correct."

Not wanting to talk about the part of the song that says love will kiss thee on the mouth, I skip over the wind section. I'm pretty sure I understand that part anyway. "Heed ye flower, bush, and tree - by the Lady blessed be means learn what various plants can do and how to use them, right?"

"Correct."

A loud bleating sound from just outside the cave makes me jump and instinctively, I move closer to Kallen. A second later, two horns attached to a large mountain goat can be seen at the mouth of our shallow cave. With a chuckle, Kallen stands up and looks down at me. "It seems we are not the only ones seeking shelter here from the snow. Unless you care to sleep with a goat, I am going to send him on his way."

"Please," I say embarrassed that I was afraid of a goat. I have lived in the mountains my whole life, why am I acting like such a pansy?

After he gets rid of the goat, Kallen and I talk for a bit longer but as the storm picks up outside I can tell he's getting concerned about something. "What's wrong?" I finally ask.

He looks down at his hands for a moment before he answers. With a deep sigh, he looks back up at me. "The rock slide that occurred last night has made for an unstable resting place for the snow. I am concerned the heavy snow that is falling may create a shift of the already loosened rocks."

Translation: I caused a rock slide because I have such poor control over my magic and have made part of the mountain so unstable that we may end up trapped in this cave by either more rocks or an avalanche. Great, now I'm worried, too.

As the snow keeps falling, so does the temperature in the cave until I'm shivering so badly that I have to crawl into my sleeping bag as Kallen and I continue to talk. Unfortunately, he starts shivering soon after. I can tell he's trying not to look as cold as he must be, but in the dim light of the lantern, I can see that his lips are beginning to turn blue.

Reluctantly, I unzip the sleeping bag, which I regret the second the cold air hits my body, and motion for him to join me. He shakes his head. "I fear that I would make you too uncomfortable after my poor behavior last night."

I'm a little worried about that myself but he can't stay out in the cold. I sigh in frustration and annoyance because the longer we argue about this, the colder I will get. "Are you planning to behave poorly again?"

A small smile tugs at his lips and he looks amused. "I am not."

"Then will you please just shut up and get over here? I'm freezing."

He hesitates about a second more and then his boots disappear as he crawls towards me. I shift in the sleeping bag to make room for him and once again, I find myself spooning with a Fairy. I never even dreamed something like this was possible just a few days ago, yet here I am.

Unlike the last time when Kallen put his arms around me, he lays his head on his arm which he has curled up and out of the sleeping bag which means that it can't be zipped all the way up and his other arm is resting on his side. I turn my head so I can see him. "You know, it would be a lot warmer if we could zip the bag all the way up but we can't because you have your arm like that." Not that I want his arms around me, I'm just making a point.

Reluctantly, he shifts again and now one of his arms is under me and the other is resting on my waist and I can zip the bag all the way up. Kallen is still trying hard not to touch me with his body which is nearly impossible in such a confined space. Part of me appreciates his efforts and the other part of me is offended.

We lie like this for a while listening to the wind. I am positive that Kallen has fallen asleep until he says close to my ear, "Who is Edgar Allan Poe?"

I can't help but laugh. Finally, something I know that he doesn't. "He was a writer around a hundred and fifty years ago or so. He wrote a very famous poem about a raven."

"An unflattering poem, I presume, from what you quoted."

"Actually, the disposition of the narrator of the poem is the central theme. The raven simply acts as a catalyst for his continued sorrow about the loss of his love. The raven is only able to say the word 'nevermore' and so the narrator keeps asking it questions that will make him feel worse and worse when the raven says that one word."

"So the raven was not a bad creature?"

"Well, it did supposedly have the eyes of a demon," I tease.

"Impossible," Kallen remarks.

"Really? Why is that?"

"Demon eyes are nothing like a raven's."

I turn my body around so I can look at him. "Are you telling me that demons are real?"

I can barely make out his expression in the dark when he says, "Do not worry; there are no demons here tonight." That definitely did not answer my question.

"Are you teasing me or are demons real?"

Kallen laughs. "Oh, so much to learn yet."

"You're laughing at my expense again."

"I cannot help that you are amusing."

I don't know why I do it, maybe it's because we have gone for hours without arguing or maybe because this whole situation is so outrageous already that nothing could really make it worse. Whatever the reason, I lift my head and find his lips with mine. He doesn't react at all for a long moment; he doesn't push me away or deepen the kiss. He is perfectly still. Embarrassed to no end, I pull back from him and I see the surprise in his eyes. Then his lips are on mine again and this time, it's a real kiss. His lips are soft and gentle as he explores mine. When I feel his tongue tease my lips, I open my mouth to him and it becomes everything a first kiss should be. Kallen shifts his body so I can lay flat and he's on top of me, pressed against me, as he kisses me the way I always imagined it would be. His hand is in my hair, keeping me close as he explores my mouth with his. My arms have weaved around his back and I love the feel of his body on mine.

As quickly as it started, it's over. He pulls back from me. "Dammit," he says under his breath as he shifts again so he is next to me instead of on top of me. His eyes are closed and his breathing is fast and raspy. I lie here wanting to die of embarrassment.

As tears form in my eyes, I turn on my side away from the pained look on his face. "Sorry, I forgot you don't kiss half-breeds," I say softly trying not to let him know how hurt I am.

"Xandra," he says as he puts his hand on my shoulder. "That is not it, I just – I cannot let this happen now."

I don't want his pity or for him to tell me again how I'm not worthy of him. I shake his hand off my shoulder. "I understand," I say and I'm so happy that my voice stays neutral.

He puts his hand back on my shoulder. "No, you do not."

"Sure I do, so let's just forget this ever happened, okay? It's not a big deal."

Kallen sighs but he doesn't say anything else. He also doesn't take his hand off my shoulder. Doing my best to ignore the fact that we are back to a position where we are spooning, I work hard to make my breathing slow and rhythmic as if I'm falling asleep to prevent any further attempts on his part to talk about the single most humiliating moment of my life. I'm more determined than ever now to gain control over my magic. The faster that happens, the sooner I can get the hell away from Kallen.

As I am beginning to nod off for real, I swear I hear him whisper in my ear, "It was a big deal to me." But I'm sure it is just my own mind trying to ease my embarrassment.

CHAPTER 11

I'm awake before the sun comes up. As my brain begins to shake off sleep, it also begins to remember how it completely shut off last night when I decided to kiss Kallen. What was I thinking? Obviously I wasn't. Put aside the fact that he's three hundred and fifty years older than I am, he has also made it abundantly clear that I am so not his type. I wish I had read a spell in Mom's grimoire that could make me invisible because I have no idea how I'm going to face him after last night.

As quietly and carefully as I can, I unzip the sleeping bag so I can crawl out of it. Kallen's arm is around my waist and I pray he doesn't wake up as I slowly move out from under it. It seems to take forever, but finally I'm free of the sleeping bag and him. I zip it back up so the cold doesn't wake him and I put my feet into my boots and lace them up.

The snow is still falling but not nearly as heavily as it was last night. Looking around, it seems as if a good foot of snow fell during the night. Great, more clean snow to pee on. Which I should do as soon as possible, my bladder is telling me.

Zipping my jacket up to the top, I pull my gloves out of my jacket pocket and I step out into the snow. I go about a hundred yards away from the cave around a small bend. I would be horrified if Kallen got to see me pee on top of everything else. A few minutes later, I am zipping my pants back up when I hear a noise, the crunch of snow under heavy feet. I crouch down behind a tree trunk and wait. I expect to see a deer or another goat show it's face but apparently, unless I find a leprechaun really soon, I am never going to have good luck again. Maurelle and Olwyn are about thirty yards down the mountain heading west.

My heart is racing as I duck back behind the tree. My jacket is bright red so I'm sure they're going to look this way and spot me. Why didn't I pick a nice white coat instead? Or maybe white with leaves and branches on it so I could blend into the scenery. I hold my breath and am flooded with relief as they keep walking away from me and the cave.

When I can no longer see them, I hurry back to the cave darting between trees and constantly looking over my shoulder to make sure they aren't following me. By the time I reach the cave, my chest is tight and if I didn't know better, I would swear I am having a heart attack. I duck into the cave and fall to my knees next to Kallen and I shake him awake.

As soon as he opens his eyes and sees the panic on my face, he sits up straight. "What is it?" he demands as he starts unzipping the sleeping bag.

"They're here, they found us!"

Kallen lets out a sigh of what sounds like relief and he rubs his hands over his face. What the hell?? "Aren't you going to do something?" I demand.

Looking back up at me, he says, "I am."

I cross my arms over my chest and glower at him. "What do you mean, you are?"

He scratches his scalp and then shakes his head as if he still isn't completely awake. "I mean, I am already doing something. I put up a circle when we first set up camp here. They can't detect us because we are between realms."

I rock back until I'm sitting on my butt. "Between realms?"

He nods as he yawns. "Yes. As I explained last night, a well-made circle sits between realms and cannot be crossed. It serves as an invisible barrier that cannot be seen and causes anyone around it to just simply ignore it and the area it covers."

"So, we're in a different reality or something?" I remember him explaining this last night but I had thought of it in the abstract, not that it was really possible.

He shakes his head. "No, reality remains constant between realms; the circle just makes certain things invisible to either realm just as it is impossible for one realm to look into the other without a gateway."

I think I'm starting to get it but I'm also still confused. "A mountain goat found us, why can't two Fairies?"

"Animals are not sentient beings, which in some ways makes them above magic. In order to be completely in a separate realm, on some level you have to realize that there is more than one realm. Animals are not capable of that and since the realms basically sit on top of each other, they are able to wander between them without any knowledge of what they are doing. So, that means they can also wander into circles that exist between the two realms."

Okay, I'm not having a heart attack now, I'm having an aneurysm. He is seriously making my head hurt. But after a second, I remember something I read once. "It's kind of like Douglas Adams' SEP field."

Kallen looks at me like I'm crazy so I explain. "Douglas Adams wrote a series of books and in one of them, he described a phenomenon called a Somebody Else's Problem field. An SEP is something we can't see, or our brain doesn't let us see or simply refuses to try to understand, because we think that it's somebody else's problem. Our brains just edits it out, it's like a blind spot. That's basically what the animals do. The concept of different realms is beyond their understanding, so they simply don't worry about it and go about their business not worrying about whether they are in the same realm they were in when they woke up that morning. But we can't do that because on a very basic level we know we have to stay in our own realm."

Now Kallen looks like his head hurts but after he thinks about it for a moment, he says, "Your analogy is convoluted but it seems to vaguely resemble what I explained."

I'm still not sure I understand the whole concept but I move on. "So, how are you holding this circle in place?"

"I am keeping a certain amount of magic within me that is helping me keep the circle."

Okay, I'm impressed. "You've done this since we got here?"

"With one exception, yes."

"What exception?"

He looks a little sheepish and has trouble meeting my eyes. "When I became angry that I was having trouble pushing your magic from me, I released the circle so I could focus more magic towards defending myself."

Oh, I'm super annoyed now. "So, instead of just telling me that you would be stronger if you weren't maintaining a circle, your pride stepped in and you had to show me even though you know I'm not hurting you on purpose. Then I end up with a broken rib. And during that time, if those two Fairies had shown up like they just did, they could have found us." His lips press together in a tight line and he nods his head.

I stand up and back away from him. "You're an ass."

He doesn't say anything in response, he simply stands up and uses his magic to make his boots appear which makes another couple of neurons in my brain fire in the right direction and figure something out. Giving him a cold look, I ask, "If you can make your clothes appear and disappear so easily, why can't you make your own sleeping bag?"

I swear I see the corners of his lips trying to move upward. He suddenly busies himself by starting up the camp stove for breakfast. "Well?" I ask tapping my foot.

Finally, he looks up at me and he's not smiling, but he does have a twinkle in his eye that wasn't there a moment ago. "Magic can protect one from many things but extremely cold temperatures are difficult and one must use a large amount of magic to ensure warmth. Using so much magic on a sleeping bag that could keep me as warm as yours would have affected the integrity of the circle I am holding."

My common sense is screaming at me that he's lying but my brain disagrees because there is no way he would have purposely chosen to sleep with me in my sleeping bag if he had another choice. Because a bigger part of me doesn't want to know which of those two is correct, I let the subject drop. "How do you think they managed to get so close to us if they can't detect us in this circle?"

His lips press into a thin line. "I should not have allowed you to test your magic outside of a circle neither the first time you tried nor yesterday morning. I incorrectly assumed that because Cowan Fairies are weaker, that a Witch Fairy would be as well. But you are not and because your magic is so strong, the runners are probably able to sense it."

"Good thing that pride of yours had to kick in so you could prove you're stronger than me, huh?" The sarcasm is dripping from my mouth almost to the point where I need a napkin.

Kallen stands up, walks over to stand in front of me and looks down his perfectly proportioned nose at me. "That is yet to be determined."

I hate it when he stands next to me. It's like standing next to a giant since he's about a foot taller than me. I have to tilt my head back to look at his face. "So, what, I could be stronger than you?"

He shrugs. "You have not come into your full magic yet. That will take years."

I feel myself pale a little. "You mean my magic could get stronger? But I can't control what I have now, what will I do if there's more of it?"

"Let us just worry about what you have now," he says evenly. Something flashes in his eyes but it's gone before I can figure out what it is.

"Can we practice with them so close?"

"Other than when I intentionally let the circle go, it held while you practiced. We should be fine."

I look at him doubtfully. I don't like that he said should be instead of would be. But, he's the one who's supposed to know what he's doing.

After we eat a small breakfast of sausage and oatmeal, we leave the cave and position ourselves where we have the last couple of days to practice. I continue to look around expecting to see Maurelle or Olwyn jump out from behind a tree. As a matter of fact, I am so worried about it that it breaks my concentration when I'm pulling magic which helps me feel past the feeling of elation and be able to tell how much magic I should be pulling. I stop when I feel it trying to seep out of me and into Kallen.

I hold the magic for several moments and then I let it slip through me back to the earth. I open my eyes and look at Kallen and he's actually almost smiling at me. "How was that?" I ask.

"Much better. Now, do it again."

So much for the fanfare for me finally gaining some control. Closing my eyes, I pull again. This time it's harder to control because the excitement of having done something right in regards to my magic pushes Maurelle and Olwyn out of my mind. As the magic flows through me and outward, though, I am brought back to my senses by having it slammed back towards me. I can feel Kallen's magic keeping mine at bay. For a second, I'm tempted to push against him but my common sense kicks in and I let it seep out of me again.

When I open my eyes, Kallen says, "Good. Now what I would like you to do is fill yourself with only the amount of magic you can hold, and then keep it at that level for as long as you can. This will help you learn to hold magic for long periods of time for things like clothes or keeping up a circle as I am."

I nod and close my eyes again. I pull the magic into me and hold it. It's hard to keep it from seeping out of me either towards Kallen or back towards the earth. Magic apparently doesn't like to be stagnant. It feels like I've been holding it forever when I finally lose my precarious hold on it. Unfortunately, instead of flowing back to the earth, it wants to be set free. I struggle to control it and I feel Kallen pushing against it to help me. But that's not how my magic sees it. As if some basic part of my nature causes it to develop a mind of its own, it becomes defensive and pushes back hard against Kallen. His magic responds by increasing in strength as well until we are back to having an invisible line of molten lava between us trying to set one of us on fire.

"Let go," I hear Kallen say but I can't. I try to push my magic back down but it simply won't go. "Xandra, you must let it go," he says again and his voice sounds strained but still, I can't make my magic retreat.

"I can't," I say between gritted teeth. "It won't let me."

"You control the magic, it does not control you."

Yeah, easy for him to say. "I can't push it out of me, it won't go."

"Xandra, I cannot keep you at bay much longer without letting go of the circle, let it go!" he barks as if he thinks that if he says it nasty enough I will just simply stop. But I can't stop. I have absolutely no control. I feel my magic pushing harder against Kallen and his defenses are starting to fail. The molten lava is starting to creep towards him and the magic he is using begins to grow stronger to keep from being completely destroyed by it.

I feel the exact moment that he lets go of the circle. It's as if the air around us is sucked inwards like a vacuum and then it pushes out in a mushroom cloud of energy seeking to destroy anything in its path. I wrench my hand from Kallen's and cover my ears to try to block out the reverberating sound of atoms exploding around us. I feel Kallen wrapping his body around mine, covering me, as we fall to the ground and are covered with an immense weight that tries to push us into the earth.

It's snow that's covering us. Piles and piles of snow. I begin to panic as a sense of claustrophobia I have never felt before fills me. I push against Kallen so I can get my arms free to start digging but he wraps himself tighter around me. "Stop," he says close to my ear. "Let me remove the snow."

It takes all of my willpower to keep my panic at bay and not move. I hold my breath and wait for Kallen to do as he promised and get us out of here. My panic starts to ebb as I feel the weight of the snow slowly leaving us. When the snow is finally thin enough to press through it, Kallen stands up and brings me with him. As soon as my face surfaces, I start taking deep rasping breaths.

Kallen turns me around and looks me over. "Are you hurt?" he asks as he shakes my shoulders to get my attention. "Xandra, are you hurt?"

My breathing starts to ease and I'm able to shake my head. "No," I gasp between breaths. My eyes are as wide as saucers and my whole body is shaking as I look up at him. "Why couldn't I let it go?"

His face is grim. "I do not know. I have never known of a Fairy who could not willing let his or her magic seep back into the earth at will."

Does that mean he doesn't believe me? "But I couldn't, I swear. I tried but it wouldn't go back!"

He nods his head but his expression doesn't change. "I know you did, I felt it. But I need you to calm down. We need to go."

I have no idea what he's talking about. "Go? Go where?"

"Anywhere but here."

"Why?"

He looks at me with raised brows and then gestures his arm around us. For the first time, I take a good look around us. Snow is everywhere. I don't mean like it was ten minutes ago when it was on tree branches and covered the ground. I mean that it's now covering some small trees completely and I can't even see the path back to the cave. We caused an avalanche, a real live avalanche.

"Xandra," Kallen says drawing my attention back to him. "It is not safe to stay here. We have to go. More snow could fall at any moment."

Dad always tried to prepare us for things like this when we'd go camping but thinking about what to do when you talk about it and thinking about what to do when it actually happens are two very different things. But as Kallen begins to move, my mind starts to clear. He's right; we need to get out of here. We also have to be extremely careful because there may be pockets in the snow that are not as dense as others causing us to fall into them and once again be covered with suffocating snow.

"What about our things?" I ask stupidly because even I can see that there is no possible way we are going to get back into the cave. Everything we brought--food, my sleeping bag, Mom's grimoire-- are all sealed under a small mountain of snow. Trying to get to them would be tantamount to trying to commit suicide.

"I believe we need to be more worried about the runners," Kallen says and I swing my eyes back to him.

"You mean they can track us now?"

He nodded once. "I let go of my circle and even though they are not strong enough to sense me, they may be able to sense you because of your Witch's blood. Also, an avalanche of this size caused by magic is hard to miss."

I hang my head and try really hard not to cry. "I'm sorry."

Kallen puts a finger under my chin and lifts my face until I'm looking at him. "It is not your fault that I keep underestimating your power and overestimating your control over it. I will not make that mistake again. But we will worry about that after we take our leave."

I nod numbly and he takes my hand leading me away from the cave. He steps gingerly in the snow, testing each step before putting all of his weight on any spot, and I am careful to follow exactly in his footsteps. Our progress is slow and each step causes me to become more and more depressed. Was it really less than a week ago that my biggest wish was that I lived near a mall? I'm certainly over that now. Now I would give anything for dry clothes and a roof over my head somewhere far away from Fairies and Witches.

We have walked for about an hour when Kallen stops so abruptly that I walk into him. I hear him mutter an oath under his breath and he turns around pulling me behind him. I'm about to ask what's wrong but the look on his face when he looks down at me tells me this isn't the time to ask him anything. About five minutes later as we stand perfectly still, I see them. A fox and a mountain lion bounding through the snow not caring about the possible after-effects of the avalanche.

As they catch sight of us, they begin to slow and the air shimmers as they transition out of their animal forms as they keep walking towards us. After living with Kallen for the last few days and his quick ability to clothe himself after he shifts, I forgot that when Fairies shift they are very much naked afterward. But this probably isn't the best time to be concerned about their state of dress.

They stop about ten yards from us. Olwyn inclines his head in greeting. "Kallen."

Kallen doesn't say a word which earns him an angry look from Olwyn which he tries to cover as soon as he realizes he is doing it. "We appreciate you keeping the girl safe for us. The King will be pleased."

"I am not concerned with the pleasure of the King," Kallen says evenly.

Maurelle cocks her head and studies him. A small sneer grows on her face. "At first, we assumed that you wanted to deliver the girl to King Dagda yourself to garner more of his esteem, but you really have come to prevent the opening, haven't you?"

"No good could come from opening the Fae realm. It will only cause death and destruction."

Maurelle grins in a way that looks more like a snarl. "But not our death or our destruction. You who has always been so careful to limit your interactions with anyone who is not full Fae should be pleased with what we can do when we come back here in great numbers."

Kallen's face is hard and unyielding. "I find nothing appealing about exerting power over a race that is not able to defend itself against us."

Maurelle laughs wickedly. "Don't tell me this little Witch half-breed has turned you soft. The King will be greatly disappointed in you."

"King Dagda knew the position I was willing to take against his plans before I left the Fae realm." I see a shadow cross over his face as he says this.

Maurelle noticed it, as well. "What position is that? Certainly you do not believe you can keep her safe forever." Kallen doesn't answer. He just stares back at Maurelle with no emotion whatsoever on his face.

Maurelle's eyes flash in anger. "But you do not plan to keep her safe forever, do you?" I have no idea what she means by that. Kallen swore on his life that he will protect me for as long as he is able.

Still, he doesn't say anything. I look at Olwyn and he seems just as confused by this conversation as I am. What is it that he and I aren't getting?

"You are determined to keep the Fae world sealed at any cost." Maurelle says as if she finally understands that Kallen is serious. Shifting her eyes to me, she asks him, "Have you explained this to her yet?"

Kallen doesn't respond, so I do. "Explain what to me?"

Maurelle laughs the wickedest laugh I have ever heard as she addresses Kallen instead of me. "Oh, this is precious. She is in the hands of the lion and she does not even realize it." Shifting her eyes back to me, she says, "You have chosen the lion over the lambs. Olwyn and I are simply messengers on an errand to retrieve something essential for our people. We mean you no harm; we will simply transport you to the gate between realms as we were instructed by our King."

"Do not believe her lies," Kallen says between tight lips.

"Oh, but what I am telling her is not a lie. No harm will come to her while she is with us but you cannot say the same, can you, Kallen?"

I expect Kallen to refute what she's saying but he doesn't. "Kallen, what's she talking about?" His eyes are burning daggers at Maurelle and he doesn't answer my question.

"Kallen," I say again. "Tell me what she's talking about."

Maurelle laughs. "Oh, but if he tells you, you will not be so willing to stay with him."

Ignoring her, I pull on Kallen's arms until he's looking at me. "Tell me what she's talking about," I demand but his eyes shift away from mine and he still doesn't say anything. Fine, then I guess I'll ask Maurelle.

"Since Kallen won't, why don't you spell it out for me. What am I missing here?"

"Oh, how I do love to spoil Kallen's plans. Don't you understand the only way for you to never open the realms is for there to no longer be a you?" She watches me with pure, evil enjoyment as her words sink into my thick head. "Ah, you understand that now, I see." Turning to Kallen, she says, "What I do not understand is why you have kept her alive this long."

What she's saying has to be a lie. Kallen swore with his life. If I die because he doesn't protect me then he dies. "I don't believe it," I say to Maurelle.

"Then ask him yourself."

Fine, I will. I stand in front of Kallen until he finally looks down at me instead of glowering at Maurelle. "Did you come here to kill me?"

He takes a long time before he answers. "I came to determine how big of a threat you are to both realms," he says evenly.

"And if you determine that I am too big of a threat, you will kill me." Please say no, please, I plead with my eyes.

"That was what I intended."

An anger like I have never felt before seethes through me. He didn't come here to teach me to protect myself. He came here on a search, learn and destroy mission.

"It is not too late for you to come with us," Maurelle says in what I imagine she thinks is a convincing voice. "We can protect you from Kallen's plan."

That I know is a lie. I believe what Kallen said about Cowan Fairies being weaker than him because of how surprised he's been at the amount of power I can pull. The thought sinks in. The amount of power I can pull. Right now. I can get away from all three Fairies. So that's what I do. I pull and I pull and I feel the magic flood me, fill me, and then overflow from me.

Kallen knows what I'm doing. He can sense it and I see honest to god fear on his face. Maurelle and Olwyn must not be able to feel my pull because they are still looking at me smugly as if I'm going to tell Kallen to go to hell and go off with them. Yeah, not in this lifetime – however short it may end up being.

My rage is fueling my power. It's not just spilling over, it's on its own search and destroy mission. I pull harder and I feel it lashing out. Maurelle and Olwyn must be feeling its effects because neither are smiling now. As they take in the fear on Kallen's face, they start to show some of their own.

"Xandra, don't," Kallen pleads. "I do not want to hurt you, I swear to you."

More lies. They just keep piling one on top of the other and they are beginning to become a mountain taller than the one we are standing on. I pull more and the magic is answering me gladly. I push it out and I see Maurelle and Olwyn fall to their knees in pain and confusion. I can feel their paltry magic and Kallen's right, they are weak. But he's not, so I direct more magic towards him and I feel him fighting me, trying to push it away but I'm determined to force him to let me go. I feel as if I could fill this forest with my magic. I can see Maurelle and Olwyn on the ground now as my magic burns through them. I remember the feel of Kallen's magic doing that to me. I remember how much it hurts but I need to show them that I will not go willingly with any of them.

The strangest thing happens. Kallen lets go of his magic. He lets it flow through him back to the earth allowing my magic to burn through him as it is Maurelle and Olwyn. Why is he doing that? He could have kept me at bay longer if not indefinitely.

He's gasping from the pain now but he looks at me with determined eyes. "I am not going to hurt you," he says.

"Stop lying to me!" I scream at him.

"I have never lied to you."

I try to hold my magic steady as I respond. "Really? Because I don't remember having a conversation with you about you coming here to kill me." He closes his eyes against the pain. Why is he letting me do this?

"The first day we met, in the woods near your home, I told you that a Sheehogue Fairy will only take a life if it is for the greater good. You said I was not going to kill you because I had not already. I told you I had not decided that yet."

Son of a bitch, he did say that. It's not his fault that I didn't take him seriously. "But you took a blood oath to protect me as you would your own life. If I die, you die."

He's on his hands and knees and he struggles to lift his face up to look at me. "Yes."

The magic flows out of me so fast that I fall to my knees as well. "No freaking way. You are willing to die if that's what it takes to keep me from opening the gateway."

He's taking deeper breaths now as his body is no longer wracked with pain. "Yes," he repeats.

"But if you decide that I'm not going to open the gate and I'm powerful enough to keep anyone from making me do it, then you'll go back to the Fae realm and leave me alone."

"No."

What the hell? "What do you mean no? Why wouldn't you leave me alone if no one can make me do it?"

"I did not say that I would not leave you alone. I meant I will not be returning to my realm."

"But you hate humans and Witches. Why wouldn't you go back?"

"Because I cannot."

Now I understand. "Because you're a traitor now for coming through trying to stop me."

He stands up brushing the snow off him and looks towards Maurelle and Olwyn who passed out at some point. "No."

I am so frustrated that I scream at him. "Stop it! Stop talking in riddles and just tell me what you're talking about for once for god's sake."

Focusing his eyes back on me, he says, "I cannot go back to my realm unless you create a way back." Pointing at the other two Fairies, he says, "Neither can they."

My mouth drops open. "You can't go back?"

"No."

"Then why did you come if you knew you had to either stay here or die with me?"

He takes his eyes off mine but not before I see the sorrow there for the loss of his world. "Because someone very important to me asked me to do it."

"Who would ask you to do something so awful?"

"My grandmother asked me to make a sacrifice for the greater good and I agreed."

I shake my head. "You're an idiot."

He laughs but not with humor. "You do keep pointing that out."

Looking at Maurelle and Olwyn who have not wakened yet, I say, "So as long as they are alive, they will keep trying to force me to open the gateway otherwise they will be stuck here." Looking back at Kallen, I ask, "Are you going to kill them?"

He shakes his head. "No, that is not the Sheehogue way."

"I don't trust you anymore."

He actually has the decency to look bothered by that. "I have never lied to you."

"No, you haven't but that doesn't mean I won't constantly be on the alert for you to decide that it's better for me to die than keep fighting."

His eyes focus with a shock of green on mine. "I want you to keep fighting."

"But wanting that doesn't change the fact you feel that you get to decide if I live or die." Wasn't I just thinking not that long ago that my life couldn't get any worse? I need to stop thinking that. It seems to be a challenge for the cosmos to prove me wrong.

Standing up, I start walking away from all of them. I don't know how long those two will be out and I don't know if I have a never-ending ability to pull more and more magic from the earth so the more space I put between us the better. Right now, I feel emotionally and physically drained and I don't know how much of that is the result of pulling so much magic and how much is the result of everything I just learned on top of how fantastical the rest of my week has been. Maybe Mom shouldn't have tried to keep me alive because apparently, I was born with a great big bullseye on my forehead.

CHAPTER 12

"Xandra, where are you going?" Kallen asks as he begins to follow me.

"Go away, Kallen. I'm going home."

"Home?" He sounds shocked. Gee, imagine that, I want to go home. What a big surprise that should be.

"You cannot go home." He says it like I'm an idiot, like he says most things to me. I certainly won't miss that.

"Watch me," I say as I keep walking, hopefully in the right direction.

"But that is not safe."

I shrug my shoulders and keep walking. "I don't know, I seemed to be able to defend myself against Maurelle and Olwyn just fine."

"Protect yourself, what about your family?"

"I'll protect them, too." What is he, a moron?

"What will you do if Maurelle or Olwyn get their hands on your small brother?"

"The term is little brother and I'll do what I just did."

"You will send your magic burning through your brother?" he asks in bewilderment.

He is a moron. "No, of course not. Will you please stop following me?"

"Do you not understand that if you send your magic searing through Maurelle or Olwyn whoever they are touching at the time will also feel its effects?" Crap. No, I didn't know that. "It is also a huge physical drain to use so much magic at once. You will become weak and then unable to defend yourself." Guess that answers the question about why I feel exhausted.

"I'll figure something out. Something that doesn't involve you."

"Xandra, please. Let me help you figure this out."

"No thanks. If I decide to off myself to protect the lowly Cowan and Witches, I'd rather do it without giving you the satisfaction of seeing it happen."

"I would derive no satisfaction from you 'offing' yourself if that term means what I believe it means." Catching up to me he grabs my arm and pulls me to a stop. Dammit, my amulet is buried under ten feet of snow.

"Will you please listen to me?"

I shake his hand off my arm. "No."

He looks to be at a complete loss. Hmm, maybe I've finally rendered him speechless. Oh, how much better the world will be because of it. I start to turn away from him and he catches my face between his hands. Before I can blink, his lips are on mine.

At first I'm stunned but now I'm mad. I push him away and he breaks off the kiss instantly with a surprised look on his face. "What, you thought you'd kiss me and then I'd go weak at the knees and do whatever you want? Maybe that works for you in Fairy land but you're not nearly a good enough kisser to make it happen here." I turn on my heel and start walking again. I hear him following me but I'm not speaking to him anymore. What a jerk! I bet he actually thought his kiss could fix everything. I guess that speaks volumes about what he thinks of me and my self-respect.

Half an hour later, I'm exhausted, drained and very lost. What I'd give for a compass right about now. And an instruction book to tell me how to use it. About ten feet ahead of me, there's a large tree lying on its side. I walk over to it and brush off the snow and then sit down to rest. Unfortunately, so does Kallen.

"I find myself again in a situation where I need to apologize to you for kissing you at inappropriate times," he says without looking at me.

I snort. "Like there's an appropriate time."

"You seem to drive me to distraction and it is the one thing that pops in my mind to do to end our continual bickering." He sounds like he has a hard time believing what he's saying. Yeah, so do I.

"So, in other words, you kiss me to shut me up. Wow, I have no idea why I'm not swooning at your feet."

"Do Cowan women still swoon?" he asks in wonder.

I give him a dirty look and shake my head. "You are too much."

"Too much of what?" He seems to realize that he left himself wide open and he adds, "Never mind, I am sure I will not like the answer you give."

"Nope, you probably wouldn't. What's it going to take to get you to go away?"

"Nothing."

My hope rises up and I have just a hint of a smile on my face. "You mean you're just going to go away? Right now?"

He shakes his head. "No, I meant there is nothing that will make me go away. I swore to protect you and I must do that."

"Yeah, well, we seem to have different opinions on what protecting me entails because in my book, I don't end up dead at the end. Tell you what; I'll let you out of the deal. You're free. Shoo. Go on your way. Fly like a bird."

The corners of his mouth lift up. "Would it make you more comfortable if I followed you in my raven form?"

"What about anything I just said made you think that I would be comfortable with you following me in any form? I want you to go away. I released you from your promise to protect me so there's nothing holding you to me anymore."

"You cannot release me from a blood oath performed by another Witch. Your mother performed the spell, not you."

I roll my eyes. "Okay, fine. When I get home I'll have Mom release you. But you can still go ahead and leave now. I promise not to get killed by anyone else on my way home. What would be the odds of more than three people wanting me dead all at one time?"

A shadow falls over his face which wipes the smile right off it. Good lord, I went and tempted the cosmos again, didn't I? "Now what aren't you telling me?" I demand.

"Nothing," he says unconvincingly.

I throw my hands up in the air as I stand up and start walking again. "You say you want to stay by my side and protect me yet you still want to keep your little secrets. You know what you should do? You should find a job because I have no intention of opening the gateway to your realm so you'll need to support yourself here somehow. Maybe you could be a bartender or something. With your looks, I'm sure you'd be rolling in the tips. I understand there are lots of bars in Denver. Why don't you go see?"

"The only way for you to open the gateway is if you are sacrificed by your father. Your dying blood will open the realm forever."

Wow, when he keeps a secret he goes all out. Why couldn't it be something like 'this isn't my real hair' or 'I'm gay which is why I don't want to kiss you unless I'm mad at you.' No, he jumps right to 'your dad wants to kill you so he can destroy humankind.'

I stop and hang my head as I cross my arms over my chest and sigh deeply. "Which is why you'd rather kill me yourself because if I'm going to die anyway it might as well not happen while opening up the Fairy realm."

"That was the reasoning I came here with, yes. But I no longer feel that way."

"Ooh, you just up and changed your mind. What a coincidence that it happened right after I found out about your plan." I start walking again. I need to get off this freaking mountain. I think the thinner air is scrambling my brain because a tiny part of me can understand why Kallen would kill me if it was the only way to stop the King from his plans. The King. My father. My father who wants me dead without even meeting me. That certainly doesn't do much for my self-esteem.

"That is not when I changed my mind."

"Please don't tell me it was after the first time we kissed. This isn't a Fairy tale. Oh, wait, I guess it is. Still, I don't see us moving on to a happily ever after. That whole death threat hanging over my head kind of puts a damper on any romantic notions I might have been able to muster for you, Kallen."

"Xandra."

He doesn't say anything else so I manage a half-hearted, "What?"

"Do you have any idea where you are going?"

Crap, I thought I was walking confidently enough that he wouldn't figure that out. "Yes, I do," I snap.

He has the nerve to chuckle. "Then are you planning to trek around the world to get to your house? Because it is in the opposite direction."

No, it can't be. I stop and turn around in a circle trying to get my bearings. It's around noon, though, so I can't use the orientation of the sun to tell me if I'm heading east or west. "So, it's that way?" I ask pointing in the direction we just came from.

"I would be happy to show you the way."

I narrow my eyes as I look at him. "Why can't you just tell me?"

"Because then I would have no leverage to use to convince you to let me come with you."

I growl in frustration. "Why are you always such a jerk?"

"You know, there are some who find me charming and witty."

"Good for you, I'm not one of them." I start walking back the way we came.

"I was just kidding, you were going the right way," he says and I can hear the laughter in his voice.

That's it. I've had it. I march over to him and putting both hands on his chest I push him. Even though he wasn't expecting it, he probably wouldn't have fallen but there is a stump behind him and he trips over it so now he's flat on his back in the snow. I stand over him with my hands on my hips. "I am so tired of you laughing at me! I am exhausted and cold and I want to go home so stop being a jerk and just tell me which way to go!"

Kallen looks up at me for a long moment and then he nods looking defeated. "Help me up and I'll tell you."

Finally, he says something I want to hear. I hold my hand out to him and he takes it but instead of me helping him up, he pulls me down and rolls on top of me. I should have figured it was too good to be true. I'm too tired to fight him either physically or with magic so I just lie here with a disgusted look on my face.

When he realizes that I'm not going to fight him, he takes some of his weight off me by resting his elbows in the snow and pushing himself up. "I changed my mind before we even started on this journey. I knew that if you were willing to leave your family and go off with a stranger because you thought it was the only way to keep your world safe, you would never willingly open the gate. That was the only reason I had ever intended to kill you if I had to. Only if you tried to open the gate of your own free will. You are correct. Your magic is strong enough to easily fight off Maurelle and Olwyn but they are determined. They would rather die than stay in this world. Unlike me, they have every intention of finding a way back home and they will use anything and everything they can think of to force you into opening the gate. Xandra, that includes your family. They will exorcise your parents as I said before if that is what it takes. They will kill your aunt and your little brother in front of you if that is what it takes. The Pooka are not peaceful nor do they have the ability to be reasoned with when they have their mind set on something. The King chose these two runners specifically because of their cold-heartedness. Please, let me help you keep any of that from happening. You have my word; there is no situation that could make me decide your death is the only answer."

Even though I'm absolutely positive that he's telling the truth, I still can't bring myself to just give in. "Nice speech, will you please get off me?"

"May I kiss you first?"

"No."

With a sigh, he rolls off me and stands up. He offers his hand out to me but I learn from my mistakes and I don't take it. Looking up at him, I cock my head and say, "For future reference, the answer will always be no to that question."

Something flashes in his eyes but I can't figure out what, nor do I want to. "Of course," he says.

I sigh loudly and look down at the ground for several moments. When I finally look back up at him, I ask, "What are we going to eat since our food is buried?"

He's smart enough to squelch the smile before it really gets going. "This is an excellent opportunity to teach you about both hunting and gathering."

"Hunting? You mean you expect me to kill an animal and then eat it after seeing it take its last breath? Not going to happen."

"Then perhaps we should follow tradition and I should hunt while you gather." I have to give him credit; he's trying so hard not to express his amusement that I think his eyes are going to start watering soon.

"Fine, just what exactly am I gathering?"

"Wood for a fire."

"Just wood? I thought you were going to tell me which berries or tree bark or something is edible."

"Unfortunately, at this altitude this time of year, there is very little the mountain has to offer as food. We will need to dine on rabbits or possibly deer. And I promise, only I will witness their dying breath."

He still doesn't laugh. I'm pretty sure he's going to burst soon if he doesn't.

"Fine, go kill a bunny and I'll pick up some sticks." I walk away from him and start looking for anything dry that would work for firewood. Out of the corner of my eye, I see him suddenly holding a bow with arrows. I really want to be able to do cool stuff like that with magic instead of just being able to hurt people with it.

I'm tempted to just keep walking and take my chances of finding home on my own, but as much as my heart wants to, my brain knows that I can't for all the reasons Kallen said. So, after gathering an armful of wood, I go back to our new little camp of sorts. Kallen is gone for about twenty more minutes and I take the opportunity to sit on the stump I pushed him over and try very hard not to think about anything. My brain needs a rest.

That's how Kallen finds me, sitting completely still on a stump and staring aimlessly off into the distance. I must be crying because he kneels down in front of me and uses his thumb to wipe a tear from my cheek. "If I could make all of this go away, I would," he says softly. I nod and try to not to cry harder. He gathers me in his arms and just holds me for a long time while I shed tears of anger, sorrow, determination, helplessness and hope.

When I finally have no more tears to shed, I pull back away from him. "Thank you," I say quietly and seeming to understand that I need space now, he busies himself with making a fire.

There's a carcass of a skinned rabbit sitting in the snow next to him. God help me, I'm going to have to eat that if I have any intention of building my strength back up. But I already feel like retching in the snow. My meat isn't supposed to have eyes or ears or a little tiny rabbit tongue hanging out of its mouth. "Next time, will you please leave the head in the woods?"

Kallen smiles and nods. "Of course."

CHAPTER 13

"Are we in a circle?" I ask as I battle a mouthful of rabbit down my throat and esophagus. It's trying really hard to come back up.

Kallen shakes his head. "Now that I know you can handle yourself, there is no need right now. When we find a place to rest our heads tonight, I will put one up so we can sleep peacefully."

I snort. "That's not likely to happen. Do you think I'll be able to make things appear and disappear like you can?"

Kallen nods. "Of course, as soon as you learn to draw only a small amount of magic instead of filling yourself to the brim you will be able to make anything you want appear."

"But you said the Cowan Fairies can't do that."

"You are not a Cowan Fairy. You are a Fairy who is very powerful. The only thing you lack is control." It doesn't escape my notice that he said Fairy instead of Witch Fairy. Suck up.

"How long has it been since there was a Witch Fairy besides me." Hey, I'm proud to be my mother's daughter. I'm not going to forget that I'm half Witch just because Kallen seems to want to forget that.

"There has not been one in my lifetime. My understanding is that it has been thousands of years because the Witches and the Fae had a mutual agreement not to create one."

"Thousands of years? My mom was the first Witch to get pregnant by a Fairy in thousands of years?" Way to go, Mom. Bring me into the world when no one else has wanted to bring someone like me into the world for millennia. My self-esteem is hanging by a thread now.

"I do not know if that is true, but yes, you are the first child of such a union to be born in thousands of years."

"Why am I so awful to have around?" He raises his eyebrows and I sigh and shake my head. "You know what I mean. Not today, I mean in the cosmic order of things."

"The prophecy says: A Witch's child of Fae is born when spirits of the realms are torn. Into the world destruction she brings while children cry and angels sing. None may survive the vengeance of she, and immortal her soul is to be to remedy the world of its natural discord."

I can't believe this. "Really. You are just now telling me that there is a prophecy? Really? Are you kidding me?"

He has the decency to look embarrassed and he's suddenly fascinated by his rabbit leg. "It did not seem important to tell you."

"There's a prophecy that says I'm going to bring destruction to the world while watching children cry and you don't think it's important to tell me that? What is wrong with you?"

Still not lifting his eyes to mine, he says, "After I met you, the prophecy did not seem to ring true so there seemed no reason to dwell on it any longer."

My mouth hangs open as I try to figure out how to respond. Do I get angry because he kept yet another secret from me or am I supposed to be pleased because I don't seem like the kind of person who could destroy the world? Or is that simply his way of saying I'm not powerful enough to fulfill the prophecy and if he is saying that should I be insulted or should I be glad that I'm not? Okay, there is no good way to respond. So I don't.

"Are you really young in your realm?"

Kallen looks up at me surprised that I completely changed the subject. "I am very young for the Fae."

"Are Fairies immortal?"

He shakes his head. "No, but it is not unusual for a Fairy to live for thousands of years."

"Hmm, I wonder how long I'll live since I'm half Witch. Guess I'll just have to wait and see since I'm such an enigma, huh?"

"It would seem so." Kallen has a slight frown on his face as he looks warily at me like he expects this conversation to be some sort of ruse to start an argument. I don't have it in me to argue with him any more today, though.

I force the last bite of rabbit down my throat. And no, it doesn't taste like chicken. Standing up, I say, "We should probably get going."

Kallen cocks his head. "Get going towards where, your home?"

I sigh a sigh that comes all the way up from my toes. "No. How long do you think Maurelle and Olwyn will be out?"

Kallen actually chuckles as he stands up. "Considering the amount of magic you pushed through them, I would assume for several hours yet."

"Okay, then let's try to put some more distance between us and them." I turn around and start walking again in the opposite direction from where we left the Fairies. I still don't know if we're moving closer to or farther away from house.

We walk a long time in silence which I don't mind at all. It starts snowing hard again and our range of vision becomes greatly diminished not to mention I am once again in a situation where even my eyeballs are cold. I hope we find someplace to get out of this weather soon. Though I don't know what good it will do us since we don't have any dry clothes or a sleeping bag to keep us warm. Maybe Kallen can use his magic to make me a blanket. And a separate blanket for himself.

After another hour, the wind picks up and it's like trying to walk against a wind machine. We have to keep our heads down and squint to shield our eyes. "I think I see a place!" Kallen yells over the wind. Thank god.

The place he finds is similar to where we had slept the first night. It's almost like a very shallow cave but not quite that big. But it is situated in a way that will protect us from the wind. The relief of stepping into it and not having the wind trying to push me over is a little disorienting. Kind of like getting off a ride at an amusement park and not being able to walk straight because you're still dizzy. Because of that, I stumble and fall against Kallen. He catches me and keeps me from falling on the hard rock.

As soon as I have my balance back, I step away from him. We are definitely not going to be sharing a sleeping bag tonight. Funny, whenever I'd had daydreams about being on a deserted island or somewhere similar with a guy as gorgeous as Kallen, I assumed that I'd want to snuggle up with him. But here I am with a guy who looks like he could be an underwear model and the idea of being attracted to him is almost ludicrous. Well, if I'm going to be perfectly honest with myself, and at this point in my life that seems like a very good idea because then at least one person in the world would be being honest with me, I am attracted to him. Physically. But that's not enough to compensate for his ego and his prejudices.

I sit down on the cold rock and curl myself into as tight of a ball as I can to try to preserve my body heat. "Any chance you could make me a blanket?" I ask Kallen with shivering teeth.

He sits down next to me. "Fairy magic is tricky with things like that. In order for a Fairy to create something such as clothes, it must be physically touching him or her at all times. As soon as the Fairy is no longer touching it, it disappears."

"How convenient you haven't explained that to me before," I say dryly. I can tough out the cold, I decide.

"It is not a matter of convenience; we simply have not talked about the finer points of Fairy magic because you are still working on garnering control over the basics." He moves so he's sitting closer to me with his leg is touching mine. I shift so none of my body is touching his.

"So, when are you going to teach me Witch magic?" I ask and Kallen looks at me aghast.

"Why on earth would you want to waste time with spells and incantations when your Fae magic is so strong? You need only think of something and draw on the earth for it to be there."

I make a face at him. "So, I'm supposed to just forget that I'm half Witch because it makes you more comfortable, huh?"

He starts to say something but he stops before any words come out of his mouth. He clears his throat and tries again. "I can see how you would want to learn about both areas of magic with your shared heritage, I was simply surprised that you would want to move past the Fae magic so quickly and begin your knowledge of the Witches."

"Why can't I learn both at the same time?"

"As they are conflicting styles of magic, it would probably become quite confusing to try to master both at the same time. But," and here his face becomes blank, "I would be perfectly willing to discontinue our work on controlling your Fae magic and beginning instruction on your Witch magic."

"How diplomatically put. Did it cause you any physical pain saying that?" He looks at me sharply preparing for an attack until he sees the teasing glint in my eye.

He leans back against the rock face and closes his eyes. "Some."

I laugh. I really do have to give him credit for trying to put his prejudices aside. After all, he has been conditioned to believe them for over three hundred years. I'm having trouble letting go of some of my beliefs and I've only had them for seventeen years. Another thought pops out of my mouth before my brain has a chance to stop it. "Why would someone as old as you want to kiss someone as young as me?"

I'm not sure what reaction I expected but I certainly didn't expect him to keep his eyes closed and smile as he says, "Because you are the most beautiful Fairy I have ever met."

"You mean Witch Fairy. You know, you could be my great great great great great great great great great great great great grandfather in human years."

He still doesn't open his eyes but his smile does get bigger. "Then it is fortunate that I am not human. Time moves differently in the Fae realm. My age is comparable to yours if assessed in human years." Opening just one eye to look at me, he asks, "Are you cold enough to share a blanket with me yet?"

"Maybe I should try to make my own blanket."

Both of his eyes pop open now to look at me. "I would rather not be buried by another avalanche at the moment, if that is alright with you."

"I wonder if my magic is that hard to control or if you are simply a terrible teacher. Which do you think it is?"

He closes his eyes again. "I am positive it is not the latter."

"How can you be so sure? Have you taught a lot of people how to use their magic?"

He nods. "Yes, I have. I am considered one of the best at it and families often request for me to help in their children's training." Shoot, I wasn't expecting that answer.

"Do you teach Cowan Fairies or do you only teach full-blooded Fairies?"

Kallen frowns. "You are quite feisty this evening. The answer is no, I do not teach Cowan Fairies but not because I will not, it is because I cannot. It would be similar to you trying to teach someone how to build a bridge but they speak a different language than you and have different tools that you have never used before."

"Hmm, I don't know how to build a bridge so that's a bad analogy."

He laughs. "So it would seem." A warm wool blanket appears over him and he stretches his legs out and wraps himself up in it.

"That's not nice," I complain.

He looks at me and shrugs. "I should not have to be cold because you do not want to share a blanket with me."

I hold out for another long five minutes but it's too cold to continue being stubborn. "Fine," I grumble and I lift up a corner of the blanket and pull it over me. The next thing I know, Kallen has slipped an arm behind my back and grabs my waist on both sides and lifts me up and settles me between his legs. "Hey!"

"It is a better use of body heat to sit like this." He wraps his arms around my waist and leans back against the rock again.

I hate to admit it but he's right; it is warmer this way. I grumble about it for a couple of minutes, which he ignores, and I finally relax and settle back into him. We sit like this for a long time without saying anything until we both fall asleep.

CHAPTER 14

I wake up stiff and cold the next morning. Kallen's arms are still wrapped tightly around me even in his sleep. I wonder if it's because he's cold or he just wants to be that close to me. I'm sure it's the former. Regardless of how he has started acting, I doubt that it's possible he put all of his prejudice aside about me being half Witch in just a few days. But on the other hand, if he's stuck in this realm forever I am the only female who is part Fairy except Maurelle. I guess that would make me the lesser of two evils. Gee, how romantic.

Now I'm super annoyed that he has his arms around me; so annoyed that I make sure to elbow him in the stomach as I wrestle my way out of his grasp. He wakes up with a loud, "Humph," and I glare at him. His eyebrows draw together in confusion as he looks at me with sleepy eyes as I stand up and move away from him.

Looking down at him, I ask, "Do you have a plan or are we just going to hide out in the mountains forever? Because this is getting really old."

Kallen takes his time answering me as he rubs his hands against his face to try to wake up. He stands up and stretches his full height with his arms above him and I really, really hate the fact that he looks so good doing it. Finally turning to me, he says with a grin, "I rather enjoy the mountain air."

I growl in frustration and turn around and start walking. "Where are you going?" he asks.

"Not that it's any of your business but I have to pee." I keep walking and if he tries to follow me, I'm going to drown him in my magic. Five minutes later when I return to the place where we had slept, my bladder feels better but I'm not any less crabby. I stand akimbo in front of Kallen who is leaning with his back against the rock. "What's your plan?"

"We need to bind Maurelle and Olwyn's magic so they are of no threat to you or your family."

I look at him like he's an idiot. Which he is. "Why didn't you do that yesterday when they were lying unconscious on the ground? It seems like that would have been the perfect time."

Now he looks at me like I'm an idiot. Which I'm not. "If it was that simple I would have done so. But it takes two powerful Fairies to perform the ritual to bind Fairy magic."

"Are you saying that I'm not a powerful Fairy?"

"It is not your power that is lacking; it is still your control. Binding Fairy magic is a delicate process and delicate is not a word I can use to describe your magic." He cocks his head and raises his brows. "Unless you do not care if we kill them instead of binding their magic as you almost did yesterday."

I feel my face blanch. "I what?"

Kallen sighs and pushes himself away from the wall. He puts both hands on my shoulders and looks down at me with something that almost mimics sympathy. "If I had not let my magic go and drawn most of your magic inside of me, you would have killed Maurelle and Olwyn. If I had been a less powerful Fairy as most are, you would have killed me. I have never met a Fairy who could send out so much raw magic and force it into others as you can. It is both fascinating and frightening to behold."

I step back away from him and he drops his hands to his sides. "Why are you saying this? Are you trying to scare me into staying in the mountains with you?"

A small smile touches his lips. "As much as I am growing to enjoy your company, with several obvious momentary exceptions of course, I am not trying to scare you to keep you in the mountains with me. I rather dislike the cold myself and would have chosen a much more temperate climate if that was the case. I am trying to make you understand that until you learn to control your magic, you are a dangerous Fairy to be around. I am assuming that no matter how badly you want to leave my company and go home, you do not want to add murder into your repertoire of skills."

I have to be whiter than the snow by now. I believe all of the blood has left the upper half of my body as I take in his words. I almost killed three people yesterday without even knowing what I was doing. "Maybe I should stop doing Fairy magic and only do Witch magic."

Kallen looks at me sadly and shakes his head. "Again, it is not that simple. Your mother explained about a Witch's mana as they choose to call it coming from the earth. Magic is magic, Xandra. It all comes from the same place whether you draw it into you using spells and incantations or you are able to draw it simply by calling to it. As I wanted to explain last night but I did not think you were of the frame of mind to hear it, the amount of magic you pull could cause a spell to go awry or become a hundred times more powerful than you meant it to be."

Secrets, secrets, secrets. I am so tired of secrets. "Last night you said you would teach me Witch magic. Was that a lie?"

"No. I will teach you if you insist upon it but I was hoping to discourage you from it until you have more control."

I hang my head. I am so overwhelmed that it's taking great effort to remain standing up. "Am I going to destroy the world like the prophecy says?"

Kallen takes two steps towards me and folds me into his arms and I let him. "No, you are not. I hold no stock in prophecies and neither should you. You are going to learn how to control your magic and we will bind Maurelle and Olwyn's magic and you will be able to return to your old life away from Fairies and gateways and other realms."

That's the first time he's talked about what would happen after I no longer need him to teach me. "What will you do?" I ask still in his embrace.

"Perhaps I shall go into Denver and become a bartender. I have been told that I am handsome enough to make excellent tips."

I can't help but laugh and I finally wrap my arms around his back. "Thank you," I murmur into his jacket. It feels really good to be in his arms like this. So good that it can make me forget about a lot of things, which is what I blame for what I say next. "Kallen, will you kiss me?"

He leans back and takes my face between his large hands and searches it to determine if I am serious or not. Right now, I am. I don't know if I will be if he doesn't hurry up and kiss me sooner as opposed to later, though. As if reading my mind, he dips his head and his lips are on mine. This isn't the gentle kiss from the other night, this is a kiss full of need and passion and hunger. I open my mouth to him and his tongue delves into its depths and I respond in kind. He wraps his arms tightly around my waist and lifts me so he doesn't have to lean over so far. He presses my back against the rock we had slept against and his mouth never leaves mine. I wind my arms around his neck and pull him closer, not wanting this kiss to end. This kiss is keeping reality at bay and that's what I need right now.

So I can't even begin to tell you how disappointed I am when Kallen abruptly stops kissing me, swears under his breath, lowers me to the ground and turns around. I'm about to make a cutting remark about him only wanting someone who is full-blooded Fairy when I see why he stopped kissing me. About fifty feet from us and looking this way with hunger in his eyes is one of the biggest grizzly bears I have ever seen. Okay, granted I haven't seen that many because they are almost extinct in Colorado, but still. It's big.

"Shouldn't it be hibernating right now?"

Kallen looks at me over his shoulder with one raised brow. "Would you care to explain that to him?"

I make a face at him and he laughs and turns back around. "I am going to give him a little encouragement to be on his way. Stay here."

"Stay here? Where are you going?" What, does he suddenly know how to wrestle bears now? "It's a grizzly bear, Kallen. He's probably as tall as you when he stands on his hind legs and he outweighs you by probably five or six hundred pounds."

Kallen smiles at me over his shoulder as he keeps walking towards the bear. "True, but he does not have magic."

As much as I think he's being stupid, I can't help but be curious how he will make a hungry bear leave us alone. Kallen stops walking when he's about ten feet away from it. The grizzly stands on its hind legs and lets out a roar but Kallen doesn't even flinch. Just as he did when he and I had our snow fight, he causes snow to start falling from the trees onto the bear. A lot of snow. The bear goes down on all fours and starts shaking its fur to try to rid himself of it. He seems to forget about Kallen as more and more snow falls on him. Finally, as if he realizes he's not wanted, the grizzly turns around and lumbers away. I can't help but be impressed that Kallen hadn't used any harmful magic against it.

"What would you have done if he attacked you?" I ask when he's close enough to hear me.

Kallen shrugs. "I guess we will find out if he comes back hungry for Fairies."

He keeps walking towards me and I want to back up but my back is still flat against the rock. When he's right in front of me, he puts his hands on either side of my head and leans towards me. "Now, about that kiss," he says with a sexy grin.

I quickly dart under his arm and put distance between us. "The other night you said you couldn't let anything happen between us. How come you've changed your mind?"

Kallen stands up and disappointment is plain on his face as he looks at me with those intense green eyes that make me want to kiss him again. So, I back up another couple of steps. "Well?"

"You had no knowledge of the big picture. It would not have been fair of me to engage you in any type of romance without first explaining to you my original intent when coming here and what the King is willing to do if he gets his hands on you."

I frown at him. "You couldn't have just told me those things that night?"

A sad smile touches his lips. "As I recall, you were not of a mind to listen to me."

No, I guess I hadn't been at the time. My feelings were hurt and I hadn't wanted to hear anything from him. "You know what this is, don't you, this sudden attraction you have for me?"

Kallen looks amused again. “Please, enlighten me.”

“I'm basically the last Fairy on earth because Maurelle doesn't really count so you have to be attracted to me.”

His eyebrows rise and he crosses his arms over his chest. “I have to be? So, even if you were spindly with warts all over your face, I would still have to find you attractive because of your Fairy blood and my lack of other Fairy options?”

Okay, it sounds stupid when he says it like that. “Shouldn't we be practicing?”

His eyes are flashing with amusement now. “Yes, we should,” he says and he removes his glove from his left hand and holds it out to me. Slightly embarrassed to be touching him again after I had asked him to kiss me, I gingerly put my hand into his. His fingers curl tightly around mine and I try to close my mind off to any thoughts of him as I prepare to draw magic from the earth.

Ten minutes later, Kallen is still on the ground trying to recuperate from my attempt to control my magic. He looks up at me and he is definitely paler than he was before. “I believe you are getting stronger with even less ability to control your magic. It should not be happening like this. You should have to grow into your powers for years, not days.” Rising to his feet, he brushes the snow off his clothes.

“Maybe I have been.” I say thoughtfully.

He stops brushing at the snow and looks at me. “What do you mean?”

“You said earlier it takes two powerful Fairies to bind another Fairy's magic. Well, I'm pretty sure my mom didn't know any Fairies when she bound my Witch magic after I was born so maybe my Fairy magic has been growing all these years. I just haven't used it until now because I didn't know how.”

First Kallen looks shocked and then he shakes his head in what looks like amazement. “Which would explain why you are having so much trouble controlling it. Fairy children begin their training when they are very young and their control grows with their magic as they reach adulthood. But you have a grown Fairy's magical abilities and a young child's ability to control it. That makes a lot of sense."

I frown. "Somewhere in there did you imply that I'm infantile?"

Kallen chuckles. "Only your control over your magic."

"Okay, what do we do now that we've figured this out?"

Kallen puts his lips together in a flat line and shrugs. "I honestly do not know."

I shake my head and sigh. "Of all the times to not have all the answers, you choose this time?"

His brows come together and he purses his lips as he thinks. "We could try to tire your magic out."

"Huh? What does that mean?"

"Maybe if we find something for your initial rushes of magic to glom onto, other than me, you will gain more control as you are able to pull less and less magic. Basically, we'd be bringing your magical abilities down to the level of your ability to control it."

I think I understand what he means. "What could I have it glom onto?" Who uses the word glom anymore? He's really showing his age with that word.

Kallen slowly spins in a circle as he looks for a target for my magic. Finally, he stops and points. "Do you see that tree right there? The one with the large knot sticking out of it about halfway up? It is already dying and will fall on its own soon. Maybe you could hurry the process along."

I look at him doubtfully. "You want me to magically cut down a thirty foot tree?"

"Believe me, if you send the same amount of magic you keep searing my insides with, you will have no problem felling the tree." Felling, glom, maybe I'll get him a thesaurus for Christmas.

I shrug. "Okay, I'm willing to try it." Kallen gestures towards the tree in an 'any time you're ready' signal.

Turning towards the tree, I close my eyes and put a picture of it in my mind. I begin pulling the magic into me and as I feel it overflowing, looking for an outlet, I imagine it flowing into the tree. Almost immediately, I hear a loud bang and I'm being knocked to the ground. I open my eyes to find Kallen on top of me with his hands over his head and using his body to shield mine. As I move my head around, I understand why. I didn't make the tree fall down, I made it explode and we are lying in a field of wooden shrapnel.

Kallen opens his eyes and puts his elbows on the ground and he shakes his head as he lifts up to look at me. "You cannot do anything on a small scale, can you?"

I don't know what to say to that so I go with, "Apparently not," which makes him laugh. Pushing himself off me, he stands up and offers me his hand which I accept.

"You need to do this several times before you will find you are able to pull less and less magic as your mind and body begin to tire. We should pick a tree that is farther away, though."

"Do you really think it's good for the environment for me to be blowing up trees? What if there are bird nests or other animals in them?"

Kallen crosses his arms over his chest. "As opposed to rock slides and avalanches ruining their homes? At least this way you are significantly lowering the number of displaced animals."

He's right. Again. I hate that about him. "Fine. Pick a tree."

He picks a tree about a hundred feet from us and I repeat the process. I do this six more times before I can finally start to feel a drag as I attempt to pull magic inside of me. Kallen gives me a relieved 'finally' look when I tell him.

"Now I want you to make the snow shake off one tree."

"Which one?"

"Any one, you pick."

I get a tree in mind and I pull from the earth. It feels like the magic is coming into me in a trickle instead of rush. I concentrate on the tree I picked and imagine it swaying softly, just hard enough for the snow to fall from its limbs.

The next thing I know, I'm being swung around in the air by Kallen. "You did it! You finally did it," he says with a grin and I can't help but smile along with him. After planting a quick kiss on my lips that I wasn't expecting, he sets me back down on the ground. I'm going to put that kiss down to his excitement and just ignore it this time. He just better not be thinking he can kiss me every time I do something right.

"Okay, do it again," he says still smiling like a teacher whose worst student finally added two plus two and came up with four instead of ten.

After a few more tries and getting it right, I'm exhausted. "I don't think I can do another one."

Kallen nods. "It is probably best to rest for a bit."

Looking out over the trees, I'm impressed with myself. I can control my magic sometimes. I'm about to turn back around towards Kallen when something catches my eye. It's brown and first I assume it's a tree but the more I look at it, the more it looks like a chimney. I squint my eyes to try to get a better look and before I know it, I'm walking towards it.

"Xandra, where are you going?"

"I think something's down there." I keep walking and I can hear Kallen's footsteps following behind.

When I can finally make out the entire structure, I turn to Kallen in amazement. "It's a ranger station!"

Of course, he has no idea what a ranger station is so he looks at me blankly until I explain. "During the summer months when there's the risk of forest fires, the forest rangers will come up and stay in these small cabins and keep watch."

"To watch the forest burn?" Kallen asks looking confused.

I roll my eyes. "No, of course not. To be able to locate a fire quickly so it can be put out before it spreads too far."

"Do Witches come and put the fire out?"

I can't help but laugh. I haven't thought about how much has changed technologically since Kallen was last in our realm. "No, they use airplanes to drop water and chemicals on the fire. Do you know what an airplane is?"

That old haughty expression comes back on his face. "I familiarized myself with the different modes of transportation when I entered this realm."

"Well, good for you," I say dryly and I start walking towards the cabin again. Maybe if I get there first, I can lock him out of it.

CHAPTER 15

The cabin is empty of course since it's the dead of winter. Peering in the windows, I can see a small cook stove, some radio equipment, a wooden table and chairs and a cot. The bare basics but after sleeping outside for more nights this week than I thought I would have to in my entire lifetime, it looks like a palace to me.

Kallen tries the door handle but it's locked. That doesn't seem to be a problem for him because within a couple of seconds he has the lock turning and the door open. I really, really want to be able to do stuff like that. I hate having to rely on him for all the magic that requires finesse and delicacy.

The inside of the cabin is dark but it only takes a moment to locate some kerosene lamps on a small shelf and get one lit with the matches lying next to them on the same shelf. Swinging the lantern around slowly, the cabin is neat and clean with only the occasional cobweb here and there. I don't care how many spiders there are, they can even sleep with me as long as I can sleep under a roof and on something other than rock. I'm grinning from ear to ear when I look at Kallen who's leaning against the doorjamb watching me. "Isn't this great?"

"Indeed."

I roll my eyes at his lack of enthusiasm. "You're more than welcome to sleep outside still. In fact, maybe that's a good idea so you can keep watch for Maurelle and Olwyn," I say sweetly.

He chuckles. "I could sense them just as easily from in here."

I give him a hard look. "Okay, but I get the cot." I add just so there's no confusion, "By myself."

He raises his eyebrows at my lack of subtlety. "Are you implying that I would want to sleep in a small cot with you? You are a half-breed after all."

I start to get mad at him but the glint in his eye lets me know he's trying to get a rise out of me. Nope, not going to happen this time. It's pretty sad that a tiny little shack in the middle of nowhere feels like heaven to me but it does and I'm not going to let him spoil my mood. So I ignore him and continue looking around the cabin.

Above the table is a cupboard with two doors and when I open it I am so happy, I almost cry. It's full of canned food. Soup, chili, stew, veggies. At least for the time being, I won't have to eat something I've seen with its head still attached.

Kallen has finally come in and closed the door and he's using some of the wood next to the fireplace to get a fire going. I take down a can of chili and find an opener in the same cupboard. I start my own little fire on one of the burners of the stove and taking a pan from a nail on the wall I dump the chili in and start heating it. I've never been a huge fan of chili but this chili smells like a gourmet meal to me.

Once Kallen has the fire roaring and starting to fill the cabin with heat, he has a seat at the table and watches me as I dish the chili out into two bowls. I hand him one with a spoon and we sit in silence as we eat. At least it's a fairly comfortable silence.

When he has scraped the last bit of chili from his bowl, Kallen breaks the silence. "How did it feel when you could control the magic?"

Hmm, how do I describe it without him laughing at me? "Well," I begin but I close my mouth and frown as I try to think of what to say. Finally, I just go ahead and let it flow out of my mouth. "It felt like the magic was as tired as I was. Kind of like it gave up the fight for control and decided to let me win that round."

Now it's Kallen's turn to frown. "You speak as if the magic is a sentient entity."

I shrug. "It kind of feels like one to me. Like when we caused the avalanche, the magic felt like a naughty child who refused to listen to its mother. It was almost as if it was sticking its tongue out at me and saying na-na, I'm going to do what I want."

I expect Kallen to laugh at me but instead he looks thoughtful.

After a few minutes, he says, "My grandmother speaks of magic like that, as if she can talk to it and reason with it."

"Is your grandmother crazy?"

He cocks his head and raises an eyebrow and I feel color rushing into my cheeks. "I wasn't trying to insult your grandmother; I was asking a serious question because if she's crazy for thinking that, then I must be, too."

"No," he says dryly, "my grandmother is not crazy. She is the most powerful Fairy alive."

Good lord, he's touchy. "Maybe she should have come to teach me," I grumble under my breath which must have been loud enough for Kallen to hear because he's giving me a dirty look now.

"I can guarantee you that she would have been a harsher instructor than I." His tone is hard and makes me want to concentrate all of my attention on my chili because I apparently hit a sore spot and now he's looking for an argument.

"I apologize if my education has not met your expectations, perhaps I should have stayed in the realm that I can no longer return to. Ever," he pushes but I'm not going to give him the satisfaction of pushing me into bickering back or letting him make me feel guilty.

Meeting his eyes, I say, "I'm sorry you had to make that choice and I'm grateful that you did." Oh, that was good. He can't get mad about that.

As if thinking the same thing, he scrapes his chair back across the floor and picks up his bowl and spoon. He opens the door and closes it loudly behind him as he goes outside to clean them. Wow, touchy much? It's not like I haven't had to give up my life plans, too.

I finish my chili slowly savoring every bite. When I'm done, I leave my bowl and spoon on the table. Kallen hasn't come back in yet and I don't want to be near him right now so I'll clean them later. Instead, I drag my chair in front of the fire and warm my hands. As the heat begins to seep into me, I find that I am actually getting too warm so I slip off my boots and jacket laying them neatly by the cot and sit back down. It feels good not to have the bulky jacket on but in some weird way it feels like I've molted because it kind of became like a second skin over the last few days.

After about half an hour or so, Kallen comes back in. He still looks kind of surly so I just ignore him and bathe in the heat that I haven't felt for what feels like forever. He pulls the other chair close to the fire and we sit like this for a long time without speaking. As he warms, his outer clothes begin to disappear until he is in a pair of jeans and a black sweater that fits him like a glove. It's hard not to stare because he looks really, really good in that sweater. He's only interested in me because I have Fairy blood and features, I tell myself for the hundredth time. Not to mention the fact that I'm the only female of any type of blood around at all.

"Do you feel rested yet?" he asks without looking away from the fire.

I groan. "Do you really want me to go back outside in the cold to practice?"

"That is why we are here." Oh, goody. The condescension is back as well as the haughtiness. This is going to be a long day.

"Fine," I grumble and I retrieve my boots and coat and begin to put them on resenting him the entire time. Kallen makes his heavy winter clothes reappear and walks out the door with a look that isn't going to win him the Mr. Congeniality award. Yup, it's definitely going to be a long day.

I join him outside in front of the cabin. "Should I try to shake the snow off a tree again?" I ask and he nods.

My magic is definitely stronger after having rested even for such a short time but it's still manageable. I direct it towards the tree I want to shake and I'm disappointed that I make three trees lose their snow instead of just one but it's better than making the trees blow up so I still consider it a win for me.

"Again, but this time try harder to control it," he says with an edge to his voice that I don't like. Jerk.

I'm so annoyed, I decide I'm not going to shake a tree. Instead, I focus on the roof of the cabin. More specifically, the snow on the roof of the cabin, and I imagine all of that snow finding its way to Kallen.

"What the hell?" I hear him yell and I open my eyes. All of the snow from the roof of the cabin is now on and around him and none of it has fallen on me.

"Is that enough control?" I ask sweetly and the look on his face makes me lose my simpering expression and back up. It only takes him a moment to remove most of the snow and the glint in his eyes tells me he's going to retaliate. I can feel him drawing a large amount of magic and I turn around and run. But I don't run fast enough to avoid the wall of snow he sends towards me and suddenly I'm covered in more snow than I had dumped on him. The force of the snow makes me fall and I go face first into even more snow.

When I flip myself over, Kallen is standing over me. "Not as good as that," he says and the corners of his mouth are possibly thinking about rising into a smile but he's not there yet.

Pulling on my own magic again, I begin to imagine the snow around me rising up but before I get enough magic, Kallen is kneeling over me. "I don't think so," he says breaking my concentration as he throws a handful of snow at me without using magic. When I try to collect some snow in my hands, he grabs my wrists and holds them still with a smug grin that he's so much stronger than I am physically.

"Okay, I give up," I say sounding defeated.

Kallen lets go of my wrists still smug that he's won and as soon as he starts to get up, I sweep my leg under his causing him to fall backwards into the snow. He's stunned into inaction for a second and now it's my turn to kneel over him. I grab as much snow as I can and drop it on his face.

He sputters as he tries to wipe the snow from his eyes and mouth and as soon as his eyes are clear, I know I'm in trouble. I scoot backwards and try to get up to run again but then he has my arms and I find myself again lying on my back in the snow with him holding my wrists. "Just do not know when to quit, do you?" he asks and he really doesn't look mad at all anymore. He actually looks like he's having fun.

"I give up. For real this time," I say but I don't think he believes me.

"What guarantee do I have that you won't simply attack me again when my back is turned?"

"I'll make all our meals if I go back on my word and I hate to cook."

He considers me for a moment and then he nods and lets go of my hands. "It's a deal," he says as he stands up. Hey, was that a contraction he just used?

Kallen offers me his hand to help me up, but I wave him off. He shrugs and starts walking back towards the cabin so as quickly as I can, I pull magic and hit him in the back with a burst of snow causing him to fall face first into the snow on the ground.

"That was so worth it," I say referring to the cooking. Kallen pushes himself out of the snow and he looks like a Yeti when he stands up and starts stalking towards me. Okay, he looks mad again now.

I turn around and start running, fully expecting him to throw snow at me so I'm taken completely by surprise when he grabs the back of my jacket and pulls me backwards causing us both to fall with me ending up on top of him. He rolls out from under me and pins me to the ground with his knees straddling mine and his hands around my wrists again. "You are the most obnoxious and aggravating female I have ever met," he says as he glowers down at me.

He looks even cuter when he's mad because his eyes shine an intense green that isn't even found in nature. "Don't hold back," I say dryly, "tell me how you really feel."

"Do you want to know how I really feel," he asks narrowing his eyes at me.

No. "Yes."

"I feel like kissing you until you can't think about anything other than my lips on yours."

"Oh." That's not what I thought he was going to say. But I can't say it sounds like a bad idea.

Releasing his hold on my wrists he leans back and this time the smile does appear on his face. "But I'm not going to because I don't want to be accused of only being attracted to you because I have no better options." Simpering, he stands up and walks away and I lie here wishing I could shoot Fairy darts at him with my eyes.

CHAPTER 16

Kallen insists that I practice for two more hours until I am so tired, I have a hard time drawing a drop of magic from the earth. But even then he doesn't let me go inside. I'm pretty sure he's just trying to torture me.

"Why can't I go inside if I'm not able to draw any more magic right now?"

Without any sympathy whatsoever for my frozen fingers and toes, he says, "Because I want to show you what it should feel like channeling someone else's magic."

I back up and cross my arms over my chest. "Uh uh, no way. You are not going to burn me with your magic."

Kallen crosses his own arms and looks at me stubbornly. "That is my point, it should not burn which is why I want to teach you the proper way to do it."

I still shake my head. "Why do I need to learn to channel my magic through someone else if I'm learning to control it?"

"So you can tell when you are close to killing someone," he says evenly.

He knows I can't say no now but I'm not happy about it. I don't believe that it's not going to hurt. This would be the perfect opportunity for him to get his revenge for all the times when my magic burned through him. Grudgingly, I take off my glove and hold my hand out to him.

Kallen takes my hand and almost immediately I can feel warmth spread through me. It's not unpleasant but I still don't like it. I don't like being at someone else's mercy and I'm starting to get agitated. I want him to pull his magic back. I try pulling my hand out of his but he holds onto it more tightly. I'm beginning to get the same claustrophobic feeling I had when we were covered by snow in the avalanche. I have to get his magic out of me but I'm too weak from all the practicing.

As if it hears me and says 'no you're not,' my magic starts to rise. It starts out weak but it gets stronger and I hear Kallen say, "Xandra, let it go." But I can't. I feel like even though his magic is coming from the same place as mine, his magic is foreign and impure and my magic needs to cleanse me of it. I try to push my magic back down but it won't go, not as long as Kallen's magic is inside of me. Finally, I have pushed his magic out and I try to send mine back to the earth but now it shifts from defense to offense and it is determined to attack Kallen who is trying to let go of my hand and is letting his own magic retreat but I hold tight and he can't pry my fingers loose as my magic begins to burn through him. Attacking him because he attacked me. I'm trying to regain control but it's as if the basest part of my brain has taken over and is reacting on pure instinct and no signals from the higher functioning parts of my brain are able to communicate with it. I know I'm hurting him and I don't know how to stop.

"Xandra, please," I hear him gasp and he's on his knees now. I try to let go of his hand but I can't and I know Kallen's trying to fight but he's not strong enough. The instant the fight goes out of him and he loses consciousness my magic retreats. It flows down through me so fast I drop to my knees next to Kallen and open my eyes. He's so pale and still that for the longest second of my life, I think he's dead. Dead because I killed him.

But then he takes a breath, a gasping raspy breath that sounds like he can't get enough oxygen, but he's breathing and I'm so happy that tears I didn't know had formed start to fall from my eyes. "Kallen, wake up. You have to wake up!" I yell and I want to shake him but I don't know how badly I hurt him, if there are physical injuries caused by my magic.

Finally, he opens his eyes but they close again immediately as I hear him trying to talk. I put my ear close to his mouth to try to catch what he's saying. "Too strong, couldn't get it out," he says in a barely audible whisper.

I need to get him out of the snow and inside where it's warm. "Kallen," I yell because I think he lost consciousness again. "I need to get you inside but you have to help me because I can't lift you on my own." I put my arm under his shoulders and hang his arm over mine and I pull. I'm able to get him to a sitting position but I can't stand him up. "Kallen, you need to help me. I want to get you into the cabin. Please, you have to stand up and walk with me."

He nods slightly and even though he seems as weak as a baby, he somehow helps me stand him up and we walk slowly back to the cabin. I almost lose my grip on him several times and I am so relieved when I can reach the handle on the door and push it open. "Just a few more feet," I tell him. We make it to the cot and he slumps down on it. I push him down and swing his legs up so he's lying on it. I feel like every muscle in my body has been strained but I don't care, I got him in here. I take a blanket from the shelf above the cot and I cover him with it.

When I have him situated, I go to the fire and stoke it. I add more wood until there's a nice blaze going and the cabin begins to feel warm. I'm so worried about Kallen that I can hardly see straight. I go back to the cot and feel his forehead and he's so cold. Too cold and he's begun to shiver. I need to warm him up.

I grab a clean pan from the wall and I go outside and fill it with snow. Back in the cabin, I light a burner on the stove and I begin heating the snow until it becomes hot water in the pan. There are no towels in the cabin so I take off my outer sweater and I dip the sleeve in the water and wring it out. I place it on Kallen's forehead. I feel him start to relax as the warmth flows into him. When the sleeve becomes cool, I bring it back to the hot water and dip it back in. I keep doing this getting more and more worried that he's not waking up.

What if he never wakes up? "Kallen," I whisper. "Please, you have to wake up. I need you. I'm so very sorry I did this to you, please come back. You are haughty and arrogant and infuriatingly sexy and you laugh at me way too much but you're so important to me. I need you to teach me how to be a better Fairy. I promise I'll never hurt you again. Just please, come back to me. I care so very much for you, I can't lose you." I lay my head down on his chest and my tears soak into the blanket as I hold the warm sweater to him.

After what feels like forever, I feel him stir. "Kallen, are you awake?" I shake him gently by the arm. "Please be awake."

He pats my hand with his other arm. "I'm okay," he whispers. "Just need to sleep."

I nod even though his eyes are closed and he can't see me. I make sure the blanket is around him snugly and I retreat to the table leaving him in peace to sleep now that I know he's most likely okay. Folding my arms on the table I lay my head down and you'd think that I'd have no more tears left by now but they keep coming. I'm never going to learn to control my magic and the prophecy is probably going to come true not because I want it to but because I won't be able to stop it.

At some point I fall asleep. It's dark outside when I wake up stiff from sleeping at the table. When I sit up and yawn, I see Kallen sitting up on the cot with his back against the wall.

"You're awake," I say with a relieved smile. He nods and he has the strangest expression in his eyes. If I didn't know better, I would say it was fear. "How do you feel?"

"Better," he says.

"Can I get you anything? Are you hungry?" I would do just about anything for him to get that look out of his eyes.

He shakes his head. "No, thank you."

"I'm sorry," I say quietly and he doesn't respond. He just nods his head once.

"At least you get the cot," I say with a poor attempt at humor. This he doesn't respond to at all.

"Kallen, please talk to me. I've been so worried."

"Why didn't you stop?" he asks and I hear the accusation in his voice.

"I couldn't. I tried but I couldn't make it stop."

"I let my magic go but you still didn't stop."

"Kallen, I swear, I tried to make it stop but I couldn't. I would never hurt you like this on purpose."

"I thought I was going to die."

My chest tightens and I feel like I can't breathe. "I'm so sorry."

"Do you hate me so very much?"

"What?" I ask in bewilderment. "I don't hate you at all. Kallen, you have to believe me. I didn't do this on purpose."

"Every Fairy but you can control his or her magic."

I hang my head and my tears start to fall again. I turn away from him and sit on the floor with my knees pulled up to my chest because I can't face him right now. I can't stand to keep looking at the fear and accusation in his eyes. "Maybe," I begin but I have to stifle a sob before I can continue. "Maybe you were right when you came here. Maybe I am too much of a threat to both realms. I don't want to destroy anything, Kallen, but I can't control my magic. I would rather die by your hand than open the gateway with my dying blood."

Kallen doesn't say anything for a long time as I continue to stare into the fire. For all I know, he went back to sleep. I continue to hug my knees not even feeling the warmth of the fire as my tears continue to flow.

"Xandra," Kallen says softly.

"Yes?" I say but I don't turn around. I'm scared of what he's going to say.

"Will you please stop being so dramatic and come here?"

My brows slam together in mystification and I let go of my knees so I can turn around. He's still sitting on the cot with his back against the wall. He's still pale but not as pale as he was. "What did you say?"

"I asked you to stop being so dramatic and come here."

I search his face trying to understand what he's saying because it's not making sense to me. I nod numbly and I stand up, walking towards him slowly. When I reach the cot, he stretches out lying on his side and he pats the empty space on the narrow cot in front of him. Is this some kind of trick?

"Why?" I ask stupidly.

He sighs. "Because I am tired and I want to go back to sleep. That will be a lot easier if I do not have to hear you cry. It is much more pleasant when you are lying quietly next to me."

"You want me to sleep with you?"

"I am always amazed by your brilliant deduction," he says sardonically. "Yes, I want you to sleep with me."

"Why?" I ask again.

"Xandra, please stop talking and lay down. You're making my headache worse."

I have no idea how to respond to that so I do what he wants and I lie down next to him. The cot is almost too narrow for the two of us but Kallen wraps his arms around me like he did when we were in my sleeping bag and he pushes my hair aside so it's not in his face. He dumbfounds me even more when he lifts his head to kiss my cheek leaving my skin tingling. "I lied to you," he whispers in my ear.

Any other time I would have been angry about him admitting to another lie but I don't care right now. "It's okay."

He chuckles softly. "Do you not want to know what I lied about?"

I shake my head. "Whatever it is, it's okay."

I feel him smile against my cheek. "I'm not sure I like you this forgiving, it takes the fun out of teasing you. I lied to you when I said I would stop underestimating your power and overestimating your control over it. You were right when you called yourself an enigma and I've been treating you as a Fairy instead of a Witch Fairy. I need to admit that I have no idea how strong you are or how wild your magic is, and that I have no idea how to teach you to control it."

"Then you should do what you came here to do," I whisper back.

He sighs. "I recall telling you to stop being so dramatic, and I did not come to this realm to end your life. I came to assess if you would willingly allow the gate between realms to be opened and I know the answer to that. You would not. Also, you seem to be strong enough that no one could force you to do it. Just because your magic is wild and untamed does not mean you are going to use it willy-nilly and cause mass destruction. You can simply choose not to use it unless provoked as you have your entire life."

"Willy-nilly?" I ask with a tiny giggle. "You are old."

Kallen nips my earlobe. "Out of that entire speech, the only thing you heard was my use of an antiquated term?"

I turn my head and kiss his lips softly. "I heard everything you said. Thank you." I turn my head back and snuggle my body closer to his pulling his arms tighter around me and feel myself begin to relax, truly relax, for the first time since we started our journey together.

CHAPTER 17

I wake up a short while later because Kallen is awake and taking a huge interest in my neck and ear. "Mm, that tickles," I complain hoping he doesn't stop. He doesn't.

"I would find you just as beautiful if there were a million Fairy women for me to choose from," he whispers making me smile. I still don't know if I believe it, but it's nice to hear. Especially after the day we've had.

"May I kiss you?" he asks as his lips graze my ear.

"You are kissing me," I can't help but saying which causes him to nip my ear as he had earlier.

"Fine," I say with an exaggerated sigh as I maneuver myself so I am facing him.

He gives me a sour look. "I would hate to put you out."

"Well, I did almost kill you today, it's the least I can do," I tease not quite sure if it's too soon to be making 'I almost killed you' jokes.

"Are you telling me a kiss from you at this point would simply be out of remorse?" he asks with a glint in his eye that tells me it's not too soon. At least I hope that's what the glint means.

"Of course, would there be any other reason?"

With a growl of annoyance, he shifts so quickly I hardly know what he's doing until I'm flat against the cot with him lying on top of me. "Tell you what," he says holding himself up by his elbows so he doesn't have all of his weight on me. "I will start kissing you and you let me know when it is no longer about remorse but pleasure."

I purse my lips as I pretend to think about it. "Is there another option?"

He's having a hard time keeping his face serious as I continue to tease him. "Yes, you could simply admit that you would find it pleasurable if I kissed you."

I feign being shocked. "I could never admit that."

"You are the most stubborn, aggravating, and mouthy Witch Fairy I have ever come across."

I snort. "I'm the only Witch Fairy you've come across."

"You do have a point. Regardless, I am afraid I must go back to kissing you for my original reason."

"Oh? And what was that?"

He grins. "To shut you up." His lips are on mine and they're demanding and sexy and I open my mouth to him and there is absolutely no remorse in this kiss. I wrap my arms around his back and he moans softly when I slip my hands under his shirt to feel the skin of his muscular torso.

"Get rid of this," I murmur against his lips and then his shirt is gone leaving my hands plenty of space to roam without being inhibited.

"I have wanted to kiss you like this since the moment I saw you," he says as he kisses a trail down my jaw to find a sensitive spot behind my ear.

"Liar," I say and then inhale shakily as I feel his hand on my skin under my shirt. I spend about half a second deciding if that is okay and I come up with the answer definitely. I pull his mouth back to mine and relish in the feel of his touch as his hands explore the contours of my body.

I groan loudly in frustration when Kallen pushes up from me closing his eyes and breathing heavily. I try to pull his mouth back to mine but he's like a slab of marble and I can't. "What's wrong?" I ask utterly perplexed. I narrow my eyes and stare hard at him. "Is this because I'm a half-breed?"

His eyes open and they're jumping in amusement. "No, it is not. As a matter of fact, I have experienced a complete turnaround in my opinion regarding the attraction of a full-blooded Fairy. It seems that I happen to prefer half-breeds."

Now I'm really confused. "Then why did you stop kissing me?"

"Because, my beautiful Witch Fairy, ironic as it may be since I was the one who initiated this, I fear that you may truly only be kissing me because of what happened earlier today."

"I'm not," I assure him and try to pull him back to me but he still refuses to budge. He chuckles which makes me want to hit him more than I want to kiss him. "You're laughing at me again."

"I assure you, I am laughing in joy for your enthusiasm," he says and he leans down and kisses me lightly. I want to deepen the kiss but he pulls back again and rolls onto his side next to me. "But it would be wrong of me to let things go any further until we both know for certain this is what you want."

I turn onto my side in frustration and mumble under my breath, "Who died and made you the kissing police."

Smoothing my hair back from my neck, Kallen kisses it lightly. "I want to continue what we were doing just as badly as you seem to right now, but I fear we were heading toward committing to something I am not certain you want and I will not take advantage of our unusual circumstances. Your emotions are running high and I'm not convinced you are of the right frame of mind to make this decision. It is important to me that you truly want to kiss me out of sheer desire, not because of some misplaced guilt."

I really, really want to be mad at him. I do. But what he's saying makes perfect sense. Less than twenty-four hours ago, I had no intention of kissing him ever again and now I'm upset because he won't kiss me. I guess I can't have it both ways. I really do need to decide what I want my relationship with Kallen to be.

I sigh and relax next to him again and he wraps his arms around me and pulls me close to him. "Just so you know," he whispers softly, "if we ever made love, according to Fairy law, we would be hand-fasted."

I remember what that means and my body instantly tenses again. If Kallen and I were to have sex, he would consider us to be married. I couldn't have gone from arousal to 'what did I almost do' faster if I had taken an ice cold shower of sleet. It seems like he could have mentioned that at least once over the last few days. But then again, when is the right time to say to someone you barely know, 'by the way if we have sex we're married by Fairy law.'

It took a long time to fall asleep after Kallen's little bombshell so when I feel him moving to get out of bed around dawn, I moan and keep my eyes tightly closed. He must have let me go back to sleep because when I open my eyes again, the sun is streaming through the windows with late morning light. I rub my eyes and yawn as I sit up.

When I open my eyes and look around, I'm surprised that Kallen isn't in the cabin. I wonder what he could be doing. I kind of appreciate the fact that he's not here because it gives me time to figure out how I'm going to act around him. Though twenty minutes later when he comes into the cabin and shakes off the snow from his clothes, I'm not any closer to an answer.

"You're finally awake," he says as he puts down several pieces of wood next to the fireplace. "Are you hungry?"

"Starving," I say realizing I had skipped dinner last night because I was so worried about Kallen.

He has a teasing glint in his eye. "Me too and I believe you promised to cook all the meals if you did not keep your promise not to douse me with more snow yesterday."

"You've been up since dawn and you haven't eaten because you were waiting for me to cook for you? That's just pathetic," I grumble as I stand up. He laughs and puts some more wood in the fire. My bladder tells me I'm not doing anything until it's empty so I begin pulling on my boots and coat.

When I come back in, Kallen has already started some soup cooking. As soon as my nose smells it, my stomach starts growling loudly in a demand to be fed. Looking up from stirring the soup, he says, "I believe I have a new plan."

Please don't let it involve hand-fasting, I think as I say hesitantly, "Okay."

He raises his brows in a mocking way at my sudden and very obvious nervousness. "It does not have anything to do with physical contact between you and me," he says dryly. I visibly relax and begin to take off my coat. When I look back at Kallen, I see a shadow of what I'm sure is rejection in his eyes. Great, now I've hurt his feelings.

Moving on to a safer subject, I ask, "Does it have to do with Maurelle and Olwyn?"

I'm relieved when he says, "Yes."

"I'm all ears," I say and I'm warring with myself whether I should give him a kiss good morning or just sit down at the table. I finally figure if I have to think this hard about whether or not I should kiss him, I should just sit down. So I do.

Kallen pours the soup into the bowls and places one in front of me. "Thank you," I say with a genuine smile. "What's your plan?"

"Since it is apparently impossible to teach you any self-control," he says and I make a face at him which makes him laugh. "I think we should go with your strength."

My mouth drops open, "You want me to kill them?"

He looks as shocked as I feel. "What did I say that made you jump to that conclusion?"

Now I feel stupid. "Nothing. What did you mean?"

Shaking his head and staring at me for a moment, he finally continues. "As I was saying, we should go with your strength and that is using your wild magic on a grand scale."

"So I can start another avalanche or a rock slide?"

He frowns at me. "Are you going to let me finish or should I just expect you to interrupt after each sentence?"

I guess he woke up on the wrong side of the cot. I'm tempted to tell him yes, that's exactly what I mean to do but I manage to keep my mouth shut and make a please continue gesture with my hand.

Looking doubtful, he begins again. "The runners your father sent here, as I explained before, were chosen because of their willingness to do anything it takes to get the job done. They would bring you to him with barely a last breath in you if they get their hands on you."

"That sounds pleasant," I mumble and he cocks his head impatiently. I grimace and make a 'my lips are sealed' motion in front of my mouth. I'm not sure if he got what it meant but he continues anyway.

"Pooka warriors are nothing better than mercenaries. They understand violence better than they understand logic so reasoning with them is almost impossible. But you have already gone a long way, I'm sure, of impressing upon them that you are considerably stronger than they are. I believe taking the fight to them is our best bet. If we actively seek them out and take up an offensive strategy rather than defensive and then you give them an even better demonstration of your magic, that may be enough for them to tuck tail and run away."

I suddenly have a vision of a fox and a mountain lion tucking their tails between their back legs and running away and I can't help a giggle which makes Kallen look at me like I'm crazy. I start to explain but I close my mouth because it was probably one of those things you had to think of yourself or it wouldn't be funny. "Okay, I understand your reasoning, but what about what you said about them using my family against me?"

"I've been thinking about it and I believe a more forceful demonstration of your power may be enough to change their minds about anything like that. I also suspect, now mind you I am saying suspect because I do not know for sure, that you would be able to direct your magic so that it only affects who you want it to affect."

Now I look at him like he's crazy. "What on earth gives you that idea?"

He shrugs. "Part of it could probably be put down to intuition but a part of it is how you acted yesterday."

"When I almost killed you without meaning to. That doesn't seem like a good example to me."

"But when you focused your magic on me, even though you could not send it back down into the earth, you also pinpointed it only on me. Not as much as a flake of snow was affected. You saw me as the threat and you directed your attack only on me."

"I didn't attack you," I say sulkily and he cocks his head and raises his brows. Okay, maybe I did. "But what makes you think they'll be so afraid of me that they'll leave me alone for good? If they still come after me after what I did to them already doesn't that prove your theory incorrect?"

Kallen shakes his head. "No, because I know you were focusing most of your anger at me, not them. They did not get a true feeling of what it is like to have your magic burning inside of them. They probably believed that it was me who was doing it."

Good lord, he makes me sound like a monster. "But you said that if you hadn't drawn most of my magic inside of you, I would have killed them."

"I believe I was mistaken."

Now it's my turn to raise my eyebrows. "You? Mistaken?"

He gives me a sour look. "You stopped focusing on them when they became unconscious and then focused only on me. I think letting my magic go only sped up the inevitable. I believe you would have been able to push it out of me eventually."

I can't help the tiniest of smug smiles. "Is that your way of telling me that even though I'm a half-breed I'm stronger than you?"

He narrows his eyes but doesn't rise to the bait. "Yesterday, when it was clear that there was no more fight left in me, your magic pulled back. I felt it. I do not believe your magic will make you kill someone but you can hurt them awfully badly." I can almost see the memory of the pain I had caused him flash over his eyes. "Unlike myself, I believe that is a lesson they will learn quickly."

I sigh and look at him ruefully. "I'm sorry for all the times I hurt you."

He shrugs as if it was nothing. "You were only doing as I instructed and neither of us knew what we were doing."

Wow, he's a new and improved Kallen. "I wish I could be as confident about this plan as you are."

"I truly believe it is the best option. I know how unappealing a life of running from them through the mountains is to you."

I can't figure out the look on his face now. "Can I think about it for at least a day? Maybe work my way up to thinking it's a good plan?" I know I keep saying how badly I want to go home but this is putting a lot of faith in magic neither of us truly knows anything about.

He inclines his head in a half nod. "That seems fair. Are you done?" he asks indicating my empty bowl. I nod so he picks up both bowls and the pan and brings them outside to wash them out.

Obviously, we won't be doing any practicing today so we're now faced with filling a whole day with something other than magic. Even though the cabin is nice and warm because Kallen has kept a good fire going, I move in front of the fireplace and revel in the heat. After spending so many freezing nights in the mountains, I don't think I'll ever truly be warm again.

CHAPTER 18

I smile at Kallen when he comes in with the dishes. He hangs the pan on the wall and puts the bowls and spoons in the cupboard. "Thank you for making lunch, I really would have done it."

He turns towards me and shrugs. "I simply warmed a can of soup." He looks gorgeous standing there. He has changed his clothes, something I regretfully have not been able to do since all of mine are buried in a cave, and he now has on jeans and a dark green long sleeved tee that fits snugly around his muscular chest. The green of his shirt makes his eyes even more amazing. What the hell is wrong with me that I don't know if I want to kiss him?

Deciding to avoid the subject, I say, "Will you tell me about the Fae realm now?"

He looks slightly embarrassed. "I am sorry I was not more forthcoming the last time you asked. I am afraid I was taking out my feelings about never seeing my home again on you when it is certainly not your fault."

"Must we do this?"

He looks confused. "Do what?"

"Analyze everything that has happened. You already gave me a blanket apology."

He smiles now so he must remember using those words himself not that long ago. "I guess I did." He sits down next to me and he's still a head taller than me. I like tall guys. Okay, I need to move off the subject of Kallen's body.

"What's it like?"

"It's different than your realm in many ways. Whereas humans have certainly come a long way with creating things by hand that

Fairies are able to create with magic, it has come at a cost. Much of your realm has become ugly because of the facilities and chemicals necessary to create these things. The Fae realm does not have any of that. For those who cannot create something on their own, there are others who can create it for them."

As much as I want to hear about the Fae realm I have to interrupt him. "Do you mean things like clothes?"

He nods but then he seems to realize his mistake as color floods into his cheeks. He actually looks contrite when he says, "Yes, I could have used my magic to make you your own blanket and myself a sleeping bag. I much preferred sharing with you."

My mouth falls open. I don't know whether to be furious with him for lying to me or be incredibly flattered that he wanted to be so close to me regardless of all his half-breed talk. Another thought crosses my mind. That means he was most likely attracted to me as early as the first night we spent in the mountains. Maybe it's not because I'm his only Fairy choice.

The thought makes me smile and then laugh and relief washes over his face. "You are not mad at me?"

Instead of answering, I rise up onto my knees in front of him and wrap my arms around his neck. I can still see a trace of wariness in his eyes as he fears retaliation of some sort. But I don't retaliate, I kiss him instead. It's a sweet kiss, not meant to be too intense. Just a promise of things that might come later. I pull back and say, "No, I am not mad at you. But you're still a jerk."

"You know, I have been told that more in the last several days than I have in my entire life. But I also never behaved as badly as I have over the last several days so it has been deserved." He smiles and pulls me towards him, not to kiss me again, but so I can sit closer to him as we talk. I sit nestled between his legs facing the fire and he rests his chin on my head.

I say the first thing that pops into my head. "Why haven't you gotten married in the last three hundred and sixty seven years?" Another thought hits me that I don't say out loud. If he hasn't gotten married, that means he's a virgin just like I am. I'm glad I'm sitting in front of him because a rush of color washes into my face.

"As I said before, time moves differently in the Fae realm. When I told you how old I was, I was giving you the equivalent of how many years had passed in your realm since I was born. But in the Fae realm, I am not considered much older than your seventeen years."

"Why does time move differently between the realms?"

He chuckles. "I am afraid I cannot answer that. It is how it is."

"Does that mean you will age differently if you are in this realm?"

I feel him nod his head. "Yes and no. When I explained to you that Fairies could live to be a couple of thousand years old, I was again referring to years in your realm. But in the Fae realm, it would only feel like the amount of time an average human life span is."

"If your realm orbits the same sun, I don't understand how that's possible."

"The Fae realm is much more magical than yours. I do not know how to explain the differences in time in a scientific way. Possibly our realm stays stagnant as your realm turns more often under the sun."

"Did you have a lot of girlfriends?"

"I had a lot of friends who were female but I am thinking that is not quite what you are asking me."

Again, I'm glad he can't see my face. "Were there a lot of girls that you kissed?"

I feel him laughing but he pulls me close. "No, there have not been a lot of girls that I have kissed. I am embarrassed to admit that I really was very much opposed to being with someone who was not full-blooded Fae and as I explained, they are not common. But I was highly sought after because of my blood status. Several Fairy families approached my grandmother about connecting our families through hand-fasting."

Okay, a sudden surge of jealousy rips through me as I think about other girls wanting him so I ignore that part of what he said. "Why your grandmother?"

"My parents died before the Fae realm was closed. They were killed by humans." Okay, that explains his prejudice.

"I'm sorry."

"It was a long time ago."

"So, your grandmother said no to all these families?" I hate to think that he has a fiancée back in the Fae realm who he wants to get back to. It doesn't sound like he does but he hasn't always been up-front and honest with me.

"Yes. She always told me that I was meant for a love match. She also told me that my destiny lay elsewhere. I never understood what she meant until she approached me about coming here."

"Sounds like she was as cryptic as my mom."

He chuckles. "Yes."

"If you wanted to be close to me that first night, why were you such a jerk?" Okay, I didn't mean to come back to this but it jumped out of my mouth before I could close it.

He takes a moment to answer. "I was angry with you."

"With me? Why?"

"Because you were not who you were supposed to be."

What is he talking about? "Who was I supposed to be?"

"The Witch Fairy from the prophecy. The one my grandmother sent me here to stop at any cost. But as soon as I met you, I knew I could not do that. Essentially, I was at war with myself. I was angry that I gave up my world to stop an evil Princess and I ended up meeting you instead."

"I'm not sure if you just insulted me or complimented me."

He chuckles again. "At the time, neither was I."

"How are we going to find Maurelle and Olwyn?"

He becomes still. After a moment, he puts a finger under my chin and lifts my face towards his. "Does that mean you agree to my plan?"

"I can't think of a better one and I really want this to be over."

"I will miss you when this is over."

I'm confused. "What do you mean?"

He smiles sadly. "I have the distinct impression that you do not want to see me again after this."

I roll my eyes. "Here I thought you had an ego big enough to keep you warm but you're just as confused as I am about all of this, aren't you?"

"It seems so."

I lift my face until I can reach his mouth and I kiss him lightly. "How about if we just take this one day at a time? I'm still getting used to the idea that I like you instead of hate you."

He laughs. "Well, I guess there is hope then."

We sit quietly for a while in front of the fire. Finally, I say, "You didn't answer my question. How are we going to find Maurelle and Olwyn?"

"I am going to call to them."

"On the phone?"

"No, I am able to project a thought to another Fairy from quite a distance away."

"Another cool thing I probably won't be able to do because I can't control my magic," I grumble.

"Control may still come with time," Kallen assures me but I can hear the doubt in his voice.

"Can all Fairies do that?"

"No, each Fairy is somewhat unique in their abilities. Drawing magic from the earth and creating something magically such as clothes is a constant among full- blooded Fairies but each of us have our own special talents as well. For instance, I am able to send telepathic messages but I am not able to receive them. I am also able to pull more magic than almost all other Fairies making me stronger and difficult to defeat in a fight." I remember him saying that the night he was super angry with me. "My grandmother has the power of divination."

I look up at him quizzically. "What's that?"

"She can see bits of the future. They are out of context and sometimes very brief but she is good at deciphering her visions. But as with all glimpses into the future, they are not certain to happen because millions of decisions and choices must be made precisely for that end result. Any shift could alter the future."

"So, when she has a vision she doesn't like, does she try to prevent that outcome?"

He's quiet for a moment. Finally, he says, "Yes."

"Did she see me?"

Again, it takes him a moment to answer. "Yes."

He's moved back to monosyllabic answers like when we first met which is making me extremely nervous. "What did she see?"

"Something that will not come to pass so it is not worth discussing."

I turn around and kneel in front of him again so I can see his face better. "Really? Come on. You're going to go with that answer and expect me to just say, 'yeah okay whatever'?"

I glower at him with my arms crossed over my chest as he stubbornly refuses to say anything else. We sit like this for several long moments. Finally, I demand, "Tell me what she saw, Kallen. It's only fair that I should know."

His eyes move away from mine for a moment and when he looks back at me I see sorrow there. Well, that's just a little bit foreboding, now isn't it? "Just spit it out for god's sake. It can't be any worse than the things that are already running through my mind now that you've said that much."

He sighs. "As much as I do not want to keep you from knowing anything else, telling you about a path that has already been altered seems moot."

"I like to hear about moot things. Then I can feel all warm and fuzzy on the inside knowing they're not going to happen."

He runs his hand through his silky black hair nervously which-- for just a quick second-- makes me think about me doing that instead of what I'm asking him to do. But I force my mind away from his numerous physical attributes. Lots of time to dwell on those later. I hope. I think I hope. I still don't know where I want this to go.

Kallen pulls me out of my mental conversation with myself by finally speaking. "She saw you forcing the gateway to the Fae realm open."

"Oh." I thought he was going to say that she saw me die a horrendous death by Kallen's hand. The thought that I would deliberately open the gateway so Fairies could come through and wreak havoc on this realm somehow seems worse. "She specifically saw me choosing to do this, not being forced?"

He nods and puts his hands on my waist as if he thinks I'm going to collapse. "She even knew the color of your aura."

Oh, yeah. I forgot that my aura becomes visible when I'm using my magic. My clashing aura.

"Where is the passageway to the Fae realm?"

"It can be in many different places. When the two realms were open to each other, a Fairy could enter this realm through anywhere there was a light."

I gasp as I completely lose track of the conversation for a second.

"That explains my name!"

He chuckles. "Defending men from light, it was rather clever on your mother's part."

"Which light did you use to get here?"

"Over the years, King Dagda continued to come through to this realm during the spring equinox and he would use those three days to hunt for your mother. She must not have used much magic in the first few years because he would come back angry and frustrated and even more determined. As you got older and were not discovered, your mother must have felt that she could begin using her magic again and the last few of your years, he was able to detect her magic."

"Because he could taste it?" I asked recalling him telling me this when we first met. Was that really just a matter of days ago?

"In a manner of speaking, yes. Last year, he was able to track her magic to the base of the mountain you live on so that is where he sent Maurelle and Olwyn through, and where I followed them. It took them several days to locate you but as your mother is the only Witch using magic in this area, she made finding you inevitable."

Poor Mom, it really was her fault. "So, when do you want to meet them?" My confidence in his plan hasn't really grown any but Kallen's right, I don't want to keep running and hiding.

"Do you still want a day to rest and prepare?"

I laugh but without humor. "Not really much to prepare. My magic has two settings, dormant and destructive."

"If you are ready, then I will call to them now. It may take them some time to find us as I cannot give them exact directions."

Now? Oh boy, am I really ready for this? My heart starts racing and I'm suddenly too warm by the fire. I stand up, moving out of Kallen's embrace and start pacing the cabin. In a matter of minutes or hours, I could be facing two Pooka warriors on the theory that I am better with my magic than they are. It's kind of like having a pop quiz on something you haven't bothered to learn and instead of failing someone could wind up dead. I miss my schoolwork. I would take a pop quiz on physics rather than this any day.

"It's done," Kallen says quietly behind me.

I bite my bottom lip as I turn to look at him. "How do you know they got the message?"

He smiles half-heartedly. "I just know."

I wish I could know things with his level of certainty. The only thing I know right now is that I am scared out of my mind. "Okay."

CHAPTER 19

Kallen covers the distance between us in two steps. He cups my cheeks in his hands and he leans down to give me a light kiss and then he leans his forehead against mine. "This is going to work," he says confidently but I'm not sure if he's trying to convince me or himself. Probably both.

I nod and wrap my arms around his waist and he folds me into his and we stand like that for a long time without saying anything. It's not even noon yet and it already feels like the longest day of my life. Or the last day. The thought hits me that if I said that out loud Kallen would probably tell me to stop being so dramatic as he had last night. I can't help but smile as I remember how sweet he was then compared to many of our other conversations. As he's opened up more, I understand his behavior better but the thought still hasn't left my mind that I am his only option of keeping a connection to the Fae. How did I go from never having had a date as of last week to now being involved in one of the world's most complicated relationships? When life makes you a dichotomy wrapped up into an enigma you gotta embrace the drama, I guess.

With that thought in mind, I move my arms from his waist to his shoulders and stand on my tippy toes as I pull him towards me so I can kiss him. He meets my lips hungrily and we both put all of our unspoken fears and hopes into this kiss. The world seems to have collapsed around us and we are the only two in the universe as we explore each other's mouths. With a swoop, Kallen picks me up and carries me to the cot without ever taking his lips from mine. He lays me down and he pulls back just long enough to study my face looking for any sign of hesitancy. He finds none.

Covering my body with his, he brings his lips back to mine. I tug on his shirt and he makes it disappear and I savor the feel of his taut muscles under my hands. "Mine, too," I whisper in his ear and a groan starting deep in his throat escapes him as he magically makes my shirt disappear.

"You are so beautiful," he whispers against my mouth as his hands explore my body. "I hate the thought of never seeing you again after today. It's driving me mad."

"I never said I don't want to see you again," I gasp as his mouth finds the sensitive spot behind my ear.

"Maybe not in those words but it comes through loud and clear in everything else you say," he says throwing my own words back at me.

Tearing my hands from his gorgeous body, it's my turn to cup his face in my hands. His eyes are dark green with desire when he looks down at me. "I know I've been kind of wishy-washy on this whole topic, but I can't imagine any more not having you in my life. You've become too important to me, even if you are the world's biggest jerk sometimes." As soon as the words leave my mouth, I know they're true. I don't know that we'll get married someday and live happily ever after, but I do know that I am beginning to care for him very much. His lips are on mine again and he lets me know how my words affected him. Apparently in a really good way.

I don't know how far we would have gone as we lost ourselves in each other. Some clothes are still on, others aren't. But everything comes to an abrupt halt when Kallen becomes stock still and lifts his mouth from mine. His eyes are suddenly glowing with a combination of passion, anger and something that almost resembles fear. "They're coming," he says and once again I feel like a cold shower of sleet has been dumped on me.

Rising from the cot, Kallen uses his magic and is completely dressed instantly. It's a little slower going for me as I pull the turtleneck I was wearing over my head. I probably could have asked Kallen to magic me new clothes, but even after what we were doing that seems too personal.

Pulling on my coat and boots with fingers that are going numb with stress, I have about a million thoughts running through my mind at once of the past, the present, and of the future. I wonder if this is what people who have near death experiences feel right before they die? Looking up at Kallen, I ask, "How long?"

"If they keep on the path they are on, it should only be a few minutes. They must have been following our trail already when I called to them." His face is grim but his eyes are flashing with confidence and anger.

Standing up, I walk into his arms. Who knew I'd be this touchy-feely when I finally got a boyfriend? That is, if Kallen is my boyfriend. I guess we haven't really discussed the details. Dragging my mind back to the more pressing matter of the Pooka warriors who want my dying blood, I ask against his chest, "Are you sure I can do this?"

His answer is strong and immediate. "Positive."

I smile at his conviction. "You have been known to be wrong before, you know."

"Very rarely and never more than once a year so I've filled my quota already," he says teasingly and I appreciate that we are both trying to ease each other's fears.

Dropping his arms from around me, he steps back with his hands on my shoulders. "Are you ready?"

No. Nope. Never. Not in this lifetime. Not going to do it. "Yes."

He holds his hand out to me and I place mine in it. He squeezes gently and then leads me outside. I don't even notice the cold as I stare at the trees where Kallen is staring and wait what feels like a thousand lifetimes for Maurelle and Olwyn to come walking through them towards us.

A big part of me is relieved that they are actually in clothes this time as they approach us. Their nakedness has always been a bit disconcerting for my prudish sensibilities. When they are close enough for us to hear them, Maurelle looks pointedly at our hands which are still clasped together and then up at me with her trademark sneer. "I see you prefer being the lion's toy rather than seeking safety with the lambs."

I can't help but snort. "Yeah, because you're so harmless."

"Your hair is quite mussed. I wonder what you two have been up to?" she says with a wicked grin. "Are you going to hide behind your Fairy lover like you did last time?"

"I did nothing to you the last we met," Kallen says in a voice of steel.

Now it's Maurelle's turn to snort. "As if a half-breed Fairy so young could hold that much magic."

Kallen shrugs. "I made the mistake of assuming that myself and it almost got me killed. I forgot that she is a Witch Fairy, not a weak Cowan Fairy such as yourself. Just how much do you know about the power of a Witch Fairy, Maurelle?"

Her confidence seems to falter for a moment but she recovers quickly. "Intimidation with lies isn't going to work, Kallen."

He shrugs again. "Suit yourself but I have warned you."

I have no idea what I should be doing. Kallen and I didn't discuss when I should, for lack of a better word, attack them. I try to inconspicuously look up at him to see if I can get some sort of hint from his face but it doesn't go unnoticed by Maurelle. "Oh, the little Witch Fairy is scared, how cute is that," she laughs. "Do not worry, little one, we only want to bring you home to Daddy."

My grip on Kallen's hand grows tighter as I listen to her lies. "So Daddy can kill me and use my dying blood to open the gateway."

"Oh my, the cat is out of the bag now, is it?" Maurelle purrs. "Very naughty of you, Kallen, sharing all of our little secrets with the Princess. You will have a lot to atone for when King Dagda returns to this realm and finds you."

"Atonement can only occur when one is repentant," Kallen says apparently unconcerned about the reaction of the King. For a second, Maurelle's eyes flash with anger at his lackluster response to her threat but again, she recovers quickly.

Maurelle shakes her head from side to side as if in pity. "Kallen, Kallen, Kallen, you are too proud for your own good. I wonder how your grandmother will feel about your lack of atonement when she is made to pay for your sins as well."

Kallen's hand tightens around mine a fraction, but that's the only outward sign that he's affected by her words. Evenly, he says, "My grandmother is the strongest Sheehogue Fairy alive; she cannot be brought down by a Pooka."

Maurelle makes a face at him. "You are just no fun to play with," she says acerbically. She turns to me. "I bet you are much more fun to play with. Do you know where we were before we came looking for you?"

I shrug. "I don't know. Shopping?"

She smiles in what she probably thinks is condescension. She misses the mark by a long shot compared to Kallen's mastery of it. "We paid a little visit to that awful family of yours. I must say, you should be grateful your features are those of the Fae because their mousy hair and blue eyes are just not attractive at all."

"My mom had protection spells around the house; you couldn't have gotten to them." Please, please let that be true. Kallen must have sensed my growing panic because he gives my hand a quick squeeze in support.

"Tsk, tsk, did Kallen not explain to you how easy it is to absorb a Witch's magic? Your mother tried to repel us but without Kallen there to provide assistance, she was not able to muster up enough power in her spirit form. It was a simple matter to relieve her of her Cowan Witch child."

I feel my face pale. "What did you do to Zac?"

"Do? Why nothing yet. We simply lured him away from the house with a song, much like the fable of the Pied Piper." She simpers towards Kallen. "A Pooka magic you did not know we possessed."

Through a clenched jaw, Kallen says, "You do not possess that power; a spell must have been created for you."

Maurelle laughs. "Oh, you are always the clever one. Alright, I admit that we did have assistance with the spell but that really does not change the outcome, now does it?"

I feel my blood start to boil as anger builds inside of me. "Where is my brother?" I demand.

Maurelle raises her eyebrows as she looks at me. "Losing your temper, are you? Now that's not going to get your brother home safe and sound is it?"

It's happening just like Kallen said it would before. This is a stupid, stupid plan that's going to get me and probably my entire family killed. "Did you hurt him?" I ask and even I can hear the desperation in my voice.

What could pass for a smile on a snake touches her lips. "Not yet. You get to decide if we hurt him or not. But if anything happens to us, you won't ever be able to find him."

There it goes. Our entire plan derailed by one sentence. It would be like trying to find a dust mote in a hay stack if they hid him in the mountains. If he is even still alive. But I can't take the risk that he's not. I have to believe they left him alive. Please let them have kept him alive. "What do you want me to do?" I say defeated.

Kallen looks at me in shock. "Xandra, you cannot give up. It is more likely than not that she is telling you lies!"

I shake my head. "I can't take that chance."

His eyes are pleading with me. "By saving your brother's life, you will be dooming the lives of this entire realm."

I look up at him sadly. "He's my brother, Kallen. I can't let him pay with his life when I can do it with mine. Your grandmother was right; I am going to willingly open the realms."

Maurelle's face is the picture of sadistic pleasure. "I knew you would see it my way. All you have to do is come with us and your brother's life will be spared above all others."

Kallen turns me to face him with his hands on my shoulders and he shakes me. "Xandra, listen to me. It does not have to happen this way. Every little decision affects the future and can change its outcome. Give us the opportunity to make this turn out a different way."

I shake my head and I feel the first of what will probably be many tears on my cheek. "I can't." Turning to Maurelle, I say, "I will go with you but you have to free my brother first."

She looks at me as if I'm crazy. "Why would we release our only leverage before you have completed your task? Would you have us believe that Kallen would not try to jump in and rescue his little half-breed lover?"

I look at Kallen pleadingly. "Tell her you won't. Promise you won't."

His face looks carved in stone as he looks down at me with fear and what just might be hatred in his eyes. I understand if that's what it is, he has every right to hate me. His voice has a hard edge to it when he speaks. "You may choose not to fight, but I will not."

"I'm not choosing not to fight, I'm choosing to save my brother's life," I reason.

"Dig deep down into your heart. Do you really believe that these two," he says as he points to Maurelle and Olwyn, "will do anything they promise? They are mercenaries, Xandra. If your brother is still alive he will be the first one they kill just because they won't want to have to deal with bringing him home!" He's practically shouting at me now.

Maybe if Kallen hadn't been focusing all of his attention on me, just maybe he would have felt the Fairy darts coming from the woods and been able to avoid them. As Kallen's face contorts in pain, he drops to his knees. I drop down next to him. "Kallen, are you okay?"

His breath is strangled as he attempts to talk. "Don't let them make you do it," he says and he drops his head as his hands fall onto the snow. He is barely able to keep himself off the ground.

With a shell-shocked look I turn to Maurelle. "How?" I ask and she knows what I mean. There are only two of them, could only be two of them, so who threw the Fairy darts?

"Kallen should have been a much better instructor because he knows that I can perform the spell of glamour. If his emotions and senses were not all wrapped up in you, he may have remembered." She couldn't look more pleased with herself, as if she had just stolen the first prize trophy at the science fair from the smartest kid in school. But this isn't school and the prizes at stake are lives, not trophies.

I feel my magic building as I watch Kallen struggling to breathe. Without even turning my head, I ask, "What's glamour?"

Maurelle laughs wickedly. "Not that you need the information for later, but I can make things appear to be here when they are not. Even other Fairies." She says a word I don't understand and when I look over at her, the figure of Olwyn is gone. I wondered why he was so quiet and let her do all the talking. It was because he wasn't really there. He was in the woods waiting for the opportunity to catch Kallen off guard. Which he did because of me.

"Now, I am afraid it will be just too risky to attempt to bring you home if you are in any condition to fight. I do not believe Kallen that it was not his magic that affected us so yesterday but no sense in taking any chances when we are this close to getting what we want." As soon as those words leave her mouth, I feel something hit my chest and half a second later, something hits my arm. I look down to find two Fairy darts that sliced through my coat and are embedded in my skin. Now that just wasn't nice.

CHAPTER 20

I wait for a long moment expecting to be incapacitated as Kallen is. His arms and legs are getting weaker and I don't think he'll stay conscious much longer by how pale he is. "Why did you shoot him with two if one would have incapacitated him?" I ask Maurelle as I continue to stare at Kallen. I really need to help him because he's dying. I wonder why I'm so calm about this. Maybe I'm in shock or maybe I'm just dreaming now because I'm a Fairy so I must be sensitive to Fairy darts and am probably unconscious.

It seems to take Maurelle a moment to find her voice. She looks so discombobulated when I turn to look at her. Discombobulated. I always wanted to use that word in a sentence just because it sounds so funny.

"Because two darts will bring a Fairy so close to death it can be difficult to tell they are really alive," Maurelle says in a voice that sounds so much less confident than it did before. I wonder what happened to make her sound like that.

"So, now you can transport us to my father without us being able to fight you off. Then he's going to kill me, right?"

"Yes," Maurelle says and I think she's trying to sound confident again. Good for her, she should stick to her guns.

I see Olwyn coming towards us from the woods. He has the strangest expression on his face. I wonder if he's going to carry me away or if Maurelle is. He looks stronger; he'll probably have to carry Kallen because I don't think Maurelle could lift him. She's so short that if she slung him over her shoulders, his head and feet would probably scrape against the ground. I get that mental image in my mind and it's the funniest thing I've ever seen and I start laughing. It would definitely be better if Olwyn carried Kallen.

"What's going on?" I hear Olwyn ask Maurelle. Okay, I never thought he was the brightest bulb in the box but even he should be able to see that they've won and they can just drag us out of here and do what they want with us. Moron.

"Hit her with another one," Maurelle says in a harsh whisper. I wonder what she means. A second later, something puts another hole in my jacket in the area of my chest. Okay, this is just getting downright rude now. I really loved this jacket. It's been like my second skin for days now. I imagine myself as a snake shedding my skin because someone has rudely put a hole in it. I'd make a pretty snake I think with black skin like my hair and pretty green eyes like mine. Oh, is that too vain of me? Kallen did say I have beautiful eyes, though, so it must be okay for me to say it.

"It's not working," Maurelle hisses. "She looks like she's drunk but nothing else is happening."

Drunk? Does she mean me? I hope not because I've never had a drop of alcohol in my life. Oh no, is that what these darts in my coat are? Did they get me drunk with them? I'm only seventeen. It's not right to contribute to the delinquency of a minor.

Turning to Maurelle, I ask, "Did you get me drunk?" Hmm, my words aren't slurring. Shouldn't they be slurring if I'm drunk? I don't know because Mom and Dad never drink but that's how it always happens on TV.

"Um, yes," Maurelle says as if she's not sure.

Standing up I put my hands on my hips as I face her. "You're not supposed to give alcohol to minors. That's against the law."

"What is she talking about?" Olwyn hisses.

Maurelle shrugs. "I do not know, just go with it." To me she says, "It is not against the law where we come from, and we need to be getting back there now."

Back there? Where? Oh, I remember now. They want to take me back to the Fae realm but there's something else. Something about me and my blood. It hits me and I start to feel really mad. "Hey! You guys are going to kill me!"

Maurelle and Olwyn are backing up because I've started walking towards them. "It's even worse to try to kill someone than it is to give a minor alcohol. You are not nice people, or Fairies, or whatever you are." I put my hand to my head because I'm starting to get a headache. It must be because I'm now getting bombarded with visual memories. There's Kallen being a jerk, that one's coming up a lot in this barrage of images scrolling through my mind. I remember Maurelle and Olwyn trying to catch me in the woods and Maurelle threw me into a tree. I remember kissing Kallen and that's so much better than any of the other memories. But the scrolling of memories stops as the last two sink into my mind. They may have killed my brother and they may have killed Kallen. Neither of those actions are forgivable.

It's as if remembering these two things clears my mind of a lot of its haziness. My eyes focus more clearly on Maurelle and she gasps as she comprehends that I'm no longer as confused as I had been for the last few minutes. "You hurt people I care about," I say as I move closer to her.

"Olwyn, do something," she hisses at him.

Like an ox, Olwyn lumbers towards me. I don't want to waste my time with him; it's Maurelle who needs to pay for what they have done. Olwyn's just her lackey. Taking my eyes briefly from Maurelle, I pull on my magic and ram it so hard into Olwyn that he flies backwards several feet. "Sleep," I order him and then his eyes are closed.

"What can I do to save Kallen?" I ask Maurelle as I focus my attention back on her. She's looking from Olwyn to me and back as if she doesn't understand what happened. Well, she should be paying attention to just me. Pulling on my magic again, I reach out for her and I feel it the second my magic starts to burn inside of her. Not too much, not enough so she can't tell me what I want to know. "What can I do to save Kallen?" I ask again.

"N-nothing," she stammers. "The poison has been in his blood too long. He's going to die soon." Oh, now that just pisses me off so I shove more magic inside of her and she screams.

"Oh, be quiet," I say and no more sound comes from her mouth for the moment. I look back at Kallen and he's completely on the ground now. "Stay there," I say to Maurelle and I hold her in place with my magic. Now I reach out to Kallen and I imagine my magic burning the poison from his body. I'm not burning him, just the poison. There's a lot of it, so it takes a moment. I wish it would hurry up because I still need to get more information from Maurelle about my brother.

After what seems like forever, Kallen coughs and then coughs again and his breathing becomes more regular and some color starts to come back to his skin. Finally. But now I have this poison hanging between us. Magic needs balance Kallen told me. The poison can't be taken from Kallen and then given no place else to go. I turn back to Maurelle and smile at her but it must not be a very nice smile because her eyes are as big as saucers. She's trying really hard to say something but I still have her gagged with my magic. "Live and let live – fairly take and fairly give," I say right before I shove the poison inside of her and she screams a silent scream as it burns a path to her vital organs.

"Speak," I say and sound is coming from her now. "Tell me where my brother is."

She shakes her head and doubles over with the pain of the poison just like Kallen had. "I can make this last a very long time," I tell her matter-of-factly because it's true. I can.

She looks up at me and between gasps she asks, "How are you doing this?"

I point at my chest. "Witch Fairy, remember? You know, a dichotomy wrapped up in an enigma." She doesn't seem to understand the big words so I roll my eyes and spell it out for her. "I'm not affected by magical things the same way a Fairy or a Witch is because I am both joined together. My magic is stronger because of it, which I'm willing to continue to prove to you if you don't tell me where my brother is."

Maurelle debates whether she's going to tell until she convulses with another wave of pain. "If I tell you will you promise not to kill me?"

I purse my lips. "Murder is pretty distasteful."

"We never had him. We went back to your house and they were all gone, even your ghost parents. I only said we had him to force you to come with us."

"Wow, Kallen was right all along. I should probably listen to him more but he just frustrates me so much it's hard to not push him over a cliff sometimes. He's gorgeous, though, isn't he?"

Maurelle looks at me like she doesn't know if she's supposed to answer me or not. I raise my eyebrows in an 'I'm waiting' way. "Yes," she finally says, "he's the handsomest Fairy in the Fae realm."

"Did he have a lot of girlfriends? You know, did he date a lot?" I ask. Why does she keep looking at me like that, I think it's a pretty reasonable question if I'm considering dating the guy. Fairy. Whatever.

"I-I do not recall ever hearing of him having any connections to a female Fairy other than friendship."

I narrow my eyes at her. "Are you telling me the truth? I don't want you to say something just because you think it's what I want to hear."

Maurelle glares at me. "I hate Kallen, I'd be glad to tell you if he did." Oh, jealous much? Sounds like she has the hots for him, too.

A sudden wave of nausea hits me and I stumble slightly. Looking down at myself, I realize I never pulled the Fairy darts out of my coat. I tug on the first one and a sharp gasp of pain escapes my mouth. Looking down at it, I complain loudly, "Hey! These have barbs in them so they hurt more coming out!" I pull out the other two getting madder each time the pain hits me.

Maurelle is on her knees and she's looking at me like she thinks she may have a chance at escape so I refocus my magic and she falls to the ground again. You know, I thought it would be more fun hurting these two but it's really not. With a heavy sigh of disappointment I stand over her. I'm distracted momentarily by Kallen who is now sitting in the snow staring at me like he's never met me before. He better not use being poisoned as an excuse not to remember that he's got a serious crush on me. I'll be pissed.

Pulling my attention back to Maurelle, I say, "What am I going to do with you two? Kallen thought that if I showed you how much stronger I am than you, you'd just leave me alone and live out the rest of your life in this realm but I think he's wrong. I think you'd just be coming back over and over and over again until just the sight of you would make me want to forget that I don't have a taste for killing Fairies. I didn't even like to eat the animal that Kallen killed for us to eat because I had to see it with its head on. Isn't that gross? It would be much grosser if it was a person." Maurelle nods her head dumbly as if she doesn't know what else to do as she holds her middle and fights the pain.

"You know what seems like the best solution?" I ask and I wait politely until she shakes her head no. This is a two-sided conversation after all.

"I think I should just send you home." Her eyes get huge as she looks up at me.

"Xandra, you can't do that!" Kallen says loudly as he picks himself up and starts walking towards me. He seems a little unsteady. Maybe I didn't get all the poison out.

I smile at him. "Don't worry, I'm not going to let the other Fae out, I'm just going to send them back in."

His eyebrows slam together and he shakes his head adamantly. "Xandra, it doesn't work that way. If you open the realm to send them back then it stays open. Remember," he says much more gently as if he's talking to a child. I really, really hate it when he does that. "You would have to die for that to happen."

I turn to face him fully. "Wow, you have no faith in me whatsoever, do you? Just because you're three hundred and fifty years older than me, you think you know everything, don't you?" He's close enough now that I can poke him hard in the chest. "You promised me that you wouldn't underestimate me anymore."

He's searching my face now and I have no idea what he's looking for. Finally, he asks, "Are you feeling alright? You are not sounding or acting like yourself."

"Well, no," I say because he's an idiot for not figuring that out sooner. "Those two," I say pointing a blaming finger at both Maurelle and Olwyn, "they got me drunk! Can you believe that?"

Kallen looks really confused. "What do you mean they got you drunk?"

"They shot me with those little darty things and now I'm all discombobulated." I giggle. "Isn't that a funny word?"

Ignoring my question, he asks, "How many of the darty things did they shoot at you?"

I hold up four fingers so I have to push one down with my other hand so there's only three. "This many," I say proudly since I got the whole finger thing right.

"Xandra, I think we should go back into the cabin so you can lie down. I can handle these two from here," he says slowly as if I'm not going to understand him if he speaks any faster.

I shake my head even though lying down sounds really good now because things are starting to spin around me a little bit. "I can't yet. I have to send them home. They're too dangerous to have here."

"Xandra, please, please don't do this," Kallen pleads. Do I really want a boyfriend who doesn't believe in my magic? I'm going to have to really think about that after I take a nap.

I remember a trick that he used when he didn't like what I was saying. I pull on his shirt until he bends down far enough so I can kiss him which takes him completely by surprise like it had when he did it to me. "Now, you have to be quiet so I can concentrate," I say and my magic flows towards him and he's trying to say something but he can't make any sounds come out of his throat. I'm really going to like that perk of my magic. I'll win all of our arguments now.

Turning again towards Maurelle, I say, "I want you to tell my father that he should do his own dirty work. If he wants to try to force me to open up the Fae realm then he should at least have enough respect for me to come himself instead of sending weak little Cowan Fairies after me. Okay?" She nods her head yes and the confidence seems to be returning to her eyes as she figures out that I really am going to send her home. Silly Fairy, it's only going to be a one way trip.

Closing my eyes, I imagine the sky splitting open like it's been torn. Peeling back the sides of it, I imagine my father. I know he has black hair and green eyes like mine. I imagine him at home in the Fae realm waiting for Maurelle and Olwyn to bring me back so he can spill my blood on the passageway between realms to take revenge on this realm because a Witch King who is long dead embarrassed him. I imagine this man who I hate all the way down to the marrow of my bones and when I open my eyes, there he is staring at me through the hole I just ripped through the realms.

He stares at me with his mouth agape. I don't know where he is, maybe his banquet room or something because he's at a huge table full of food and the furnishings are gold and tacky and everything I would have expected from an egomaniac. When he finds he is able to speak again he says in a voice that sounds like liquid velvet, which helps me understand how he tricked my mother, "You did it. You've set us free."

As I stare at this man who rises from his chair, this man who has made my mother's life hell and in turn mine, the only thing I can think to say is, "I thought you'd be taller."

Confusion washes over his face as he walks towards me. "How is this possible? It is supposed to be your blood that opens the realm." When he's close enough to the tear, he reaches out his hand to touch it. It shimmers like water and his hand blisters as soon as he makes contact with it and he snatches it back. "What have you done?" he asks with accusation, anger and disappointment all rolled up nicely in that smooth voice of his.

Everything about him makes me laugh, which I do. He looks so betrayed that I wasn't willing to die for him. Seriously, I have this man's DNA inside of me? "What's the matter, Dad? Not happy with the way I opened up your realm? Oh well, you've been a real disappointment to me, too, and I just found out about you a few days ago. But I have something for you." Without closing my eyes, I lift Maurelle and Olwyn from the ground with my magic and I shove them through the tear. Maurelle screams as she feels the burn of the passage but Olwyn is still asleep so he doesn't feel a thing. He'll probably be pretty sore when he wakes up again.

The world is starting to spin around me and I know my strength is failing but I have one more thing to say to my biological father whose face is contorted in anger and I'm pretty sure some fear, too. "If you push me, if you send more after me, if you do anything I don't like, I will become the prophecy. I will rip your realm apart and this one too if that's what it takes to stop you. You don't get to decide if I live or die but I get to decide if you do." Turning to Kallen, I say, "This is your chance to go home if that's what you want. My biological father won't hurt you and I can protect you from the pain of passing through the torn realms if that's what you choose to do."

He looks at me for a long moment. "Is there another option?" he asks.

"Yes, you can stay here with me."

With the happiest smile I've ever seen on his face, he says, "I choose to stay."

"Okay, then." With that, I slam the folds back in place and the tear becomes nothing but sky again. That's the last thing I remember before everything goes black.

CHAPTER 21

"Xandra, please wake up," a voice is saying in my ear. I remember that voice, I wanted to wrap myself up in it before. I like that voice a lot. "Please, you have to wake up."

It's a struggle to open my eyes and even more of a struggle to focus them but eventually, Kallen's face becomes clear. "You didn't go home," is the first thing I think to say. I'm in the cabin again lying on the cot and he's kneeling next to me. He must have carried me in here after I passed out.

He smiles. "No, I did not. I chose to stay."

"But you could have gone home and lived with the other Fairies. My father wouldn't dare to hurt you."

"No, after your little conversation with him, he probably would not."

"Then why didn't you go?"

"Why would I go back to the Fae realm when the Witch Fairy I want to be with is in this one?"

"What about your grandmother?"

Kallen smiles again but maybe a little sadder this time. "Somehow, I suspect my grandmother knew I wouldn't want to go back. I think she changed some of the details of her divination to get me to come here knowing what I would actually find. I believe she knew why you opened the realm and that it was only one way. I feel foolish for ever suspecting you would do it any other way. I'm sorry I did not trust your judgment earlier."

"Huh. The people who raised us kept a lot of secrets from us, didn't they? Did you really stay here for me?" I ask and I try to sit up but a jackhammer starts up in my brain and I have to lie back down.

"Wow, my head hurts."

"Yes, I really did. And I believe your headache can be attributed to a hangover."

"A hangover?" No way. "But I didn't drink anything."

He chuckles. "No, but you absorbed an awful lot of Fairy poison into your bloodstream which you seem to metabolize as others would alcohol. I should have suspected that you were not affected by things the same way as others of the Fae because you were able to wear your amulet without harm."

I groan. "I can't believe I lost Mom's amulet. And her grimoire. Do you think you remember where that cave was so we can go back there in the summer and look for them?"

"Of course," he says and there's something in his eyes. Hesitancy, maybe? I can't quite figure it out.

"What are you thinking?" I ask knowing that it's the question that guys hate to be asked the most.

"Nothing that can't wait," he says.

I glower at him as much as my headache will allow. "After everything we've been through you're really going to give me that crap of an answer?"

He looks like he's not going to say anything but then he starts talking without quite meeting my eyes. "I made the decision to stay based on my desires but I hold no knowledge of how you feel about it."

I roll my eyes. "Kallen, if I wanted you to leave I would have shoved you back to your realm like I did Maurelle and Olwyn. Though, it may be a shock to Mom and Dad when I ask them if my boyfriend can stay with us because he just gave up his entire realm and everything he knows to be with me."

His face pales a little. "I had not thought everything through as you have apparently. Do you honestly believe your parents will accept me into your home? I did not make the greatest impression when I was there last."

It's my turn to laugh. "No, you didn't. But you did teach me how to use my magic and helped me get rid of the Fairies who wanted to kill me. I'm pretty sure they'll overlook your rude behavior. But you'll have to stay in the guestroom because we're not getting hand-fasted any time soon."

He laughs again. "As I would expect. You know, you were a sight to behold earlier. How did you figure out you could do the things you did?"

I think about it before answering. "I think the Fairy poison had a lot to do with it."

He looks surprised. "How so?"

"Because before I was thinking too hard about everything so I couldn't accomplish anything. When the Fairy poison entered my system, my thoughts became scattered and I didn't think about any one thing for any amount of time, my thoughts were all over the place."

I can see his lips curling upwards as he says, "Such as when you asked Maurelle about my history with Fairy women?"

Color rushes to my cheeks as I remember all the things I said while under the influence of the Fairy poison. I thought he had been unconscious at the time. "Are you going to keep interrupting? And don't think I don't know you're laughing at me."

"I would never do such a thing," he says and he makes the same gesture of keeping his lips sealed as I had when I kept interrupting him.

Choosing to ignore him, I continue. "Because I wasn't so afraid of my magic, I was more in tune with it. I knew what I had to do and it's almost as if I knew instinctively how to do it. Does that make sense?"

He inclines his head and nods. "I believe so. Apparently, if I had thought to infect you with poison sooner we would not have had to spend so many nights in the cold together."

I make a face at him. "Kallen."

"Yes?"

"Shut up and kiss me."

"Gladly," he says and his lips graze mine in a gentle kiss which my head appreciates because anything more would make it start pounding again.

"Can we go home now?" I murmur against his lips.

He sits back and pushes a stray strand of hair from my cheek. "It's very late. It would be better if we got a good night's sleep first."

"Okay, then come lay with me because I'm really tired."

He doesn't need any more encouragement. He lies down with me after I scoot over to make more room and he wraps his arms around me pulling me close. I'm getting really used to sleeping with him. I'm going to miss it because I know for certain that Mom and Dad would have serious issues with me continuing to sleep with him at home but I'm so glad he stayed.

CHAPTER 22

The next morning, we start back for home. Kallen uses his magic to make me a new coat since mine has three holes in it now. I went ahead and asked him to make a whole outfit for me after he gave me some privacy to clean up and it felt great to wear clean clothes. He made the sweater the same color green as my eyes.

Our trek back to my house is very different from the one we first embarked on. The biggest difference being that Kallen and I actually get along. We even hold hands for the most part and I'm still getting used to the whole thing but having him stop every once in a while to kiss me is so much nicer than him being condescending and haughty.

We walk most of the day to get to my house. I thought we were farther away so when I learned we weren't I didn't care if we walked for so many hours as long as I could sleep in a warm bed tonight. As we get closer to my house, both Kallen and I are getting anxious about talking to my parents and Aunt Barb. I keep reassuring him that it'll be okay, but I'm just as nervous as he is. I believe it will work out but things will probably be a bit strained at first. To distract us from our nervousness, I spend a lot of the time telling Kallen about all of the changes in technology and communication that have occurred over the last three hundred and some years. Some of it he knew about and some he didn't.

Just as night falls, we are at my house and I give Kallen's hand a squeeze in encouragement as we get close. Kallen stops about fifteen feet from the house and I look at him questioningly. "Fairy trap," he reminds me.

Oh yeah, I forgot about that but as I look closer I can actually make out a faint haze in the air surrounding the house. With a wave of my hand, the trap falls. If it had not been my mother's I don't know if I could have done it so easily. Kallen hesitates for a second but then he begins walking again and he walks right up to the house with me without anything happening to him.

I open the back door and we come into the kitchen. "Mom, Dad, are you here?" I call. Please let them be here.

Almost instantly, both of my parents come through the wall. "Xandra! You're okay!" They surround me in a group hug of sorts and my body temperature drops a few degrees as their ghostly skin touches mine.

Finally floating back from me, they look back and forth between Kallen and me. "What happened? Are the other Fairies coming?"

I give them the condensed version of what had happened. "My magic is stronger than theirs and I was able to tear open a hole through the realms and shove them back through it." Both of their mouths hang open as they take in what I said.

"You did what?" a deep voice says from the doorway of the kitchen. I turn to find an older man with thick gray hair and a round middle. He's dressed in a dark gray suit and the jacket buttons are just beginning to strain around his stomach. His face is lined with age and right now it's facing me and it's covered with an expression made of shock, disbelief and anger. Those are pretty strong emotions to be directing towards me without ever having met me.

"Who are you?" I ask probably less politely than I should have.

He straightens up to his full height and puffs out his chest like a rooster. "I am your grandfather, King of the Witches."

I look at Mom questioningly and she nods. "I contacted my father to ask for help protecting you."

Before I get a chance to say anything, he turns his angry face towards my mom. "Quillian, you didn't tell me how powerful your daughter is." Turning to me again, he asks boorishly, "Why are you in the company of a Fairy?" He said Fairy like it was a dirty word.

Heat flushes to my face. "Because he's my boyfriend," is all I can think to say.

"Are you telling me that you are powerful enough to split open the realms at will?"

Well, actually I was telling Mom that but it's probably not best to bring that little point up when he's already so mad. "Yes."

He's shaking in anger now. Rounding on my mother again, he growls, "You should have let us kill her in your womb! But it's not too late." He turns towards me and starts speaking, "From ancient times of rhymes and runes this witch calls upon the power of the moon to scourge the earth of magic black and within its womb to take mercifully back this one born in heresy and shame..."

"Father, no!" Mom screams trying to make him stop but he just ignores her.

What the hell? Why is my biological family so dysfunctional? First my real father wanted to kill me and now my grandfather? I really think I should only get to know Dad's family from now on.

Kallen has moved in front of me as if he's going to take the brunt of my grandfather's spell but I push around him as my grandfather finishes. "...all this I ask in the goddess's name."

I am always so disappointed by Witch magic because it's not as visible as Fairy magic. I wait a minute for the spell to kill me but after a few seconds my grandfather's eyes get huge so I'm assuming that something went wrong. Now I move from shock to anger pretty quickly at yet one more person wanting me dead. Other girls my age don't have to put up with this crap.

Pulling on my magic, I push my grandfather with it through the kitchen door into the living room and then I open the front door with a wave of my hand and push him out of the house as I walk. "I am so tired of people being mean to me!" I yell at him. "I don't care who you are, I am not going to sit idly by and let you people do whatever you want with my life. I choose if I live or die and I choose to live so you can just go right on back to wherever you came from and forget all about me."

He was struggling at first against my magic but when he figures out that he can't do anything about it, he just stares at me wide-eyed with fear. Good, I hope he is scared. I stand in front of him now with my arms crossed over my chest waiting to see what he does.

Giving me a last long hard look, he turns to my Mom because

everyone had followed the two of us outside. "Quillian, you have truly brought destruction into this world. I will be back with the Witan and we will do what we should have done seventeen years ago."

I roll my eyes. "Yeah, yeah, heard it all before," I mutter. "Say it walking, okay?" With that I push him towards the car in our snowy driveway that must be his. It's a black Lexus and as soon as his body hits it the alarm in it starts going off. My grandfather digs his keys out of his pocket and hurriedly shuts off the alarm and almost dives into his car. If there was pavement, his tires would have squealed as he put the car in reverse and slammed his foot down on the gas. If he's not careful, he's going to end up just like Mom and Dad.

When I can no longer see the car as it careens at dangerous speeds down the mountain, I turn around to find Mom and Dad staring at me like I have two heads. Kallen is smiling at me as if he's not surprised in the least that I could do this. That makes me like him just a little bit more. Looking at my parents, I say, "Mom, Dad, Kallen stayed in this realm to be with me and he's going to be living with us because he doesn't have any place else to go. I'm pretty tired after walking all day and then using my magic to yet again keep a relative from killing me, so after I eat something I'd like to go to bed. Kallen will be sleeping with me but we won't be having sex because to him that would mean we're hand-fasted and I'm not ready to marry him at this point in my life. I'm way too young. Tomorrow we can talk about what we should do about Grandpa getting his Witch council together so he can come back and try to kill me again. Okay?"

Both of my parents nod numbly. I give them a grateful smile and I take Kallen's hand and walk back into the house with him in tow. Being seventeen is a lot harder than I thought it was going to be.

ABOUT THE AUTHOR

Loves:

1. People who read my books.

2. My children. (Please don't tell my kids I listed fans before them. You may cause a riot in my home. They're pretty feisty kids.)

3. My cats and dogs when they're not making me sniffle, sneeze, rub my eyes or irritating my asthma. (Scratch that, they always do and I love them anyway.)

4. Writing. (I would have listed this first, but it would have looked bad. Worse than putting fans before my kids.)

5. Good friends. (Fortunately, I have several.)

6. Quiet evenings at home in front of the fireplace reading a good book.(Please, like that's going to happen with five kids in the house - but I can dream can't I?)

7. I got stuck here so I asked a couple of friends to tell me their fondest memory of me. This is what I got:

Deb: It was when you used to babysit Michael and rode the horse in Meijer so he could ride with you. Also......my first trip to TX for a wedding. You were at my house and said you would put my clothes in the dryer when they were done. Needless to say, the next morning I had to pack wet clothes in my suitcase. The airline lost my luggage for 4 days so when I finally got it back, my clothes were all mildewed. (Okay, in my defense – I was twelve at the time. The sad thing is, I still forget to put clothes in the dryer.)

Michele: I have too many...but one of the first that popped in my head was how you drove all the way to Chicago to look at my apartment for me because I was too hung over, and then gave me all the details so I could pretend I was there. You are a good friend... (It was only a seven hour round trip. What are friends for?)

Joe: A particular Domino's pizza delivery and you invited the delivery guy inside...(I'm going to stop there because my ex-husband thinks he's funny.)

For obvious reasons, I didn't ask anyone else.

Hates:

1. Puppies, kittens, babies, sunshine, peace on earth, goodwill, recycling, education, gifts, and sweets of any kind. (Really, I do.)

2. Being facetious. (I would never dream of it!)

3. People who don't read my books. (Well, maybe not all of them. But, most of them.)

4. People who always manage to stop by the house when I look terrible.(You know who you are…)

5. Lumberjacks. (Don't know why, just do.)

Now that you know everything about me, you should drop by my Facebook page at https://www.facebook.com/pages/Bonnie-Lamer-Author/129829463748061 to tell me all about you.

Made in the USA
Columbia, SC
05 November 2017